# Fou....y ...

## by

## Heather Carver & A.K. Layton

*Heather Carver*

Found by You

ISBN: 978-1-949300-16-1

Edited by Pamela Tyner

Cover Art by JM Walker

This book is a work of fiction and any resemblance to persons, living or dead, or places, events or locales is purely coincidental. The characters are productions of the author's imagination and used fictitiously.

Published in the United States of America by Beachwalk Press, Incorporated

www.beachwalkpress.com

# Dedication

*Heather Carver*

I hope everyone out there has a friend that you can share everything with and experience the ups and downs in life with. True friendship is hard to come by, so when you find it cherish it!

*A.K. Layton*

I want to dedicate this book to my co-author and good friend, Heather Carver. Without you this book wouldn't have been possible. Thank you for choosing me to go on this journey with you!

# Acknowledgements

We are so excited to share this book with you. It's been a project years in the making, and we are incredibly grateful to Beachwalk Press and Pam for helping us share it with the world. We cannot thank Beachwalk Press and their staff enough!

And to Cattigan, thank you for taking time to beta read our book; it wouldn't be what it is today without you!

Thank you to our cover artist JM Walker with Just write. Creations, who worked with Heather on this amazing cover.

To our families who've supported us while we sat around beating up our computers, talking to ourselves and working into the wee hours of the nights, thank you for loving us just the way we are.

And lastly, to you, the person reading this right now, you are why we write. Thank you for reading our story, and we hope you love it as much as we do.

# Chapter 1

*Kenslie*

"You really want to do this now?" I ask, shaking my head, forcing the angry tears to stay put.

"When else should we do it, Kens? When you're halfway around the world, or when you've moved to Connecticut?"

Everett Langley is the love of my life, and right now I can see his heart breaking, but it's as much his doing as it is mine. If he'd just give me a chance to explain, a moment to talk, calmly, but calm was never our strong suit. No, we are passion and fire; impulse and need.

"What are you getting at? Have you forgotten that I asked you to come with me to Connecticut?"

"But not Europe?" Everett says with a huff that visually vibrates through his body.

His green eyes meet mine, and the sadness is clear; hiding just behind it is the hopefulness that he will win this one. Nothing else gives away his emotions. They don't flow as easy as they do for others, but I know he loves me. He's as stubborn as an ox, and I've told him so on many occasions. To which he calls me 'crazy in a loveable way'. I smirk at the thought, but then a sorrowful pang hits me.

Everett is that gruff man—a man's man type. And I'd be lying if I said I didn't think that was sexy as hell, coupled with his good looks and I was done for at first sight. His dark hair, shaved short on the sides, paired with his five o'clock shadow. He's taller than I am by about five inches, but he's as wide as a house, with muscles that stretch against the t-shirts he wears; muscles that aren't very well hidden under the button-down shirts he wears on date nights. But it comes with his laborious job. A career I'm asking him to leave so I can follow my own ambitions.

He's right, this discussion needs to happen now, and I can see this *talk* is killing him. But I can't back down, and yet the thought that this might end us has my heart already breaking.

"No, not Europe." I stand my ground. "You know that Anna and I have been planning this since freshman year of college. It's our graduation gift to each other—our goodbye gift to each other before we go our separate ways."

"What about us? Where is our goodbye gift to each other?"

*Ooof.* His words hit me hard, knocking the air from my body. My heart drops to my stomach, and I feel sick. *Goodbye?*

"What do you mean *goodbye*?" I pause, startled, then I quietly ask, "Does that mean you've made up your mind?"

I watch as Everett paces our small living room, rubbing his hands over his short hair. *Our living room.* I swallow down the hard lump in my throat. It's been our home for more than a year, and Everett has been *mine* for almost two.

He's known about the Europe trip forever, but what I hid from him were the applications I'd been sending in to hospitals around the country. Having completed my nursing degree, I'm ready to start living my dream. I want to work in a major hospital, in the ER, where my contributions make an instant impact, right then and there. It has always been my dream, and Everett is fully aware of that.

And then it came true. Three weeks ago I received the letter in the mail from the Hartford Connecticut Hospital, offering me a position. It never works out this well, not for nursing students straight out of school, but I've put in my time. I got straight A's, volunteered, interned, completed all those extracurricular activities that aren't necessary but *encouraged.* And this wouldn't have been possible without letters of recommendations from a few teachers. I worked my ass off for this job—this job that I've been reminded is on a trial basis due to my lack of my hands-on experience. I must be perfect. I need to come into it with a level head and a positive attitude. And with my world falling apart, my dream is quickly turning into a nightmare.

"I know you want this job, but do you want it more than you want *us...me*?" He stops, and his eyes, full of hurt, meet mine.

"That's not fair! You know I love you. And if you loved *me*, you'd support me." I fight back against the hurt.

"Now who isn't being fair?" Everett crosses his arms over his chest, rocking back on his heels.

It's true. He has a great job here in Oregon doing geology work for construction companies as an independent consultant. But why does his happiness come before mine? But shouldn't it come before mine? If you love someone shouldn't you put them first? *Fuck.* I give my head a hard shake. I don't know what I'm doing anymore, and the more I think about it, this European vacation seems like another stressor, not a getaway.

"Everett, do you want to marry me?" I ask flatly. I need to get to the bottom of this. I need to know where he stands. Two years together and no proposal...doesn't that mean something?

I'm not exactly eager to get married, but I want to know what the future holds for us. Is that the direction we're going? Isn't that the direction couples in our situation would be heading? Would this decision be easier on both of us if we were engaged? I sigh inwardly, now regretting the question.

"Uh. Well…" Everett shrugs his shoulders, breaking our eye contact before he continues. "I don't know, Kens. I guess I haven't given it much thought. I love how things are right now. Why would I want to change that? I don't want anything to change!" he says adamantly.

*Now you know. Happy?* I berate myself.

"Then that's that." I manage to croak out the words as the unabashed tears fall hot and fast.

"What?"

I force myself to look up at his wide-eyed expression. His mouth opens to speak, then shuts again before he finally says something.

"Just because I don't know if we will get married?" His voice goes up an octave, and he clears his throat.

But it takes just a minute for Everett to close the distance between us, and I can feel his mood change. His arms encompass my body, cradling me while I cry. I tuck my head into that familiar spot on his chest, desperate to burn it into my memories, because soon that's all Everett will be. The memory of the first boy I ever really loved.

"Kenzie. Hush, baby. It's going to be okay." His strong

hands smooth my hair, comforting me. "I love you. I don't want to fight. Now isn't the right time to talk about this, you're right."

I can hear the desperation in his voice. He knows just as well as I do where this is going, and I love him for wanting to spare my pain for as long as possible.

Pulling back out of his arms, I wipe my eyes on my sleeves and blow out a brave breath.

"It seems love isn't enough for us, not right now at least. I can't give up my dreams to stay here, and you feel the same way about not leaving. If one of us gives in, we'll just end up resenting each other in the end. I love you too much to ever want to hate you."

I pause, steadying my voice, as I look up at Everett, only to look quickly away. The foreign tears hiding in the corners of his eyes are going to have me a complete, utter wreck any moment now.

"I'll have most of my stuff out by tomorrow night. I'm sure Anna will let me keep it at her place. You can have all the furniture."

"You're the one leaving me, for the record," Everett says sorely.

"For the record?" I roll my eyes. "Yeah, well, for the record, I'm the one who's a crying mess, I'm the one who's said *I love you* a dozen times, I'm the one who thought about marriage and our big picture, not you."

"I don't want this. I love you too. Tell me what I can do to make you stay?"

I can hear the desperation in his voice as he takes a hesitant step toward me, and it makes me want to rethink my decision. Maybe I can find a hospital locally, even though I was turned down for my top choice local jobs I'd applied for months ago. I'd have to start small and work my way up, but I could do it, I tell myself hopefully. But a voice in the back of my head tells me that I deserve more. That I've worked hard for *more*.

"You can't," I finally say.

"Then what good would chasing after you do?" Everett says with a scoff. Turning, he slams his hands on the table, and the loud thud bounces off the happy memories and pictures hanging on the walls.

"Thank you." I pause, trying to stay collected. "Now we've both broken my heart."

*Asshole.*

Grabbing my purse off the kitchen counter, I head for the door, my chest heaving as I attempt to control the sobs. I vaguely hear something like "*I'm sorry, wait,*" as I step out the door, slamming it behind me, but the whooshing in my ears makes the world around me blurry as I take off running for my car, seeking the comfort of a quiet space.

Climbing in, I sit. I don't know for how long. My mind, my face, my body, all numb. I'm confused. What in the hell just happened? Then it hits me, and the tears rush down my face again. I feel like a silly girl, crying over a silly boy. There are far more important things in the world to cry over, yet so much of Everett was my world. The fact that he wouldn't support me and move with me hurts the most. Maybe he thinks I'm being selfish for not supporting his work, but jobs like his are easy to get. He could move anywhere in the world and be just fine. That's not the case for me; a green nurse getting a position in the emergency room isn't typical. And I've worked for this. I deserve this. *I deserve this,* I tell myself again.

I need my best friend right now; I need Annaliesa.

*Me: Are you home?*

*Anna: Yep.*

*Me: I'm on my way over.*

*Anna: Okay, girly.*

*Me: I just broke up with Everett.*

*Anna: WHAT?!*

*Me: I'll tell you about it when I get there.*

# Chapter 2

*Annaliesa*

*What the hell happened between them? It must have been bad.*

I can't believe Kens sent me a text instead of calling me. She is in love with Everett, so I have no doubt she's breaking down. Not wanting her to drive if she's hysterical, I decide to call her.

"Hhhhellllo," Kens stammers out between sobs.

"Hey, love. Are you okay to drive?" My heart is breaking, knowing she's in need of comfort and I'm not there. "I can come get you if you need."

"I'm good. I'm just leaving now. I'll be there soon," she replies.

At least she's calming down a little. "Okay. Drive safe. I love you."

"Thanks, Anna. You too."

Abandoning the daunting task of packing, I go in search of beer, praying I still have a couple that Kens likes. Beer is gross, so I only keep it around for her. Though I had some left over from a guy I was hanging out with. But that went nowhere fast considering he was swiping away on

Tinder while hanging out with me in *my* apartment.

This conversation will require alcohol. Later we'll stuff our faces with ice cream and watch some chick flicks.

It doesn't take long before Kens is barreling through my door. "He's such an asshole. I can't believe him," she says, wasting no time.

"Here." I hand her a Stella beer that she loves. "Now let's sit, and then you need to tell me what happened, because I thought he was coming around to the idea of moving to Connecticut with you."

"Well, he still doesn't understand why our trip to Europe is important. He got pissed that you and I are doing a goodbye trip and I don't want to do one with him. Why would I when I thought we were moving together?" she says with tears in her eyes.

I'm surprised she isn't bawling. "I don't understand why he's so bent out of shape over this trip. He's known about it since you guys got together a couple of years ago. It's not like you have to do everything with each other."

I sigh. This is why I'm happy to be single. I want to focus on me and my career. I received an offer to work for a top architecture firm in Chicago, and I don't have to worry about whether my boyfriend can come with me. Job opportunities in architectural drafting and design engineer aren't easy to come by right out of school. Guys spell *drama* for me. They say women cause all the drama, but I beg to differ.

"He also said if I loved him I'd stay here with him and find a job close to home."

"Oh no, he didn't." *What an ass.* "You need to follow your dreams. If you don't, you'll end up resenting him. You also can't force him to move, because he'll resent you. I know you love him and want to marry him, but that saying 'If you love something, let it go. If it comes back to you, it's yours forever. If it doesn't, then it was never meant to be' is true here. You need to do you and let him do him. If it's meant to be, you guys will find your way back to each other."

"I know. It's hard though. I want him with me. I don't want to choose between him and my dreams, but I'm greedy and want them both." She sighs and covers her face with her hands. "It probably didn't help that I was telling him he didn't love me if he wasn't ready to move, but then I wouldn't stay for him."

"This is sucky timing, but we're not going to let it ruin our trip. What can I do to help you?"

"Will you help me get all my stuff from his place? I'll need to store it here."

"You still have a room here, so that's fine with me. But I'll only have this place through July before I have to move to Chicago."

"Most of it is going with me, and what isn't I can take to Mom and Dad's house or ship it," Kens says.

"Now that that's settled, let's start finalizing plans for this trip."

"Yes!" Kens shouts.

"Wait, we must have some chocolate chip cookie dough ice cream first. It'll help improve both of our moods," I suggest.

"You sure do know a way to a woman's heart. Beer and ice cream," she says, hugging me before I can make it to the kitchen.

I really hope talking about Europe will help her get excited for our trip. I know she feels guilty going without Everett. It was a huge debate between us last year when we were buying the tickets. She wanted him to come, but since I'm single I really wanted it to be just the two of us like we'd planned. I want that goodbye trip. I know we'll only be about fourteen hours away from each other, so it isn't like we'll never see each other. It just won't be every day like it is now.

With our snacks in hand, we settle down on the couch

to discuss our upcoming adventures. When I glance at the clock I realize several hours have passed and it's after midnight. We've been talking about all the sites we want to see while we're traveling through Europe for two weeks. There is so much to see and not enough time. I tried to talk her into taking a month off, but with our new jobs and her not wanting to be away from Everett that long we compromised on two weeks. We've had to cut out some things, but we're trying to hit everywhere we want.

I'm most excited to see the Leaning Tower of Pisa and the Pont des Arts. I'm bummed I'll never be able to have a lock put on the bridge and throw the key into the Seine River. Couples in love used to put a lock on the bridge with their names carved into them then throw the key in the river as a way to show their commitment. But just going and seeing this bridge will be amazing. To see all the love stories. I wish there was a way for me to see how many of these couples are actually still together.

"Hey," I say for the third time before she finally acknowledges I'm talking to her. "What are the places you're most excited to visit?" I ask, trying to help take her mind off Everett.

"I'd really like to see the Devin Castle in Ljubljana. I've always wanted to see a real castle. It was built in 1864!

Nothing these days seem to last that long," she says with a heavy sigh, but recovers. "There is also a hike I'd like to take up to Mount Saint Mary in Bratislava. I bet the view up there is just amazing. What about you? What places are you most excited to visit?"

"Well, the number one place is the Leaning Tower of Pisa. I also really want to see the Spittelau District Heating Plant, the Kaiser Wilhelm Memorial Church in Berlin, the Louis Vuitton Foundation, the M by Montcalm building, the Pompidou Centre, Inntel Hotel, the Dancing House and the Pont des Arts. I know boring to you." I can't wait to see all these places. Kens is amazing to be willing to go to all these places with me, but she doesn't share the same excitement over buildings as I do. Good thing we both love the outdoors.

"Geez. You're lucky I love you. This trip is going to be all buildings," she says, laughing.

I know I've been very blessed in the friend department. While I'm excited to be moving to Chicago and pursuing my passion in architectural drafting and design engineering, I'm also scared. I won't know anyone, and it'll be the first time in years that I won't have Kens by my side. I like to think I'll be open to meeting and making new friends, but I tend to be a homebody.

I haven't had good luck with men, but when you've been cheated on you learn to grow on your own. I don't ever want to rely on someone to take care of me. I only need me, but if I can find a guy who wants the same things as me, then I wouldn't be opposed to a relationship. It's just finding that person that's hard.

"Anna, where'd you go?" Kens asks, waving her hands in front of my face. "Earth to Anna."

"Sorry. I was lost in the land of Annaliesa. I was thinking about how I can't wait for this trip to happen, but I'm also sad because it's the end of the Anna and Kens show. I know we'll still be besties, but we'll live so far away. It's hard to not get sad when I think about it. I know it's for the best and we're both following our dreams, I'm just scared we'll fall apart." I hate that I'm getting emotional when she needs me to be strong for her right now. "Hey, forget I said anything. Tonight is supposed to be only happy thoughts."

"Don't belittle your feelings because I've had a rough night. Yes, it sucks that Everett and I broke up, and yes, my heart is hurting, but I have to move on. I have to follow my dreams. I wish that I could have him and my dream, but it just isn't in the cards for me right now. I don't want you to be sad or scared. We are lifers—there's no way you're getting rid of me."

"Is that a threat or a promise?" I ask playfully.

"Both," she replies.

This is why we're so good for each other. We are willing to always let the other vent. We're honest with each other, and we don't hide our feelings.

"Well, you ready to call it a night? We have a busy day tomorrow, and I still need to pack. You know me and my last-minute packing. I'll be packing as we walk out the door. Should we take a bet on how many things I'll leave at home?"

"You'd lose that bet. I know you. Just don't forget your bras this time. We aren't the same size anymore, Ms. Big Tits," Kens says, laughing.

"One time. It was one time that I forgot my bras. I will never live it down. I would gladly give you my boobs. I hate them."

"No thanks. I'm perfectly happy with my boobs."

"Well, me and my boobs are calling it a night. See you in the morning," I say, giving her a hug.

"Good night. See you in the morning."

Walking into my room, I get ready for bed, and once there I have trouble sleeping. I feel bad that Everett and Kens can't work things out. But I have a feeling that everything will work out once we get home. They are meant for each other. Not that I know what that feels like. I've been single for far too long, but I'm glad I'm not in their situation, tied down...and dealing with a man-child over a trip that was planned before they were even together.

Everett loves it here and doesn't want to move, but I think he will for Kens. He was being difficult tonight because he's being a baby about Europe. He's been standoffish about it for the last year, saying he should be able to take his girl there for her first time. I almost wonder if he was planning on asking her to marry him there. But this has been our dream for four years now. Maybe it is wrong of me to keep him from coming with us. I just don't want to be the third wheel on a trip that's been on my bucket list for as long as I can remember.

I finally fall into a blissful sleep, dreaming of all the love stories that can be told from Paris. Wondering if one day I'll create my own love story.

# Chapter 3

### *Kenslie*

I sure waited long enough to pack my things from the apartment. We leave for London tomorrow on the red-eye. Anna thought it'd be a good idea to travel that way, so we could sleep and save on needing a hotel for the night. This way we get a full day before we have to transfer to our next destination. But it also means that we're going to have to pack *somewhat* lightly.

I'm relieved when we pull up to the apartment building and I don't see Everett's truck.

"He's not here," I tell Anna.

"Is he at work?"

His work schedule varies. He's an independent consultant, which means he sets his meetings and can work what hours he wants and will often work from home. I've wanted to text him the last two days and see how he's doing, but I assume he's pouring everything he has into work to avoid thinking about us. That's what he's done in the past to avoid talking about his feelings. But he usually comes around.

*Not this time, dummy*, I scold myself. This isn't a fight

or an argument. This is a break-up. And I'm moving out of state. It's not like I'll have the chance to bump into him at the grocery store accidentally-on-purpose.

"Probably," I answer. "But let's hurry."

"All right, love. Let's go."

I let out a huff as we get out of the car. Taking the short hallway down to my apartment, my heart pounds harder in my chest with each step. I'm walking back into our memories just to leave them again.

"So, girly. What kind of stuff are we packing? You said none of the big stuff goes, but are you taking pots and pans, dishes, any of that type of stuff?"

I unlock the door, leading us into the living room and shutting the door behind us. The place is just as I left it.

"No. Just very basic stuff. I think the biggest thing we are taking is my grandfather's cedar chest. We should be able to fit it in the truck. Other than my clothes, luggage, and toiletries, I think I'm good."

"If you say so." Anna gives me a sad smile.

I can see she wants to say more, that she's holding back and staying strong for me, and I love her for it. She liked Everett, and I like to think that we were all friends. I don't think she ever felt like the third wheel, and if she did, she was quiet about it. Just another sign of a best friend being supportive. But it's not like we didn't try to set her up. She's stubborn, but being hurt can do that to a person. Looking back now, it's a good thing we didn't set her up with Everett's cousin like I wanted; it would have made putting the past in the past harder.

It takes us no time at all to move the trunk into the truck before we begin stuffing all my clothing in the nice three-piece luggage set my parents bought me as a graduation gift.

"How many pairs of shoes do you need, woman?" Anna teases, lightening the mood.

"I can't help it. I walk around in ugly flats for twelve hours a day, so it's nice to put something sparkly on every now and then."

We both laugh at my ridiculous answer. But the laughter turns to silence as we hear the front door open, and the soft rattle on the walls as the door closes. My heart stops. *He's here.*

"Let's go." I scramble faster to force the shoes into the bag.

"Calm down, sweetie. It's going to be okay." Anna places her hand on mine. "Want me to go out there and talk to him?"

But there isn't a chance for me to respond as a large,

dark shadow fills the bedroom door.

"Kenzie?" He gives me a sad look before realizing that Anna is with me. "Oh, hey Anna." He recovers, acknowledging her, only to leave the doorway again.

I stare at Anna, stunned, and she only shakes her head at me. We pack faster as we listen for the front door, wondering if he'll leave now that he knows we're here. Anna and I grab the luggage totes and wheel them out of the bedroom, toward the front door.

Everett sits at the dinner table with a cup of coffee, not looking up at us. The sight of him sitting there looking so dejected sends goosebumps inching across my body, and tears well in my eyes. I love this man. And yet, we have no future together. And the past is already too far behind us to go back.

Anna reaches the door before me, and I'm relieved that we'll be able to make a swift exit. Being this close to him is dangerous. I've spent the last couple of nights trying to figure out how I could be happy staying here, what compromise would work for me so that I *can* have everything I want. But every time I come up short.

"Anna," the deep voice calls from the table behind us.

"Yeah, Everett?" she responds, not missing a beat.

"Can I talk to Kenslie alone for a minute?" he asks, still

looking down into his coffee.

Anna looks at me, raising her eyebrow in question, making sure that it's okay with me before she responds. I give her a reassuring nod, pausing to collect myself. If he wants one more talk, it's the least I can do.

"Sure. Kens, I'll be in the car."

Anna shuts the door behind her, and I move closer to the table, taking a seat. I'm sure I'll need to be sitting for this conversation.

It's quiet, and uncomfortable. It shouldn't be like this. Just because we aren't going to be together anymore doesn't mean I don't care. I can't stand the silence and the pain sucking the life out of the room. I will myself to stand up and walk around to his side of the table. There is just enough room for me to step between his legs, and I allow him to wrap his arms around me. He squeezes me tight, and I rest my head atop his, taking in his scent. Taking in the way his strong muscles hold me, and the way he *needs* me.

We stay like this for I don't know how long before Everett breaks our connection by standing up. I take a half-step back, then I'm pulled right back into his arms. It's my turn to nuzzle against his body, my face resting gently in the nook of his strong chest as our breathing becomes one.

"I don't want you to go," he finally says.

"Everett." I pause, pulling back enough so I can look up into his sad eyes. "I have to go. I've had this trip planned for years."

"That's not what I mean."

*I know.* I let out a heavy sigh. I don't know what to do. I don't know where to go from here, but the tears do, as they stream down my face without permission.

"I love you, Everett" is all I can manage to say. He knows the rest. He knows that I can't stay.

His hands are in my hair, holding me, as he studies my face. I look back at him, trying to memorize every feature on the face of the man I love. And then he kisses me. A hot and needy kiss. I relax into him, opening to him, letting him lead the way. I want to stay. I want to be here. I want to live in the world of Everett and Kenslie. My arms wrap around his neck so I can pull myself closer.

It's the familiarity of the embrace that hits me like a bucket of cold water, and I pull back. We can't be this any longer. Feeling this way only means that the pain will last longer.

"Come with me," I plead, looking up into his eyes.

With a wistful groan, Everett pulls away, pacing in the small dining area.

"Why do you have to leave? This is your home. Our

home. Is leaving everything you know and love worth a job?"

I wipe the tears from my eyes, frustrated at his words. I can't have this conversation again. It's a battle not won by either side. I shake my head and sigh inwardly. All I can do is rip the bandage off quickly.

"Everett Langley, I'll love you forever. But I can't have this conversation again."

I take a step toward the door. I can't risk him taking me into his arms, or even a goodbye kiss.

"I know where you stand, and you know where I stand. We've discussed this and haven't been able to find a middle ground," I say earnestly.

I open the door before looking back one time.

"As cliché as this sounds, I hope you find happiness. I wish you nothing but the best, because you deserve nothing less," I say wistfully.

I hold back the tears as I shut the door behind me. I walk down the cool hallway to the car where Anna is patiently waiting for me.

I hop into the passenger side.

"Wanna talk about it?" she asks.

"No," I say simply. "I need to get over this. We're going to Europe!" I smile at her.

I don't want to be a downer, for her sake, and mine. It's a once-in-a-lifetime trip!

"Let's get the fuck out of here." The smile's gone from my face, but I hope the forced excitement in my voice covers my agony.

"All right, girly. Let's go!"

And with that we're off on our adventure.

\* \* \* \*

It's early morning, and I'm still groggy from the valium I took on the plane ride as we pass through customs with no issues.

"I can't believe we're here!" Anna squeals, hooking her arm through mine.

There are lots of things I'm having a hard time believing as of late. I return her wide smile. Life has been crazy, but this trip is exactly what I need.

"Me either! This was a brilliant idea!"

"All of my ideas are brilliant." Anna snickers, playfully bumping her hip into mine.

We'd decided not to pack full luggage. Since we're traveling at night mostly to avoid hotel stays, we needed to pack light.

We work our way through the crowd, looking for the Heathrow Express to take us downtown. The airport is extravagant. We stop every so often to take it in, to point out the large statues, and even pass by the Queen's Terminal. Eventually we make it to the enormous train platform, and only have to wait a few minutes before it arrives.

My stomach gurgles as we board the train. "Oh, girl, I'm gonna need some breakfast and coffee pronto."

"Yes! I bet we can find some awesome bistro, with buttery croissants and espresso!" Anna offers enthusiastically.

"Perfect."

I'm shaking with excitement, and a silly smile pulls hard across my face as I look out my window as we approach London; words escape me.

"Can you even believe it? It's a dream. We are really doing this," I tell Anna with amazement.

"We sure as hell are!"

# Chapter 4

*Annaliesa*

*London to Amsterdam*

Picking a red-eye flight might not have been the best idea, but with school I've pulled all-nighters before. I'm too excited to sleep. Kens is out for the count due to her having to knock herself out to fly. My mind is spinning with thoughts of all the amazing sites we'll see and what my life will be like once I get to Chicago. I'm excited for the next adventure of my life.

I often wonder if I'm capable of finding love. I haven't had a long-term boyfriend since high school. In college, it was hard because a lot of guys are into partying or only want in your pants, and they make that known. I'm that girl who wants a connection before I spread my legs. I've been called a tease and many other names I don't wish to repeat. There are times that I wish I had what Kens and Everett had, but other times it seems like a lot of work and heartache. But there is that saying that love isn't all roses and sunshine.

I'm shocked the flight went as fast as it did. I didn't sleep a wink. I hate the getting off the plane part, because it seems to take people forever. A red-eye flight is worse since people are just waking up and moving slow. I just want to shout *Get the hell out of my way, London is waiting for me!*

"Ugh, I wish people would just stay in their seats if they're going to be so slow," I mumble loud enough for hopefully only Kens to hear me.

"What fun would that be?" She laughs.

She knows I'm not patient, so she loves to tease me any chance she gets. She has the patience of a saint. I guess we balance each other out.

Once on the train I'm grateful we didn't have to wait at the carousel for checked bags. That's the plus side to only having a backpack. It was easy for me to leave with a few things, Kens had a little more trouble. Hopping off the airport train shuttle, we head straight outside, taking in the view of London.

London is breathtaking, just like I knew it would be. There are so many quaint, cute bistros, cafés, and restaurants that we can stop at. It isn't all fast food like it is back home.

After we eat our yummy breakfast of buttery biscuits, bacon, pancakes, and lots of coffee we decide to explore before we take the Eurostar. The Eurostar isn't something I'm excited to take. The first reason is it goes up to 186 miles per hour, and second is that we spend twenty minutes in an underwater tunnel. I'm not a fan of tunnels on land, so

I doubt I'll like one underwater.

"Anna, quit stalling. Everything will be fine on the Eurostar. They wouldn't be operating it if it wasn't functional," Kens says.

"Ugh. I know. It's an irrational fear, just like my damn fear of elevators. It doesn't matter how many times I tell myself they won't get stuck, I still freak when I have to ride one. It doesn't make sense. And I know if it does get stuck that someone will get us out and fairly fast."

Why can't I get over these fears? Why must I always think of the worst possible thing that can happen? I wish I wasn't always like this, thinking about the negative in everything.

"Let's go. Who knows, maybe you'll meet your prince charming on the train and you'll be too caught up in him to notice anything else," Kens says, laughing.

"Haha. You're so funny. Just wait. Paybacks are a bitch." I wink and turn to get our tickets.

\* \* \* \*

The ride through the tunnel wasn't as bad as I thought it would be. It went a lot faster because of the speed of the train. Amsterdam is one of the top destinations on our list because we're staying at the Inntel Hotel. It wasn't originally on the itinerary, but since it is houses stacked upon houses, I'm curious about it and want to check out how it was done. When I showed pictures to Kens and told her I wanted to stay there she agreed it'd be fun. The only issue is we'll lose some time in Germany, but it'll be worth it.

The first thing I notice in Amsterdam is all the canals. I swear there is one on every street. I can't wait to take the canal cruise planned for today.

As we are flagging down our first cab I pray that we can speak clearly so they know where to take us.

"Greetings," the driver says as we get in.

"Good afternoon," I say.

"Where are you headed?" he asks.

*Thank you, Lord, for letting him speak English.*

"Hotel Inntel, please," I reply.

And off we go.

"Holy shit, the pictures didn't do this place justice, Kens," I say as we pull up to the hotel, pay the driver, and head inside.

"You were right, this place is amazing. Even I can see the beauty here. Are we going to take a tour?" Kens asks.

"I believe so. I've been emailing them about it, and they said they didn't see any issues with that." This is going to be a kick-ass vacation. It's already starting out great.

"*Hallo*. We are here to check in," I say to the gentleman behind the desk.

"*Hallo*. Can I get your name, please?"

"Annaliesa James and Kenslie Walker," I respond.

"Awe yes, here you are. We have you in a Craft Deluxe Room, is that correct?" he asks.

"Yes, we were told the Craft Deluxe Twin Room was sold out."

"Well, let me see what I can do for you," he says as he pounds away on his keyboard.

"This is amazing, Kens. Are you seeing all the beauty in here?"

"Yes, you'd have to be blind to miss it." She rolls her eyes at me.

"Not true. A lot of people miss the way buildings look on the inside. They're too wrapped up in themselves and what they have on their agendas," I reply.

"Sorry to interrupt you, Ms. James, but we have a Craft Deluxe Twin Room available. I can upgrade you for free. Would you like me to put you in that room?"

"Yes," Kens says.

"Will you need two room keys?" he asks.

"Yes, please," I respond to the kind man.

"Here you go," he says, handing us our room keys.

"You're going to be on the fourth floor. The elevator is right over there." He points behind us toward the elevators. "Have a wonderful time."

"Do you have stairs we can take?" I ask.

"Sorry, ma'am, but they are locked on all floors for going up. You can come down them though since they have to be available in case of a fire."

"*Dank u wel. Doei,*" Kens says.

We walk to the elevator, and luckily, it's open when we get there, so we don't have to wait for it.

This is absolutely amazing seeing all the different culture here. I really wish we had more time to explore everywhere on our list, but we're on a tight schedule. And I'm anal about staying on schedule. I like everything to go as planned. One of the things that bothers people about me is that I'm a stickler for staying on schedule. I don't usually fly by the seat of my pants. I've actually had boyfriends break up with me because I'm not spontaneous enough. It used to bother me, but now if someone wants to be my friend they have to accept me for who I am. I won't change for anyone.

"Are you ready to put our bags in the room then head out on the canal cruise?" Kens asks, pulling me out of my thoughts.

"Yes, we don't have a lot of time, and there's no use wasting it sitting in our room. We'll have to rush back though to make it for a tour if we can, otherwise I'll just stay up late exploring the hotel and sleep on the train tomorrow."

"Sounds good to me. I won't be missing my beauty sleep though," Kens says.

Opening the door to our room, I let out a gasp. The pictures of the room don't do it justice. The mural alone on the wall is enough to take all my attention. It isn't just a white room. There is color spread throughout the room. I could sit in this room and read a book all day and be content, but that isn't going to happen.

"Wipe your mouth, Anna, I think I see drool," Kens says while she wipes tears from her eyes because she's laughing so hard. "You'd think you just had an orgasm from walking into a room."

"Oh, hush. This is a dream for me."

"I know. Now let's leave for that cruise before we miss it."

"Fine," I huff. "Let's go."

* * * *

This has got to be one of the most educational cruises I've ever been on. We go by the Anne Frank House Museum, the Red-Light District, and the old Heineken factory, the Westerkerk Church, the Nine Streets District and the Skinny Bridge on the Amstel River. We also see a few more canals.

It was nice that it was just the two of us and the guide on the boat. I think it gave the guide more time to point things out since we didn't ask a lot of questions. I can only imagine how many questions some people have.

The guide reminds me of my grandpa. He loved to tell stories, and this guy told some great stories about things he's seen and done.

When it's time to say our goodbyes to the guide he gives us each a big hug and tells us to enjoy our journey and to not let anything get in our way of having fun, especially a schedule. Kens made it a point to tell him I was a stickler for a schedule.

"He was an amazing guide. I'm so happy we got him. I didn't want to get off the boat," I say.

"He was. We really couldn't have gotten any luckier with who we got. Though we could have had some hot guide."

"Then neither of us would have paid any attention to the scenery."

"Yes, we would have." She winks at me.

I swat her arm. "You know what I mean. Looking at

man candy isn't the scenery we came here to check out. But it is a nice bonus."

"Party pooper."

"Yep, that's me. I think we should make this a trip we do every other year. This is something that wouldn't get old because we'd learn and see new things each time."

"Yes, but I don't want to promise, because once we get home we'll both be moving and starting our new careers. But I do agree we need to do a yearly trip where we get together and do a vacation," Kens says.

"I guess that'll have to do for now. Who knows, maybe I'll meet the man of my dreams on this trip and never go home," I tease.

"Oh, that'd be the day. I would love for that to happen. You need some love in your life."

"Whatever. I don't need a man's love to be happy. I just need you and my family for now. One day I'll let a man into my life. But I don't have any plans on that happening anytime soon."

We spend the evening exploring Amsterdam, and all too soon we're heading back to the hotel to sleep. One thing I'm beginning to see is that Europe is full of romance. Everywhere you turn there are couples in love. They are embracing, kissing, holding hands, laughing, and some just staring into each other's eyes. It really is making me second-guess my thoughts on wanting a man to spend my time with. Kens is amazing, but having a man is different. One day I'll find myself someone who can love me for who I am.

We've been back in our room for all of ten minutes and Kens is already in bed, ready to sleep. That girl can fall asleep anywhere, and she falls asleep almost from the moment her head touches the pillow.

"Are you going to stay up all night, or are you going to crawl into that comfy bed and sleep?" Kens asks.

"I don't know yet. I really wanted to do that tour, but it's too late now. I feel like I'm wasting time sleeping when we can sleep on the train in the morning."

"True, but then you'll miss all the scenery. Which I know is something you enjoy," Kens says.

Well shit, she does have me there. I guess my bed will win for now, because I don't want to miss any stops on the way to Germany.

"You go ahead and sleep now. I'm going to shower, and then I'm going to crash," I say.

I grab all my things and head to the bathroom. I'm excited to try out this rain shower. I've never used one before, but I've heard they're amazing.

"Oh my, Kens, we need to get a rain shower at home,"

I scream out after standing under it for a few minutes. Oh crap; hopefully I didn't wake her up and scare her.

"I know. They are pretty amazing," she responds from inside the bathroom.

*When did she come in here?*

"What are you doing in here?" I ask.

"I had to pee, and I knew you were going to take forever."

"I'm usually an in-and-out girl."

"I know, but you've never had a rain shower. I knew you'd love it," Kens says.

"Get out of here and go to bed or you'll be crabby tomorrow and blame it on me keeping you up all night," I say.

"Night," she says.

"Night. Love you."

After she leaves the bathroom I rush through my shower so I can get some shut-eye. Tomorrow is going to be a new day with new adventures.

I'm so happy we decided to do this trip. I'm learning things about myself that I didn't know. There really is a part of me that craves a man who loves me and wants to be my partner in crime. I now understand why Kens has been so emotional about losing Everett. One day we'll both find the men of our dreams.

# Chapter 5

*Kenslie*

*Germany*

Tiptoeing into the bathroom, I shut the door gently behind me, before turning on the water, letting it heat up. Knowing Anna, she most likely stayed up late, and I can't blame her. This whole trip has been surreal. I close my eyes, trying to burn the memories of the first day in my mind. All the places we visited, the people we saw, the smell of fresh-baked pastries. This is truly the trip of a lifetime.

Today we are off to Germany! That is if we can get our butts moving. I slip off my pajamas and step into the hot shower, letting the water wash over my tired muscles. Standing on my feet for ten hours a day at the hospital is one thing but being cramped on an airplane just to take another trip on a train is a different story. *They* say traveling is tiring, and the jet lag hasn't even set in.

I squeeze the hotel shampoo in my hand and start cleaning my hair. Suddenly, from out of nowhere, the image of Everett's face fills my mind, our last words to each other replaying over and over.

I'm here on this most amazingly beautiful trip with my

best friend in the whole world, but the reality of life hits me. I no longer have someone who cares for me waiting at home. *Shit.* I don't even have a home. Connecticut is going to be my new home, and it might as well be a foreign country. And unlike here, I won't have Anna to lean on.

I shake the thoughts from my head before the tears have a chance to prick at my eyes, and hurry with my routine. We don't have any time to waste. We'd planned on doing most of our sleeping on the train rides, but last night was a delightful exception, and now I can enjoy the scenery on the ride. I can hardly contain my excitement.

Stepping out of the shower, I wrap myself in a lush towel before I pick up my cellphone. I know there won't be a message or missed call waiting for me, but I look nonetheless, and my heart flutters with the spark of hope that I might be wrong. But I'm not wrong. Nothing. The heavy release of air deflates my body, and I continue to rush through the rest of my morning routine. I slap on a hint of makeup after brushing my teeth. From the clock on my cellphone I see it's only taken me about twenty minutes to get ready. I grab my tote and head out of the bathroom to find Anna rustling around in the small room.

"Good morning, sunshine!" I say with a chipper tone. "It's Germany day!"

"Yes, it is!" Anna replies, more awake than I expected.

"We need to leave here in the next forty minutes. Will that give you enough time?" I ask. "Sorry I didn't wake you sooner."

"No, that's fine. I showered last night. Just let me change and get cleaned up and I'll be ready to go."

"Great. I'll call the lobby and have them get us a cab to the train station."

\* \* \* \*

"Wanna talk about it?"

"Huh?" I ask, pulling my gaze away from the window.

We'd quietly settled into our seats a couple of hours ago. The little sleep last night and the fact that our eight AM train time would be eleven PM yesterday, our time, was starting to take its toll. The cool glass of the window was soothing, just as the soft gray sky opened to the day, and here I was, stuck in my own head. I'm like a child watching her parents' fight—my heart and head still can't figure out where it all went downhill with Everett. Or if there even was a downhill. It was more like a cliff we didn't see coming.

"Don't *huh* me. Have you heard from him?" Anna asks with a gentle concern.

"Nope. You'd know if I had," I say, trying not to snap the words at her.

"Well, it's only been a few days. He'll realize what a stupid mistake he's made soon enough."

It's all I can do to smile at Anna. She's so strong and supportive, but she hasn't had many strong relationships. I don't know if that makes her more or less jaded, but unfortunately, I don't think she's right this time.

"So, what's the first thing you wanna do in Germany?" Anna asks, changing the subject, and I love her for it.

"Since you won't let us go to the zoo, we have to go to Handwerkerhof. You'll love it! It's craftsman buildings and cobbled streets. Ye Olde Time Germany." I giggle. "It's the perfect place to get souvenirs. And I know they'll have huge beers and great food."

"What! You're such a foodie. We're both going to leave this trip fat!" Anna protests.

"No, we won't. All the walking we're doing will counteract all the food. Just wait and see."

"Fine, but then we're going to the Chain Bridge," Anna demands.

"Sure, that *doesn't* sound scary," I tease.

"It's the oldest chain bridge in the European continent. It was built in 1824!"

*Oh, Anna.* She loves her work, and she's going to be an amazing architect one day, I just know it.

"That sure restores my faith." I playfully roll my eyes.

"You're going to love it. Besides, it's not that high above the water, so if it breaks, you won't die."

I gasp, and it's her turn to laugh at me.

I pause as a voice from overhead starts speaking German. Luckily, the words repeat in a few languages before coming over in English.

"Next stop Frankfurt. All transfers please exit on the right side."

"That's us, girly." Anna smiles.

I stretch my arms overhead. The four-hour train ride wasn't as bad as I expected. The chairs for the economy seating were very nice, and since we had no one sitting by us we were able to spread out.

We each grab our bags, following the slow pace of other travelers off the train.

"I gotta pee." I giggle as we make our way to the train flat.

"Why didn't you go when we were on the train?"

"I didn't have to then." I shrug.

"What? Are you four years old?" Anna teases me.

I look around, and it takes no time at all to recognize the universal sign for bathroom.

"I'll be right back."

"Want me to go with you?" she asks.

"No. I'm good. Just don't get kidnapped."

"Yeah, yeah." Anna shakes her head. "I'm not waiting for you though. If you miss the train, just meet me in London." She laughs.

That girl loves her schedules and being on time and having a plan. That's why I put her in charge of the itinerary. Researching this trip was more work than finals, but we're here now and it was all worth it.

I rush to the bathroom, making it back to Anna in record time.

"Miss me?" I say, bumping my body playfully into Anna's. She flinches and jumps back.

"What the hell! You scared the crap out of me!"

"I'm sorry," I apologize between my laughs.

"I'm serious!"

"Hey, did something happen while I was gone?" I ask.

"No, not really. There's some guy who keeps looking at me. It's not a big deal, it's just that we're in a foreign country, and I don't need any weird drama."

I nod, agreeing with her. There are TV shows and murder files about young women traveling who meet the wrong guy and it's all downhill from there.

"Which guy is it?" I ask out of curiosity.

I should probably know what he looks like to keep an eye on him too, just in case.

"Right over there. The guy with the manbun." Anna gives a discreet head tilt.

I stretch my arms over my head, trying to draw the least amount of attention to myself as I get a sly eyeful of the man. "Damn. He's good-looking."

"Kens!" Anna scolds.

I giggle. She hasn't had a serious boyfriend in I don't know how long, and I like to razz her about guys every now and then. I think it keeps her on her toes. And what kind of friend would I be if I didn't give her hell?

"Come on, Anna. I'll protect you. And it looks like our train is boarding."

\* \* \* \*

The gray sky overhead, and the soft whooshing of the water underneath us is soothing. The Chain Bridge, while intimidating, is beautiful. I didn't trust it at first, but it appeared to be well maintained over the past, almost, two hundred years. I'm glad Anna insisted on us visiting it. But it's moments like this, quiet moments, where my head and my heart battle over Everett, and my future. I feel so lost and unlike myself.

"Hey. When we're done here can we walk over to St.

Lorenz?" I ask. "It's this really cool medieval church."

"Yes. of course. Churches have some of the most beautifully detailed structures." Anna agrees easily. She'd never pass up an opportunity to admire architecture.

"Great. I mapped it, and it's only about a ten-minute walk from here."

"Perfect. Lead the way."

As we make our way through the neighborhood streets of Nuremberg, Germany, it's almost funny how much it reminds me of home. Little row houses, kids playing. This isn't the tourist spot, this is just Germany. It's their *home*. A pang in my chest reminds me of my lack of *home*. One day though, one day I will have this. I'm done with the self-pity; it's unbecoming.

"Oh my," I gasp. The church steeples are perfectly etched with almost gothic details. Brick by brick all the way up to the green mast. It's one of the most beautiful places I've ever seen. It just might make me cry.

"It's beautiful," Anna manages after moments of silence.

"Let's go inside." My words are hushed by my amazement.

"Totally," Anna replies, leading the way.

As we make our way into the church my breath is taken

away by the great hall entryway. I look up the tall walls, and the light shines through the many stained-glass windows. I notice Anna out of the corner of my eye, inspecting every inch of the structure, enjoying herself, of course.

I see the church pews, and I wonder if they still hold service here. It's been years since I've been to a proper service. I wouldn't say I'm exactly religious, but many of us who work in a hospital have a belief that traditional medicine can only take a person so far before divinity steps in, for better or worse. And I've seen my fair share of miracles.

I wander down the aisle a few steps before taking a seat in the solid mahogany pew, captivated by the glorious sight of the altar. And for a minute I wonder if the powers that be have brought me here. I'm lost and confused. This trip is the last piece of my old life. We've been planning this trip for years, and once it's done I have to leave Anna, our home, and I've already managed to leave Everett.

*Dear God, a sign would be nice. Just something little to let me know I'm moving in the right direction. In the name of Jesus, Amen.*

I reach my hand around and squeeze the back of my neck, working out some of the tension. Then a burst of giggles echoes through the building, and I turn, looking back to see a little girl running around, being chased by her mother. The girl is all smiles and laughter. And there is my sign. I'm overthinking this. I'm not living in the moment that I've planned and waited for. I'm done moping on this trip. I'm going to have a kick-ass time, starting right now!

With my new determination I get up, ready to find Anna and see what else we can pack into our limited time here. Maybe even something fun, like a club?

* * * *

I check my phone again. Five PM, that's eight AM home time. Which means we went to bed at two PM home time. *Ugh.* My head hurts, the full effect of jet lag has set in. I know where I am, barely, but I have no clue *when* I am. The exhaustion is real. With our second full day of Germany quickly closing behind us, I'm ready for Prague, and a nap.

I lean my head against the glass window and look across at Anna. Her arms are wrapped around her bag on her lap, her head tilted back on the head rest, her eyes closed. She has the right idea. I give the train platform one last look. People are scurrying around, trying to find their trains. But there is something odd. There's a man standing still, just staring at me. I blink again, and once again. I must be dreaming.

"What the fuck?" I say, the words a whisper, before

panic sets in. I'm hallucinating! "Anna! Anna, wake up!" I shriek.

"What?" She bolts upright in her chair. "Are you okay?"

"I'm... I'm...not sure," I say, trying to find my words. "Look at that man standing outside the window. Tell me, does he looks familiar?"

"Oh no. It better not be that guy from the other day," Anna says sternly, and then goes silent.

"Say something," I beg.

I can only watch Anna. I can't bring myself to look back out the window again. If it's him, I'm going to be crushed, and if it's not...I'm going to be crushed. It can't be him. He won't move across the states with me, he sure as hell wouldn't travel to Europe to try and track me down. Would he?

"Anna!" I demand.

"If that isn't Everett, he has a twin brother that he's never mentioned." Anna shakes her head, the disbelief written across her face.

I let out a hard sigh as my mind tries to wrap around the fact that Everett is *here*. I want to consider not talking to him, to continue the trip as planned, but I can't. He's come too far.

"I have to go talk to him," I say, abruptly getting up from my seat and making my way down the aisle.

"Don't! Kens!" Anna hollers after me. "The train..."

I can no longer hear her words, just a throbbing in my ears of the blood rushing through my veins. I must have answers, nothing else matters. I fling my bag over my shoulder as I hop down the train steps, walking with determination toward Everett.

He's wearing jeans, his broad shoulders covered in a fitted black t-shirt, looking like the day I left him. But with each step closer I notice little things out of place. The five o'clock shadow, while it suits him, has never been his style, and the faint circles around his eyes are also a new addition. His mouth sits in a flat line. I stop a couple of feet in front of him, just looking at him. I open my mouth to say something, only to close it again. I rub my hands over my face. I don't even know where to begin.

"That was a dumb move." Everett's deep, familiar voice is soothing, but it takes a minute for me to register what he said.

"What exactly was dumb? Because if you came all the way out here to fight with me, you've wasted your time," I counter, my hand on my hip.

"To be clear, the dumb move I was talking about was

getting off your train."

Shit! The train! Anna! I turn just in time to see Anna frantically waving at me from her window seat. She's holding something up to the window. I squint my eyes only to realize that she's holding my cellphone. I left my phone on that damn table.

"Fuck!"

# Chapter 6

## *Annaliesa*

*Prague*

"You've got to be kidding me. She really got off the train for that asshole," I mutter under my breath. "I can't believe she'd do this to me. No, to us."

I don't believe Everett came all this way to...what? Get Kens back? Or ruin something that meant the world to me? I understand he wants to do something with Kens, but this was supposed to be our thing. How could she let him ruin this? If he really wanted to talk to her, wouldn't he have gotten on the train?

What am I supposed to do now? We were going to sleep on the train so we could enjoy all the sites tomorrow. There is no way I'll be able to sleep now while I'm alone on a train in a foreign country.

"Is everything okay?" some guy asks me.

"No," I say before even thinking.

Why am I telling some guy this?

I raise my eyes and look into the stalker's face. But holy shit does he have the most mesmerizing green eyes ever. He also has a deep, sexy voice. It isn't as sexy as a

European accent, but it's close. I can't quite place his American accent, but it sounds like he's from the Midwest.

"I just saw your friend get off the train. What was she thinking?"

"That's the problem, she wasn't. She saw her ex-boyfriend and jumped off to go talk to him. I haven't a clue why, because if he wanted to talk, he should have gotten on the train himself."

I can't believe I spewed all that. I need to learn to have a filter. I don't know this guy, yet I'm telling him the story. The next thing I know he's going to kidnap me and they'll never find my body.

"Does she have any way to contact you, or do you guys have a plan in place to find each other if you get separated?"

"Why are you asking me these questions? You're freaking me out. First you stalk me at the train station in Germany, and now you're here asking me all these questions."

"Whoa. Hold up. I wasn't stalking you anywhere. I may have been at the Germany train station at the same time, and I remember seeing you, but stalking? No. I'm only trying to help you so you aren't alone in an unknown place. Sorry for freaking you out. I'll leave you to it," he says and walks away to find a seat.

What did I just do? Why do I always have to think bad about everyone? Oh, that's right, the fucking media has everyone scared of their own shadows half the time. I need to go apologize, but I don't know if I can risk being nice right now.

I put Kens's phone in my backpack, so I don't lose it, and head to the back of the train, hoping to find a big enough space so I can try to get some rest before arriving in Prague and starting my venture to find Kens. Though I'll be there before her. The first thing I need to do is find out when the next train will be arriving.

"Excuse me, ma'am," I say, walking up to a nice-looking lady who reminds me of my grandma.

"Yes," she responds.

"Do you know when the next train leaves the station to go to Prague?"

"This is the last train until 5:49 tomorrow morning."

"Thank you for your time."

"You're welcome."

Well, that just sucks. I'm going to be stuck in Prague for several hours waiting on her. I definitely need to get some shut-eye now, because I won't be getting any when I get to Prague.

It seems everyone else has the same idea of sleeping on

the train. I do manage to find an open seat, but it's next to the green-eyed, gorgeous man, and I don't know if I can risk sitting next to him. Something about him has me spewing whatever I think.

"Sit, I won't bite," he says as I walk by him again in hopes of finding a place to sit.

"I don't want to interrupt your peace."

"You're annoying other people by walking up and down the aisle, looking for a spot."

"That wasn't my intention. I just wanted to find a spot big enough so I could try to sleep," I say as I sit down, but as I scoot around him to get to the seat by the window my bag knocks him in the head.

"Fuck, what's in that bag?"

"Oh shit, I'm sorry," I say. Crap, I should've taken my backpack off before trying to sit. "Are you okay?"

"I'll be fine, but I may have a broken nose and a couple of black eyes," he mumbles through his hands. "I hope you like raccoons."

"What?" I ask, confused about why he's talking about raccoons. "You're not okay. Maybe you have a concussion. You need to go to the hospital. You're bleeding," I say, trying to get out of my seat to stop the train.

"Sit down. I don't have a broken nose or a concussion,

and if I did, they wouldn't stop the train. They can't. But I may have two black eyes tomorrow."

Duh. That's why he was asking me about the raccoons. I don't believe I didn't catch that at first. Normally, I'm not that slow, but I was too preoccupied with the thought of him needing medical care. Plus, the stress of being split from Kens isn't helping.

What a craptastic day this has turned into.

"Are you sure your nose isn't broken? It's bleeding," I say again.

"It's fine." He pulls a shirt out of his bag and wipes his nose. "It was an accident, unless you're just trying to show me you can defend yourself," he says with a laugh, showing me his shirt to prove he wasn't bleeding that bad. "Really, I'm good. Sit down and relax. Maybe I can help you come up with a plan to find your friend."

I really shouldn't get close to him, but he seems nice, and I could use some support right now. Maybe he can calm me down a little, so I don't feel like murdering Everett the next time I see him.

Sitting down, I set my backpack under my seat and take a couple of calming breaths. "Thank you," I say, even though I'm not really sure why. "Before you ask, I don't know what I'm thanking you for."

"You're welcome. Maybe it's my good looks," he smirks at me.

"Har har har. There are a lot of good-looking men on this train, and I'm not sitting next to them thanking them."

"Fine, it's because I'm the only one who'd let you sit with me. Or maybe it's because I offered to keep you company while you're separated from your friend. The one who should never have gotten off the train like that. Or could it be that you want to have a whirlwind romance in Europe?"

"I happen to agree with you about my friend. She tends to do some crazy things when it involves her ex, Everett. I guess that's what happens when you're in love," I respond to that part of his questions.

He gets a look in his eyes like he knows what I'm talking about, but it's gone before I can tell for sure.

"I've heard love can make people do some stupid shit," he says.

"Sounds like you have some experience there?"

"Not personally, but I've seen my cousin do some pretty crazy things for love. When I say crazy, I mean over the top. He recently split with his girl, and he's determined to win her back. He'll be lucky if he can actually win her back and not scare her away."

"What is it with men doing crazy shit? Why can't they just leave well enough alone and move along? Men are so infuriating. Grrrrr."

"Did you really just growl?" he asks with a grin.

"Yes, just thinking about Everett and the shit he pulled makes me want to go postal on his ass. He knew this was our goodbye girls' vacation that we've been planning for years. He couldn't get Kens to let him come along, so he made her feel guilty and they broke up. Then he shows up to ruin our trip. Oh look—he got his way, and now I'm stuck in Europe without my best friend."

I can't believe I just spewed all that to a stranger, but it felt nice to get it off my chest. I don't want to harbor bad feelings toward Everett just in case things work out between him and Kens.

"Please say how you truly feel about men," he says.

God, is he offended I lumped him into that category?

"Sorry if I offended you. I wasn't talking about you. I don't know anything about you, and here I am telling you all this stuff, and you could be plotting my murder, and now I wouldn't blame you."

I need to go to the restroom before I let him see my tears. I'm having a hard time staying in control of my emotions. I'm one of those weird people who cry when I'm sad, angry, or upset.

"I'll be back," I say, getting up and walking away.

What the hell am I going to do? I don't know what to do. I never really thought I'd get separated from Kens. I jinxed us by saying I'd leave her if she wasn't out of the bathroom in time.

I hurry up and use the restroom and head back to my seat. I don't want to be rude and end up passing up the generosity of this man. If he's willing to help, I should let him. Maybe then I won't be a target for other men to hit on me.

Sitting down, I start speaking so he doesn't have a chance to say anything. "Hey, I'm really sorry about earlier and the way I've been acting. I'm not normally a bitch, but I'm scared and alone. I don't know when I'll be able to meet back up with my friend, and you hear horror stories about women being kidnapped and sold into slavery. I don't think you'd do that, so I'm going to try and get to know you on this train ride and hope we can form a connection," I say, taking a deep breath. "My name is Annaliesa, but my friends call me Anna."

"It's a pleasure to meet you, Annaliesa. I'm Ryker," he says. "And to respond to your rant before you told me your beautiful name, I can't even begin to imagine what you're going through. I wouldn't want to be in an unknown country alone."

"But you are alone, or at least I thought you were since the seat next to you was open. Oh my God, are you here with someone? Is your girlfriend going to get pissed you're talking to me?" I'm freaking out now that I'm going to be left alone again.

"Calm down. I'm here alone. But I'm not in an unknown country. My parents and I have been touring Europe for years. We usually pick one place in Europe to stay at a time, but since this is most likely my last trip for a while, I decided I'd tour all my favorites."

"Why exactly is this going to be your last time for a while? Getting hitched and the wife won't let you off the leash?" Ouch, that's harsh of me. I don't know where this bitchy side is coming from. "I'm so sorry. Do not answer that. I don't have a clue what's going on with my brain-to-mouth function." I'm embarrassed that I'm coming off as a bitch.

"For the record, I'm not getting married, nor do I have a girlfriend, and I'd never let my wife or girlfriend dictate to me what I'm allowed and not allowed to do. I finally got my dream job, and I know that I'll have to work hard to get to the top of my field. I want to prove that I'm willing to work for it and that I deserve it."

"Again, sorry. I know I've been saying that a lot. Now I need to put it into action so you actually believe me," I say, praying that I can lose the stick that somehow got lodged in my ass. "So, can I ask you what your dream job is?"

"I graduated from the University of California, Berkeley, and finished my internship to be an architect. The tests about kicked my butt, but I passed, so now I get to work my dream job."

"No way! You're joking. Where are the cameras? Did Kens really get off the train? Is she punk'ing me?" I ask all the questions so fast, frantically looking around.

"Umm, I'm pretty sure that you're not being punk'd. Why would you think that?"

"I must be imagining you then. I'm not lucky enough to be stuck in a foreign country with a man who has the same passion as me. I just got my dream internship for architecture. I ended up getting my BA in three years instead of five. Plus, I have two years of my internship under my belt. Just one more year and I'll be able to take the exam and get my license. I love designing buildings. Though some things can be tedious, and I feel like they should leave those tasks to the minions."

"Wow! I'm impressed. Not many people can get their

BA in three years. How did you do that?"

"My high school offered an associate degree program along with your diploma, and I really wanted to be an architect but didn't want to wait eight long years after graduating high school to make my dream come true. Figured if I could get two years done while in high school I could possibly have my dream career in five to six years after graduating high school." Who really wants to spend five years getting your bachelor's degree and then three years working before they can start their career? Not me.

"This is kind of like a dream come true. When I planned this trip, I didn't expect to meet a woman, let alone one with the same interests. Though I'm now intimidated that I'm with a Miss Smarty Pants. So, what were you planning to do on this trip?" he asks.

"Well, I have a whole list of all the amazing buildings I want to see, but I had to scratch some off the list because I didn't want to bore Kens. She's a nurse and doesn't always appreciate a building like me. I'll be drooling and talking nonstop about one, and her eyes will be glazed over." I laugh.

"Sounds like some of my friends. You have to go see the Dancing House while you're in Prague."

"Yes, that's the main one on my list for Prague. I love

that there is so much uniqueness to the Dancing house. The house was meant to look like two people dancing around each other. The 'dancing' shape is supported by ninety-nine asymmetrical shaped panels of concrete. Did you know that there's a large, twisted, metal sculpture on the top of the building that is nicknamed *Medusa*?"

"Now that's my kind of talking there," he replies breathlessly.

"And you're becoming more my type of guy," I say before I can think.

"Then we should make the most of this stop while we wait for your friend. If I remember correctly, this is the last train until morning, and that puts her here around ten-ish if she leaves on that first train."

"You'd be correct. We could probably go to the Dancing House and be back at the train station before she even arrives," I say with a squeal.

Oh my God, this is a dream come true. One where I get to experience this magnificent building with someone who actually understands my need to know everything about a building.

"Maybe, but I'm not positive. I'd hate for you to miss her," he responds.

"We can do it. It's not like we know for sure she'll be

on the next train. What if it's full or she falls asleep and doesn't make it? I will be here, but I just hope she is too."

I can't believe this is happening, but I'm happy I have Ryker here to spend time with.

"Since we have a plan for when we arrive in Prague, would you mind if I get some shut-eye?" I ask. "I didn't sleep much last night, because I planned to sleep on the train today."

"Sleep, beautiful," he says.

While he takes out his phone and headphones I drift off to dreamland.

\* \* \* \*

"Holy shit, will I ever get used to how beautiful it is over here?" I ask Ryker. I hurry to grab all my stuff so I can get up and stretch. Sitting cramped on a train isn't the most comfortable way to sleep.

"No, because once you start to you're leaving the beauty behind. Then you go back home and forget how amazing the rest of the world is because you get caught up in everyday life."

"You're right. Plus, at home we don't stop to smell the roses and enjoy what we have. We are always go, go, go. We all need to learn to enjoy what we have and learn to take better care of it."

"I agree. Everyone is more worried about themselves and how they can make more money and have more things."

"Enough about the depressing stuff. Let's grab some food and head toward the Dancing House," I suggest. I didn't come here to get into all the issues of the world. I came to take a break and enjoy the beauty that is Europe.

"Sounds good. But I need coffee more than food. Do you have any preferences?"

"I'm pretty easy. Just feed me," I say with a smile.

It feels so nice to not have to worry about things. But I need to not just rely on Ryker to make all the plans for me. I need to step up and think on my own.

We end up eating at a hole-in-the-wall café with the most delicious pastries. I don't think I've ever tasted anything that literally melted in my mouth and made me salivate for more. Now this is something I'd give up sex for. I never understood that saying until I ate this chocolate éclair. Though it's not like I've been having sex anyway, so it's not that much of a loss.

"Can we just stay here all day? I don't want to be without these éclairs. How have I lived twenty-two years without them?" I moan as I take another bite.

"No, we aren't staying here all day. You'd be sad to miss out on the Dancing House. Plus, you can get an éclair anywhere."

"Yes, but not these ones. These are the best I've ever had. No one can beat them. Maybe I can buy stock in this business and they'll send them to me in the US."

"It can't be that good. I'm sure you can find someone in the US close to where you live that makes them," he says.

"You must try this and see for yourself," I say, holding the dessert up to his mouth. "Take a bite," I taunt him.

"If you insist." He takes a gigantic bite. I know the moment he knows I'm right, because he can't suppress the small moan that escapes.

"Told you these are the best. How many years have you gone without these in your life?"

"Twenty-five."

"Wow, you're an old man." I laugh. "Now back to these delicious éclairs, I'd even venture to say they're better than sex." I grin at him.

What the hell am I doing? Am I really flirting with him? Yes, because I haven't been able to get those green eyes out of my mind. I dreamed of them and everything he could do to me when I fell asleep on the train.

"I wouldn't go that far, but they're good."

"We'll just have to agree to disagree on this topic."

"Oh, we will," he says, and then I swear I hear him say,

"But I'll show you I'm right."

"Let's head over to the Dancing House and take a quick tour. Then we need to hurry back to the train station, so I can meet up with my friend and you can get back to your trip without babysitting me."

"I'm actually enjoying my time with you. It's not every day I get to show a beautiful lady around Europe."

"To be honest, I'm enjoying my time with you too. It's nice to have someone to talk to and enjoy the scenery with. Even though this was supposed to be a girls' trip."

We pay for our food and leave the small café.

"Do you know how to get there?" I ask.

"Yes, follow me," he replies. "Do you mind walking, or would you like to grab a cab?"

"We can walk. I don't mind a little exercise. I've been neglecting running since we've been on vacation, and I miss it."

"It'll be a little bit of a walk, but we should be able to see some other historic sites."

The first building that drew my attention was the National Museum. "This building has been through some extensive repairs. I really wish it was open for us to tour."

"How about when you meet up with Kens later I'll bring you both here to tour it. It should be open then."

"I'd really like that, but I don't want to keep you from doing what you want, and I don't know if Kens will want to come to this museum when there are other sites we have planned to visit. Being the planner that I am, I have our days all mapped out, so we can both do stuff we want."

"Sounds like you need to learn to live a little. Don't map everything out. Have you ever heard the saying 'fly by the seat of your pants'? You should really try it every now and then. Especially while on vacation."

"This is an issue I have. I have to be fifteen to thirty minutes early to everything or I'm late. I can't stand it when people get to their appointments right on time, because it makes everyone one else run late. I'm working on learning to be more flexible."

"Over there is the New Town Hall," Ryker points out as we get close to it.

"I read about this building and the Gothic tower that is seventy meters high. I'd love to see the view of the Karlovo Square from up top. Though I hear you need to get tickets online to ensure you can take the tour."

"That isn't necessarily true. I think it's more for people like you, who want to keep a schedule. I'm sure if you wanted to do it when it opened you'd be able to."

This is why being such a planner is a pain in the ass.

I'm sure I miss a lot of things I'd love to do because I don't *fly by the seat of my pants* as Ryker said. I really need to learn to let up on the reins a little.

"Well, maybe you'll rub off on me a little, and I won't be such a stickler for time while on this trip," I say.

"I'd rub myself on you all right," he says.

Oh my God. Did he really just go there?

"I guess I set myself up for that one."

"Sorry, I couldn't help myself. I'll help you loosen up a bit on this trip, but it won't be much if we only have hours," he says. "Oh, and look where we are now."

"Holy shit." My mouth drops open.

"You better close your mouth before you drool all over yourself," he says between laughing at me.

"Oh, shut it. This is amazing," I say in awe. "I would have loved to spend time working on designing this building, watching it come to life. One day I'd love to have people coming to our country to see something I designed."

"Isn't that every architect's dream?"

"I would hope so, but like all things, some people are forced by their parents into a career field or they do it for the money. If everyone could work in a career they loved, the world would be a much happier place."

"Very true," he agrees. "Shall we go inside and see

what's open?"

"Yes," I scream in excitement. "Sorry, I didn't mean to be so loud."

"It's good. I love seeing your excitement for the architecture. It really does put into perspective that when you see things regularly they don't have the same impact as when you first see something. This building still is amazing for me to see, but seeing it through your eyes makes it even better."

"Wow. I'm happy I can make you see this hotel in a new light. I don't think I could ever get bored of this place. I'm sure there's always something new we could find in here. It would take us months to explore every room. I'm sure a lot of them are similar, but it would be amazing to tour the whole building."

"Well, I can't promise that, but I can promise to show you all I can." Grabbing my hand, he pulls me inside.

I'm in heaven. I have to pinch myself to make sure this isn't a dream. I can't believe my lifelong goal of coming to Europe has actually come true. And getting to see some amazing structures built by some of the greatest architects makes it even better.

While I miss Kens, I can't say I'm sad I'm experiencing this with Ryker. He's just as into it as I am.

Though his excitement isn't as great, but this isn't his first time. He also understands what I'm saying and my love for everything architecture.

"Let's see if we can go out on the balcony I saw when we were entering the building. I don't remember how far up it is, but I'd love to see what the view looks like."

"Let's go. I'm not sure if we'll be able to get up there, but let's try," he says, grabbing my hand and pulling me through the lobby.

* * * *

While I didn't get to see every thing I wanted, we did see a lot. I'm sad that we have to leave now, but we're already running late for the train station. Something I should be freaking out over, but I can't, because I wouldn't trade this experience for anything—even being on time. Maybe it was meant to be that Kens got off the train. Was it fate?

"Thank you so much for letting me experience this with you, Ryker. I don't think it would've been the same without you."

I really think he added to the experience. He knew things I didn't, and he shared in the excitement with me. I could get use to this.

"You're welcome. As I said earlier, it was like seeing it for the first time again. I want to kidnap you and take you around to other sites, so I can experience them again for the first time."

Be still my beating heart. Does this mean he wants to be around me more?

"Maybe we can arrange for that. But you may have to fight Kens for my time. Though I'm sure she's going to be tied up with Everett when we meet back up." I should be sad about this, but if I have Ryker, it won't be so bad. I wouldn't be the third wheel. Also, we'll have to see if he really means it or not.

We walk up to the train stop fifteen minutes late, and there aren't many people walking around inside. If Kens was on that train, she should have waited inside for me. Or would she have left to look for me? This is a clusterfuck. This isn't good, because I can't contact her, and I haven't a clue where she'd go first.

"I don't see her," I mumble.

"Hey, it's going to be okay. I'll stay with you as long as you want. I will get you connected with her. Do you know her phone number?"

"I have it programmed into my cellphone, but she left hers on the train when she got off. So, that really is a moot point." Silly for him to ask this now when he should have mentioned it on the train.

"Do you have her ex's phone number?"

Shit, why didn't I think of that? "Yes." I pull my phone out to call him. "I hope he got the international plan," I say to Ryker as I scroll through my contacts to Everett's info and press *send.*

It rings once and sends me directly to voicemail. I bet he didn't think ahead to get the international plan.

"No luck here." Maybe he just has it off.

"Sorry, we can try again later," Ryker says, grabbing my hand and squeezing it.

"Thank you for suggesting I try his number. I didn't even think of that."

"No worries. Let's think. What is the one place she wanted to see really bad while here in Prague?" he asks.

"Church of Our Lady before Týn," I respond.

"Why don't we head there and see if that's where she went first?" he suggests.

"Okay. We should probably get a cab. That way we'll get there faster."

Once we secure a cab, we head to the church. As I get out of the vehicle, I pray that I find Kens here, but in my heart, I know she isn't going to be here. I don't know how I know it, but I do.

"I don't see her or Everett. I don't know what to do.

How long should I wait here? How many places do I search looking for her? I don't know," I say, holding back tears.

"Hey, it's going to be okay." Ryker pulls me into his arms. "I don't know the answer to those questions either. Why don't we just try to hit all the places you guys wanted to see and hope for the best. Maybe we'll run into them."

"Okay."

I can't let my disappointment ruin this trip for me. I want to continue enjoying things like I did this morning. I need to learn to let go and live a little. Kens would be so proud of me for actually enjoying myself and not making a schedule for the day.

Tomorrow is a new day, and I can only hope if I don't find her in Prague I can find her on the train to Bratislava or while we're there.

# Chapter 7

*Ryker*

*Prague*

Oh shit, I hope I didn't mess everything up by making Anna late to the train station. I know how she feels about being late. I really thought we'd have enough time. But I guess when you have two architect nerds looking at historic sites you tend to get lost in the beauty.

"Anna, I'm sorry again that we got here late," I say.

"It's not your fault. We both got caught up in the magnificent sites. While I'm bummed I missed her, I also wouldn't trade in my experiences thus far to have been here on time," she says and stops to look over at me. "And who's to say she even made the first train? What happens if she got distracted by Everett and is still back in Germany?" she asks.

"I wish I had an answer for you. Since I don't know how she'd react to the situation I can't answer you."

I can't believe Kenslie actually got off the train to go talk to her ex. Who leaves their best friend alone like that? I'm still unsure what to think of Kenslie. I want to not like her for ditching Annaliesa, but if she hadn't, I wouldn't have had the chance to talk to her. So, maybe I should be thanking Kenslie for this gift. Her loss, my gain.

Annaliesa isn't like anyone I've ever met. She's into the same things as me, and we both want to explore the architect here in Europe. My buddies always want to come and party and see how many girls they can hook-up with. I'm not into one-night stands. I know that's unmanly to say. I love sex just as much as any guy, but I like to have a relationship too. I like to know where I'm sticking my penis. I don't want to end up with an STD.

"What else did you guys have on your list for today?" I ask.

"Well, we had the zoo, the Lennon Wall, and Kenslie had a church or two she wanted to see."

"I can tell you now you'd have better luck finding a needle in a haystack than finding her at the zoo. So, I'd suggest we leave that one out and head to the Lennon Wall and the churches. Maybe even squeeze in some food," I reply.

"That sounds like a good plan, but where do we go first? Should we go back by the places I wanted to see in case that's where she goes looking for me?" she asks.

"Do you think that's where she'd go first? Or would she go where you both wanted to go?"

"Gah. I have no clue. While we made plans for if we got split up, we never really thought it would happen. If it wasn't for Everett, I'd still be with her." She sighs.

"Well, what's on your agenda for tonight and tomorrow?" I ask, hoping to come up with a plan to get them back together tomorrow if it doesn't happen tonight.

"We planned on spending the day in Prague then taking the train to Bratislava around seven tonight. Kens has a hotel room reserved in her name since we wanted to sleep in a bed because we slept on a train last night," she replies. "Oh crap. I just realized I don't have anywhere to sleep tonight. If we can't book a room, how do you feel about staying in a hostile?"

"Let's plan on being back to the train station tonight at six. If you can't find her here, we'll take the train to Bratislava and you can look for her at the hotel, assuming you have the name of a hotel she made reservations at."

"Shit!" she yells. "I can't believe this. I don't have the name of the hotel on my itinerary. It was Kenslie's turn to pick where we stayed, and she wanted to surprise me. I knew it was a bad idea for her not to tell me." She sighs. "This is the reason I'm so OCD about planning stuff. This is a clusterfuck."

I don't want to tell her to calm down and get her even

more pissed. I know that much from dealing with my sisters. But what can I do to help her relax a little?

"Hey, let's walk and look around for a place to eat and make a plan of action. Maybe mapping areas around the train station will help." Maybe if she plans it'll help her feel more in control of the situation.

"Sounds good. Do you have a place you like to eat when you come to Prague?" she asks.

"I know just the place. Is there anything you won't eat though?"

"I'm open to try anything once. Lead the way."

I love a woman who's open to trying new things. Maybe she'll be open to giving me a chance to wine and dine her while we're in Europe. There's something about her that makes me want to continue getting to know her.

# Chapter 8

*Everett*

*Germany to Prague*

*God damn it!* I scold myself. This wasn't how it was supposed to go. None of this was part of the plan. Life had hit a fork in the road, and at every turn I seemed to be on the wrong path. I need Kenslie, and all I wanted to do was show her that. Instead, I'm giving her more reasons to walk away.

Kens whips her head around, leveling her eyes at me, her face pale.

"My cellphone was on the train. I left my fucking cellphone!" she screams, throwing her arms up in the air.

Turning quickly on her heels, she heads over to the ticket booth, and I follow silently behind her. I've done enough to fuck things up; words are probably the last thing she needs from me. Not that I've ever been good with words. *Obviously.*

"English?" I hear her ask in a hopeful tone.

I post up against the counter next to her as the man behind it motions for a woman to come to his station.

"Yes, madam?" the woman asks.

"I just missed my train to Prague. When is the next

train? And do I have to buy a new ticket?"

"Yes, a new ticket. And the next train is at, uh, 5:49 AM, arriving in Prague at 9:50 AM."

"Shit." I hear her swear under her breath as she shakes her head. "Fine, I'll take one, please."

I clear my throat. "Make that two, please," I interrupt, pulling my credit card out of my wallet and slapping it down on the counter.

"What do you think you're doing?" she demands with a death stare.

"I might be the reason you got separated from Anna, but I'm sure as hell not letting you on that train by yourself. Once we find her, then maybe I'll let you go off on your own."

"*Might* be the reason! *Maybe* let me go off on my own?" she shouts, her words echoing through the train station.

*Damn it.* I rub my hands over my head and down, pinching the stress out of the back of my neck.

"The timing is bad, but I'm not sorry."

"You arrogant son of a bitch." She shakes her head at me before turning back to the woman at the counter.

"*Danke,*" Kenslie thanks the woman, snatching up the tickets before turning sharply.

I follow her in silence, sitting down next to her as she finds a seat on one of the hard, wooden benches. We sit in silence for several minutes before she pushes my ticket at me.

"You're picking now to be the strong, silent type? Typical," she says.

"I *am* the strong, silent type. Have you forgotten me already?"

"It's been a week. Have I forgotten you?" She shakes her head at me, her eyes welled with tears meeting mine. "How will I ever forget you? Especially now that you've ruined my trip with Anna. You know this is something we've been planning forever. One last hoorah before we go our separate ways now that college is over."

"I never meant to ruin your trip. You have to know that," I tell her earnestly.

I really didn't. But how could I not chase after the woman I love? In hindsight, maybe this wasn't the right way. But for some reason I pictured it going better, more romantic. Her running into my arms under a ridiculously romantic European tourist attraction. Not a dingy train station staring at her like a creep.

"Why are you here then?" she asks, her voice just a whisper.

"Because I love you."

"You love me enough to travel across the world, but not enough to come with me across the states. Makes perfect sense, Everett." She huffs. "Fuck it. I'm tired. I had a long, beautiful day in Germany. I was supposed to sleep on the train, with seats much more comfortable than this bench."

I press my lips together, contemplating telling her that I have a room in the neighboring hotel, but it might not be the best idea. But I sure as hell don't want to sleep in a train station, especially since I have a bed I already paid for.

"I…uh… I have a room next door. I wasn't planning on getting on the train until tomorrow. I was going to try and meet you in Paris."

Kens lets out a heavy sigh, and the smallest sensation of relief comes over me. She's considering my offer.

"It's only four and a half hours until I have to be back here to make the train," Kens tries to reason.

"Until *we* have to be back. But you'll be much more rested in a bed. And I promise to get you back in time. Don't overthink it, come on."

"Fine. Let's go," Kenslie says, standing up and grabbing her bag.

\* \* \* \*

It was less than ten minutes before Kenslie was

slipping into bed next to me, and nothing over the past week had made me feel more like the man I used to be. The only reason she was next to me was a combination of the lack of sleep, lack of sofa in the crappy room, and more importantly, the lack of a second bed. And thankfully, she hadn't insisted I sleep on the floor, which I wouldn't have agreed to anyway.

"Did you set the alarm?" Kenslie asks from her side of the bed, facing away from me.

"Yep, two on my cellphone and the room alarm clock."

"Thank you." Her voice was a whisper. "Good night, Everett," she says with a soft hiccup.

That sound made my heart ache in a place that it hadn't since the day she walked out on me. I imagine the pools of tears in her eyes, or maybe they were already running hot down her cheeks? I'd done all of this; I caused this.

Over the past week, I tried to figure out why I couldn't just agree to move with her, to let her pursue her dream job. It wasn't like uprooting my self-employment would have been an issue. But my ego told me that she would choose me over a job, and when that didn't happen I was too stubborn to go back on my word. And *that* was exactly what landed me in this situation.

My soft side isn't one that shows itself often. In fact,

Kenslie is the only woman who ever meant enough to me to see it. And now I'm about to press my luck. Scooting past the imaginary line that separates us in the bed, I pull Kenslie into my arms. Thankfully, she comes willingly, turning into my body. Tucking herself into the nook of my arms, she presses her face against my chest as tiny sobs shake her body. I run my hands down her back, trying to soothe her hurt.

"I love you, Everett," she says, not looking up at me. "I want to be angry with you, for so many things. But I can't. And I hate myself for being happy to see you. This was supposed to be about me and Anna, and the whole time all I've thought about is you."

It's my turn to be taken aback with emotion. Kenslie and I have never been the break-up to make-up couple. I have no clue what I'm doing.

"I'm sorry, babe. I wasn't thinking straight. You chose your job over me, over us. And when I realized how dumb I had been, forcing you to choose, I had to see you. I had to tell you in person."

"What did you have to tell me in person?" She looks up at me with puffy eyes.

"I had to tell you how much I love you. How I always want to be with you, no matter where you go. That I will *never* again hold you back from your dreams. I have everything I want, but without you, none of it means anything. You are everything."

Leaning down, I press a kiss to her soft lips. "Let's get some sleep."

"That sounds good. Besides, I'm not the only one who has a big day tomorrow." Kenslie gives me a devious smile. "Anna just might rip your balls off. She's gonna be pissed."

*Shit.* If that isn't the truth, I don't know what is. Anna is going to be furious, probably for more than one reason. And I can't blame her. I give Kens an easy smile before pulling her closer to me as we drift off to sleep.

\* \* \* \*

"Not again! Not a-fucking-gain!"

The screeching words cut through my head, and I run my hand over my face, trying to figure out where exactly I am and what the hell is going on. *Shit!* I bolt up out of bed. I'm in Germany with an extremely angry Kenslie pacing the shitty motel room. I reach for my cellphone and see that it's just after 8 AM. *Fuck.*

"You did this on purpose, didn't you? Why, Everett? Why?"

I open my mouth to tell her it was an accident, that we *both* slept through the alarms, but I decide to keep my mouth shut. Telling her that she's wrong is not going to help anything.

"You know, when I left the first time there were things I wanted to say. Angry words on the tip of my tongue that I didn't want to regret saying, but now I can't think of a better time."

*This ought to be good.* I think. At my much slower pace, I find my jeans and pull them on.

"You're a selfish man. You're a taker. I've given you years of my life. And I've asked you for so little. I've never pushed the idea of marriage, although after two years together it's something people at least talk about. I supported you when you started your business, but now that I have a career to pursue you can't find it in you to support me. And now—not once, but twice—you've taken this trip away from me."

The feeling of my jaw hanging open startles me, and I try to quickly recover.

"Why are you just bringing this up now? Why didn't you say it when you left?" I ask bitterly.

Has she always felt this way, or is it a combination of exhaustion and me fucking up again that's causing her to say this? I need to know. I couldn't have been selfish all this time? We are in love, she's the only one, she knew that. She must have seen it. *Sure, asshole.* I clench my jaw. I sure showed her, proved my feelings, right, that's why she left.

"Because I love you…I loved you…" She pauses, and that last statement feels like a punch to the stomach. "I wasn't about to taint all the beautiful things we had in our relationship. It was ending, and I was going to make damn sure it was ending on a high note. I thought that much of you. I thought that we deserved that much. But now. Now I don't even…I can't even…"

In one swoop, she picks up her bag and storms out of the room, and I need a wall to punch.

# Chapter 9

*Kenslie*

*Prague*

I curl up on the shitty coach seat of the 8:40 AM train to Prague. It was sheer luck that the woman working last night was also on duty today and gave me a discount on my ticket, seeing as I have purchased three of them. Third time's the charm, I tell myself, angry that I have to see the bright side.

This is all Everett's fault. That man makes me crazy. I wrap my arms around my legs and rest my head on my knees as the unkind words replay in my head. I hate myself for each word, but if Anna was here I know she'd ask me: Were your words truthful? Did they serve a purpose? Can you take them back now?

I sigh inwardly. They were mostly true, part of their purpose was to hurt Everett, and I can't take them back now. And frankly, I don't want to. It's not my style to be mean and hurtful, but looking back, he needed to hear how I was feeling in that moment...unfiltered. Maybe it was his turn to feel bad. God knows I've been hurting for weeks.

I love that brute of a man, but I wish he was less of a

brute and more of a gentle giant. I do recall him saying something about meeting me in Prague for a romantic moment. He confessed he loves me and wants to be together, but I'm not sure that's enough anymore.

*Oh, Anna, where are you?* I need her for so many reasons right now, and as selfish as I've been, I've really started to wonder if she's okay. A lone woman in a foreign country—if that's not a movie of the week, I don't know what is. I hope to hell she's waiting for me at the train station. That makes the most sense. That's what I would do. But then again, I did miss the last train. Would she just wait for me there? And for how long?

I drop my legs down, settling in my chair as I feel the pull of the train begin. I don't know what in the hell I'm going to do if she isn't at the station. And then a reassuring thought hits me: Anna's need for over preparation. I dig through my bag, searching for our itinerary, thanking God that I wasn't dumb enough to leave my bag on the train along with my phone. This paper is gold. If she isn't at the station, this might help me find her.

"Okay, Anna. Where'd you go first?" I say, talking to myself.

"I'd scratch zoo off that list. It'd be more difficult finding her there than finding a four-leaf clover in the desert," a deep voice says next to me.

I shake my head, not having to look—I'd recognize that voice anywhere: Everett. I was too wrapped up in what I was doing to realize someone had sat next to me.

I clear my throat, working up the courage to look at him. His wide shoulders fill the tiny seat and stretch his basic t-shirt, showing off those massive muscles that my fingers still remember every detail of. I'm fighting a losing battle with myself. I'm so angry with him, but my body misses him, especially last night, those arms wrapped around me in familiarity.

Last night. Ugh. *That's right. Angry, Kens, remember!* I scold myself.

"Did you purposely make me miss the first train? And tell the truth. I can't be madder at you than I am right now."

"Isn't that the truth?" He snickers.

"Yeah. Lots of truths coming out lately, aren't there?" I spit out.

I watch as he opens his mouth just to close it. His face pales for a flash of a second, and knowing that he was hurt by my words, hurts me. I want to hug him and tell him I'm sorry, but I'm not. I might be sorry for hurting him, and maybe not saying it sooner, but nothing else.

"No, Kens. I might be selfish, but I'm not a bad guy. I

wouldn't do that. And you know that."

It's my turn to pale. The blood pumps hard through my body, and I feel like I'm going to be sick. Deciding I can't sit here any longer, I get up. I need a drink. Standing up abruptly, I push past him, not looking back as I head toward the bar car.

\* \* \* \*

"So, all American girls drink like you?" the bartender asks, his distinct German accent not so thick that I can't understand him.

And I'm thankful he understands my English enough to keep serving me.

"Maybe just the lost and heartbroken ones?" I muster up a half-smile.

"Heartbroken?" He tests the word.

I nod and place my hand over my heart and frown. His soft eyes meet mine, and he nods with understanding.

"And *heartbroken* what is name?"

"I'm Kenslie. You?"

"Elias." The slightly older man, with salt and pepper hair, places a hand on his chest.

It must be the alcohol, but he has almost an avuncular vibe. His English isn't great, but I find myself wondering how many languages he has to learn. At least a small amount of many in order to get by, I imagine.

"Kenslie, on me." He places an empty shot glass in front of me as he grabs a bottle from the back. "German schnapps heals all."

I hold up the shot glass, giving it a sniff. In the States, all I've ever had is peppermint schnapps, but this one smells fruity. I toss back the liquor in one swoop, unsure if that's the right etiquette, but I'm in need of a buzz. The sweet taste of pear on my tongue distracts from the liquor burning down my throat, but it's a nice interference either way.

"*Danka*," I reply, hearing the slur in my words.

I twist my half-liter of beer, letting the fuzzy thoughts fight in my head. I decide I'm going to put on a smile. I'm in Germany, or maybe in the Czech Republic in route to Prague by now? This is a trip of a lifetime! And one hell of a story to tell. Sure, it's not great in the moment, but once I find Anna, man, the people back home aren't even going to believe it! Yes, we are going out with a bang!

"Hey man, you got food back there?"

I roll my eyes as the formerly unoccupied chair next to me rustles around, and I know it's *him*.

"Yes, sir," the bartender replies.

From the corner of my eye I see the bartender slide a menu over to him.

"Bretzel and beer cheese, *danke*," Everett orders.

"Elias, can I have another schnapps, *bitte*?"

"I'll have one too, and one of those giant beers."
Everett points to my drink.

Elias eyes me, obviously picking up on the familiarity
between me and the man next to me. I return a soft smile
and place my hand over my heart, and he nods in
understanding. He brings out both drinks before turning
back to what I assume is the kitchen.

I let out a huff. I don't even know what to say. I don't
know how I'm feeling. Only moments ago, I'd decided to be
positive and enjoy this ride, and then Everett comes out of
nowhere. His mere presence scrambles my emotions, and
right now it'd be really nice to be in control of at least one
thing in my life. I bite down on my bottom lip, waiting for
him to say something, and when he doesn't I take a large
gulp of my beer.

"I've decided," Everett says, "when we get to Prague
and you meet up with Anna, I'll go home. Back to *my*
home."

"Fine."

"Fine is all you've got?" he asks.

"Everett..." I turn to him—whoa, a little too fast—and I
brace my hand on his strong thigh.

"How much have you had to drink?"

"What? Listen. I'm too tired and tipsy to argue with you. Let's not make a big deal out of this. Please. For me. Not now."

My eyes plead with him to not push this conversation right now. I know he's trying to get a reaction out of me, but I'm not in the mood. And luckily, Elias comes back with his food.

"For you, sir." He places the food down in front of Everett.

"Elias, how long until we stop in Prague?" I ask.

He looks down at a sheet of paper and back up at me. "About three hours."

"Great. Thank you. I'd like to pay my bill now."

"I've got it," Everett interrupts.

"Fine," I say.

I hear the harsh tone in my voice; I sound like such a bitch. I'm tired, crabby, and confused, but this isn't me.

"Thank you, Everett," I say, placing my hand on his arm.

I see a blush hit his cheeks, and it's the first warm moment we've had together since last night.

"Eat with me?" he asks.

My stomach rumbles and the answer to that question is

easy. "Okay, but then I want to nap before we get to Prague."

"Deal."

* * * *

"Fuck, fuck, fuck!" I mumble. "Where in the hell could she be?" I ask no one in particular.

There are a million questions and scenarios racing through my mind. Is she okay? Did someone take her? Did she miss her stop? Did she get off early, trying to catch me? I take a deep, calming breath before exhaling, finding a bench to sit on to collect my thoughts.

"I have a thought..." Everett offers, and right now I'm desperate.

I turn, looking at him with wide, questing eyes. "Go on."

"What if she saw that you missed the first train and decided to see some of the sights before trying to come back for you? You have that itinerary, maybe we can go to some of the places and try to find her?"

I consider it. "We had planned to take the train from Prague to Bratislava around seven. It's only a three and a half-hour trip, and that way we can check into our room for a good night's sleep before sightseeing. I could for sure meet her at that train and if not there, at the hotel!"

"See, if she missed you at the train station, I bet she has the same idea as you do. You will meet up one way or another today. But I don't want you to miss out on anything else, at least see something other than the train station while you're here."

"I guess you're right."

"Hell yeah, I'm right. And maybe part of this trip could be our last hurrah too," Everett says with a flat smile.

*Last hurrah?* Hadn't he offered to move with me? *No.* He'd admitted he was dumb for not agreeing to move with me. That he loves me and he's sorry, and that once he reunites me with Anna he's going back to *his* home. My heart sinks into my stomach. With all the anger and fighting we've done, I'd convinced myself that he'd changed his mind about coming with me. But those were words I put in his mouth, my interpretation of what his apology meant, yet he'd never come out and said that he would come with me.

\* \* \* \*

"What is it with you and churches?" Everett asks, pulling me from my awe-stricken state. "You've never gone to a Sunday service, but you've always been fascinated."

"I have my own beliefs, and I don't think God needs me at church to know where we stand." I let out a heavy sigh as I look up at the remarkable gothic church. "I've always wanted to help people. That's why I became a nurse, but there's only so much doctors and nurses can do. The rest is left up to Him."

Goosebumps tickle across my body from the overpowering effect this place is having on me. I've always wanted to help people, always, and becoming a nurse held a certain allure. In a few months I'll be working in an emergency room, trying my damnedest to help as many people as I can, to keep people safe, to keep families together. I'm not so naïve to think every case is going to work out perfectly, but I know that I get the chance to try, and that's better than nothing. I shake the thoughts from my head, taking a deep inhale before letting it out.

"And," I say upbeat, hoping to lighten the mood, "knowing how much Anna loves architecture, it was easy to convince her to visit places like this. I mean, look at those steeples, and the stone work. This structure was built in the fourteenth century, doesn't that just blow your mind?"

"That is pretty impressive," Everett agrees, taking my hand in his. "Let's go take a closer look. Maybe we'll even come across Anna."

"I sure hope so," I say softly.

I'm missing my best friend dearly. I should be here with her now, rolling my eyes at her technical terms of this lovely structure. How she breaks it down piece by piece, no detail going unnoticed, while I lamely swoon over it like any tourist would.

"What do you want to do after this?" Everett asks as we start to walk toward the front doors.

"Well, if Anna isn't here, we had planned on seeing the Lennon Wall, and then I could use some lunch."

"The Lennon Wall?" Everett asks curiously.

"Yeah. It's this giant wall full of beautiful graffiti artwork that has reference to John Lennon and the Beatles. It's pro-peace and love."

"Wow. Did you girls pack this much stuff into each day? How are you not exhausted?"

"I am exhausted. But this is the trip of a lifetime, and we didn't want to miss anything. There will always be time for sleep, but who knows how long these sites will be around? Nothing seems to last these days." I shrug.

My face goes hot at the implication of my last statement. I didn't mean it as a dig at him and I; I've done enough of that in the last twenty-four hours.

"Maybe...maybe not. You say this church has lasted fourteen centuries, so that's something." Everett's thumb soothes over my hand, but the expression on his face is firm.

My stomach sinks, and I know I can't do this right

now. I can't try to unravel what he is thinking. I can't pretend to know his intentions, and I'm not ready to ask him. I just want to stay here in this almost platonic moment and hope to hell that I find Anna.

"Come on, let's go," I say after a moment. "We have lots to see, and not very much time to do it. I have another train to catch in six hours."

"*We*, you mean," Everett says as he pulls us closer to the building.

"Maybe," I say softly.

# Chapter 10

*Annaliesa*

*Prague to Bratislava*

Ryker took me to the most amazing place for dinner. I'm having trouble enjoying myself because my mind is on Kenslie. I can't believe we haven't met up with her yet. I'm trying to have fun, but I'm also stressing out. I just want to reunite with her, so we can finish our trip. Though I'm not ready for my time with Ryker to end. I'm enjoying getting to know him and wish I wasn't worrying so much about Kens and how she's handling everything.

"What time are you planning on leaving Prague?" Ryker asks, then quickly adds, "And where are we off to next?"

"We're going to Bratislava next. We were going to try to take the seven PM train and get there around ten thirty-ish. But I have no idea if Kenslie is still planning on being at the station then. I also don't know if we can meet up after the station, because the hotel is in her name, and if hotels are the same here, they won't give me any information."

Why didn't we put both names on the rooms? Oh, that's right, because we didn't plan to be separated. We more joked about it because neither of us thought it would become a reality.

"Bratislava is a beautiful place. We must go to the Devin Castle," Ryker says.

"That's on my list of places I want to see. Kens wants to see the Roland Fountain, and then we plan to go see the Wooden Churches of the Slovak Carpathians."

"You guys did your research before coming on this trip. You seemed to pick all the best places to stop and see."

"Well, I wasn't sure if I'd ever have the chance to take this trip again, and I'm determined to make the most of it and see as much as we can while we're here. I'd hate to regret not seeing everything because we wanted to sleep and lounge by a pool."

"I'm happy you don't just want to sit by a pool. This isn't the trip for that. And you're going to enjoy Bratislava even if we somehow miss Kenslie again. Though I hope we don't," he says.

"I hope so too." I sigh. I can't imagine doing this whole trip without her.

"What do you think of getting out of here and heading to the train station now?" Ryker asks. "Maybe Kenslie will show up early."

"That'd be great. You wouldn't mind sitting at the train

station with me?" I ask.

"No. Let's go. I want to see a smile on your face all the time. When we're just sitting around you look sad, and I don't want you to waste the trip being sad. When you're immersed in architecture you have this smile on your face that reaches your eyes. You're in heaven then, and I want you to feel that happiness the rest of this trip. The sooner you and Kenslie meet up, the better it'll be for you."

How can he read me so well? He hasn't known me long.

"Yes, but then you'll be going your separate way, and that'll make me sad too. I don't understand my feelings for you yet, but there's something about you that makes me want to get to know you more. It may be like Stockholm syndrome, but instead of you kidnapping me you rescued me when I was in distress."

"The feeling's mutual. There's something about you, besides your beauty, that makes me want to get to know you more. So let's continue the journey, and when Kenslie meets up with us maybe I can tag along since I'm guessing her ex will be with her."

*It'll be like a couples' trip.* Shit! Where the hell did that thought come from? We aren't a couple.

"Let's cross that bridge when we get there," I say.

The train station isn't that far from the restaurant we ate at. We have plenty of time to spare. We decide to buy our tickets now, so we don't have to worry about a long line forming.

"How can I help you?" the ticket agent asks.

"Can we get two tickets to Bratislava, please?" Ryker asks as he places his card on the counter.

"You don't have to buy my ticket," I say, pulling my wallet out of my purse.

"It isn't that big of a deal."

"The train is set to arrive and depart on time this evening. But the weather forecast is now predicting some thunder and lightning showers," the ticket agent informs us.

"What does that mean?" I ask.

"Well, sometimes if it's bad enough, the train will be delayed. Or if the train is running early, it may take off early to avoid having any delays."

"Thank you for that information," I say as Ryker grabs our tickets and leads us to some chairs where we can wait.

"They just take off early if the train is already here? What about the people who have tickets for that train?" I say to Ryker.

"I'm sure they let those people take the next train if they do that. I would have to assume that it's to get the people already on the train to their destination instead of having them stranded at a train station," he says. "Chin up. I'll make sure you get reunited with Kenslie."

I really hope he can make that happen, but I also know that I have to make it happen too.

"Let's hope Kenslie makes this train with me. If not, I wouldn't really be shocked, because she tends to run late when it isn't work related. I don't mean that in a bad way. She just gets caught up in the moment and loses track of time."

"Sounds like you need to do that more often," Ryker says. "You can't take life seriously all the time. You need to enjoy all the moments you're given and not let any pass you by because things aren't going the way you planned. It's hard to give up some control, but it'll be more fun if you can get over not having to be in control all the time."

I want to do what he's saying. I've tried, and it hasn't worked for me. I ended up planning anyway. Maybe if I trusted the right person it'd be easier. I tried with Kenslie to not really plan this trip, but we both wanted to see so much, and I wanted us both to be able to see all that we could, so we planned, or more like I planned.

"I'm trying. I even tried to not plan this trip, but it was hard, and I eventually ended up planning everything to make certain the trip ran smoothly. At least I didn't plan everything to the minute," I say in my defense.

"Nothing wrong with a little planning. I just want you to have a fun vacation, and I see you stressing because it isn't going as you planned and you don't have your friend with you. I don't want you to have regrets about this trip. You can still worry about your friend, but have fun and really enjoy the sites Europe has to offer you. You said yourself that this may be the only time you make it out here, so make the most of it. Give up some of the control. Let me help you shoulder some of the burden of being here alone."

*I can try*, I tell myself. "I will try," I say out loud with a firm voice to Ryker.

"We'll now begin boarding to Bratislava," a voice says over the intercom.

"What? They're going to leave early? I'll definitely miss Kenslie."

"I don't think they're going to leave early. It's already after seven," Ryker says.

Where has the time gone? I guess when you aren't stressing about everything the time goes by a lot faster.

"I can't believe it's already after seven. I for sure thought they'd be leaving early since they warned us they could be."

"I think they like to warn people about it, but I don't think it happens often. I've never had it happen the times I've been here."

I hope this means Kenslie will be on the train with us. I'd love for her to get to finish the trip with me and also to meet Ryker, so she can give me her opinion on him.

"Let's find a seat and wait for Kenslie on the train. That way we can spread out a little and not be cramped if it's a full ride," Ryker says, grabbing our packs off the floor by our feet.

I don't want to get on the train without Kenslie, but I don't want to miss the train either.

"I can see the wheels turning in your head. What about *try to have fun* did you not understand?" he asks.

"I understood it all, but it's hard to break old habits," I say, then I stand up and proceed to lead the way to the train.

"Can I please see your boarding pass, ma'am?" asks the train attendant.

"Yes, sorry I forgot to get it out and ready," I say to the attendant. "Ryker, where did I put my ticket?" I ask as I'm scouring through my pack, not finding it anywhere.

"I have them both," he says and hands them to the attendant.

"Thank you, Ryker. I don't know what I'd do without

you here by my side."

That's the truth too. I'd probably still be back in Prague at the train station waiting for Kenslie and praying we didn't miss each other.

"Safe travels. Have a good time in Bratislava," the attendant says as we board.

I can't believe that we're halfway through our trip. Time is flying by. I can't wait for the adventure that awaits us tomorrow.

It doesn't take long to find two open seats since there seems to be a lot of open spots. I'm constantly looking out the window for Kenslie.

"Last call for those going to Bratislava," a voice says over the loudspeaker.

"Where is she?" I quietly ask myself. This can't be one of the times she's running late. She should be early to make sure that she finds me.

"Take a deep breath. You don't want to hyperventilate and end up in the hospital." I hear Ryker say close to my ear.

Closing my eyes, I take a couple of deep breaths then count backward from ten. Feeling a little more under control, I look up at Ryker and thank him. He's done way more for me than most would. I don't know how to repay him. Well, I do...he wants me to live a little on this trip and give up some control, so that's my new priority for this trip.

"Welcome aboard train C5 to Bratislava. We should have a clear path from the storm on this journey. It seems the storm has gone around us. This trip should take around three and a half hours," someone says over the train speakers.

The doors have closed as I see Kenslie running toward us screaming, "Wait. Stop. You can't leave yet."

"Open the doors," I shout, though the conductor can't hear me from this car.

I run toward the windows facing Kenslie, and our gazes connect. I recognize the look of defeat because I see the same look on my own face reflecting back from the window. How do we keep missing each other?

*I'm sorry*, Kenslie mouths to me as the train pulls away from the platform.

"Shit, that wasn't how I was hoping tonight would go," I say to no one in particular. Why does this keep happening to us?

"I know you don't want to hear this, but it will be okay. We know that she'll be on the next train. We can just stay at the station and wait for them."

"What do you mean *them*?" I question.

"It looked to me like she was with a guy when she walked in and he followed her to the train. I would guess she's still with her ex," he answers.

"That would explain why she was late. Those two have never been able to keep their hands off each other and actually make it somewhere on time. I don't know how they ever made it to work on time."

I don't believe she is still with him. Well, actually I do. She loves him and is going to give him a second chance. How did I forget he was with her? I guess the stress is making me forgetful.

"Did you really think she'd leave him? I mean, would she want to be alone in a strange country without a phone or someone she knows?"

"No. Yes. I don't know. I want to say she wouldn't, but I don't know anymore. I do know that she loves him and wants him with every fiber of her being. She was devastated when they broke up. She didn't want to lose him, but she isn't willing to give up her dream for him either. She knows that it'll only cause more pain and heartache farther down the road. She deserves to be happy in all areas of her life. If he makes her happy, then I'm happy for her. I want the best for her, and I wholeheartedly believe he is the one for her."

"You're an amazing friend. I haven't known you very

long, but I can see that her happiness outweighs yours. Not many people are like that. A lot of them would be pissed she's with her ex, and they wouldn't try to connect with her every step of the way. They'd blow her off and do what they wanted and not even think about Kenslie and her feelings."

"I feel like I'm being a whiny, little brat about the whole thing. I'm mad that she got off the train to go talk to him, but at the same time I know that this is something she needs to take care of. I know it was weighing on her a lot, and it was hindering her ability to have fun. She wouldn't have said anything because deep down she feels the same way I do. She'd give up her own happiness to make me happy."

"That's a friendship you want to hold onto and cherish," Ryker says. "Not many people have one that strong."

"Thank you, for everything," I say, swiping at my eyes. I'm an emotional mess. "I really appreciate you taking time away from your vacation to show me around and make sure I'm not alone. You didn't even know me until a couple of days ago, and yet I feel like I've known you for years."

"You're welcome. It's been more fun showing you around than it would have been on my own. Plus, I think it's you who's showing me around. You have the list of places, and even though I've seen them before, it's like seeing them for the first time. Watching your face light up and the excitement when you talk about things makes me look at it from a new perspective."

If I'm not careful, I'm going to fall for this guy. I'm not one to believe in insta-love, but he's making me rethink it. *Kens, where are you? I need advice on how to handle Ryker and my feelings.*

"We're almost to the train station. Where would you like to stay? I probably should have told you I have a room at a hotel close by. I'm not sure which one, but I have the confirmation in an email. Or we can go to a hostel for the night. I know that's a cheaper way to go."

"I don't want you to lose money, so if you don't mind a guest, I can sleep on your couch."

"There's no way I'm letting you sleep on the couch. You can have the bed, and I'll take the couch or ask for a cot," he says. I open my mouth to protest, but before I can say anything he says, "Don't even argue with me. I will not sleep in a bed while a woman is sleeping on the couch. Not happening. No way, no how."

See, he's making it hard for me not to fall for him. How many men still have these types of values? Most would say they're paying for the room, so they should get the bed, and they'd expect me to share my body with them too.

"We'll see about that," I say, trying to hide my smirk. I don't want to let him think he's won.

* * * *

Why does morning always seem to come so fast when you're having the most amazing dream? And then when you fully wake you can't even remember what you were dreaming about.

Trying to snuggle back into the covers, I burrow into my pillow only to realize it isn't a pillow. *Oh shit.* I'm all over Ryker. My head's on his chest, arm slung over his stomach, and my legs are twisted up with his. I guess I wasn't just dreaming good things.

How do I talk myself out of this mess? We'd agreed to share the bed since it was a king and we could each stay on our own sides.

"Mornin'," Ryker says in a deep, husky voice.

He can't use that voice if he doesn't want me to pounce on him. It makes me think of the sounds he'd make as he pounds into me. Of all the times to think about that, it definitely isn't when I'm wrapped around him like a sheet.

"Morning," I respond.

"I can hear the wheels turning in that beautiful head of yours, and it's giving me a headache. Quit overthinking our current position and go back to sleep. I'm not ready to get up yet. It's only three AM, and I plan to get a couple more hours of sleep."

How can he act like this isn't a big deal? That's right, he flies by the seat of his pants and doesn't overthink every little thing he does or that happens to him.

"Okay. But I do need to go to the bathroom before I fall back to sleep." I slowly slip out of bed and try not to sprint to the bathroom.

"Hurry up, will you?" Ryker yells. "I've lost my blanket."

I can hear him laughing, but it's just what I need to make myself stop over analyzing not having boundaries. I don't even bother giving him a response. Instead I decide to jump farther out of character and head back to bed and right back to the spot I vacated.

"Ummm. This feels nice," he murmurs in my ear once we're situated.

"It does," I whisper back.

That's all I say before we both fall back into a peaceful sleep.

"Annaliesa," Ryker says. "Time to join the land of the living."

"Ugh. Go away. I'm not ready for this dream to end." I

push him away.

"Oh, darling, this isn't a dream."

"Shhhh. Go away or you're going to make me lose this incredible feeling."

Suddenly, I'm flipped onto my back and he's hovering above me.

"No woman is going to be dreaming of another man while draped over me," he says then instantly gets up off me and stalks to the bathroom.

*What the fuck was that?*

I feel like shit now, but I wasn't dreaming about another man. If I'm being honest, he was the star. But apparently it wasn't all a dream, because from the looks of it, I was all over the poor guy.

Deciding not to linger in bed any longer, I get up and dressed before he comes out of the bathroom so I don't feel so naked and exposed.

"Sorry about the way I reacted. It won't happen again," he says, walking out of the bathroom.

Damn, he looks fine with his hair pulled up into a man bun. And don't even get me started on those jeans that fit him like a glove.

Shaking my head, I pull myself out of my thoughts and respond to him. "It really isn't a big deal. I get where you're coming from, but maybe you shouldn't jump to conclusions. You don't have a clue who or what I was dreaming about. For all you know, it could have been a vacation or my happy place."

"If you moan like that on vacation or in your happy place, I want to have those kinds of dreams. And you were practically humping my leg."

*What!* I scream in my head, and I can feel my face turning red. Was I really humping his leg?

Ryker starts laughing. "I wish you could see your face right now."

"What?" I ask, confused.

"It was a joke, beautiful." He's still laughing but not as hard.

"Men," I say, stomping toward the bathroom.

"Beautiful," he says, making me turn around. "Don't be mad. You were the one practically molesting me last night. I'm not complaining though. You can use me in any way you want any time you want."

There has to be some truth to what he said though, because of his reaction when he stormed off to the bathroom after saying 'no woman is going to be dreaming of another man while draped over me'.

"I'm not mad. I'm just excited to start our day. Hurry

up so we can go have the time of our lives, giving you something to dream about tonight. I'll have to put pillows between us tonight to keep you on your side of the bed."

"Keep dreaming," he says. "Now hurry up and brush your teeth. I can smell you over here."

"Is that how I can keep you away from me?" I ask.

It sounds like he whispers, "Nothing can keep me away from you," but all I hear is "Yep."

I rush into the bathroom and take care of business and come out ready to start the day. "Let's go," I say excitedly.

"I've been ready. Let's go," he says.

"Do you have anywhere you want to see while we're here?" I ask.

"Well, I was wondering how you would feel about me planning where we go today. I know some really cool places, and I'd love for you to just enjoy the day and not stress."

While that sounds awesome I can't not look for Kenslie all day. Or can I still have fun and look for her? I don't know when she'll be here or if she's even here yet, and I also don't know where she's going to go. To just sit in one spot waiting for her would be a waste of my time.

"Yes," I nervously respond. "This should be fun. Where to first?"

"First place is some coffee and food, then it'll be a surprise where we end up after that. No more questions. Just relax and enjoy what I have in store for you."

He really wants me to have fun and not stress. He thinks that if he plans it all I can have the time of my life while here. So, for him, I'm going to do everything I can to give this to him.

"Yes please to coffee and fuel. I'm still not sure how to give up control for the whole day, but if I can give it up to anyone, you're a good choice, because we like the same things."

* * * *

"Holy smokes, I don't think it's possible for me to walk another step," I say as I plop down onto a bench.

"You're done?" he asks.

"No. Yes. My poor legs haven't got this much action ever. You've had us walking all over town." This is where I need one of those fancy watches that track how far you've walked. I bet I'd have the highest step count ever.

"Are you complaining now?" he asks, feigning hurt.

"Haha. No complaints from me. You've shown me more than I would have ever seen had we not met. Everything was amazing. I'm sad though that you didn't take me to Devin Castle yet."

"That's on the list still. But first I need to know how much longer we have here."

"Well, we can stay another night here and then leave for Vienna tomorrow morning, or we can hit Budapest and Vienna this evening."

"Why don't we stay here tonight, then hit Budapest first thing tomorrow morning and do a couple of sites there, then hit Vienna late morning, early afternoon tomorrow?" he suggests.

"Sounds amazing. A girl could get used to all this pampering."

"If you were my girl, you'd have more pampering than you could handle," he mutters.

"Did you say something?" I ask.

"I said every girl deserves to be pampered."

"Well, pamper me and get me to Devin Castle stat."

"Yes, ma'am. It'll be our next stop before we have to leave for our last adventure of the day," he says as he flags down a taxi.

The cab driver holds open the door for me and asks, "How is your day going, miss?"

"Very good. Thank you for asking," I reply as I climb into the cab. Once he shuts the door I turn to Ryker and say, "Why can't people back home be as friendly as the people we encounter here? That wouldn't happen in New York or any big city back home."

"I don't know," Ryker responds to my first question.

"It's because people back home are on time schedules, and they don't know how to let loose. I'm one of those people. But there's something about being over here and having you take control that's opening my eyes to the fact that I stress way too much. Life is so much easier if you just give up the reins a little."

I don't believe I'm even saying this. I've never thought this way before. I guess it takes seeing it and actually giving it a try to make you see the up side. Kenslie isn't going to know what happened to me.

"You are right about that. Everyone is always in a hurry to get somewhere, and they don't take time to smell the roses anymore. It's always a shock traveling out of the country and seeing how other people live. Even Hawaii is laid-back. I still can't believe I just moved to a big city a couple weeks ago. The things we do for our jobs."

"Where is your hometown?" I ask, curious to know more about him.

"I was in California the last several years, but before that I lived in Eastern Oregon. Small town, and I miss it."

"I'm from Oregon also, but I live northwest of

Portland. What city are you moving to? I just got a job in Chicago," I reply giddily.

"You're joking?" he asks, looking shocked. His mouth is slightly open and his forehead is creased.

"Um, no. Why?" I ask hesitantly.

"You won't believe me, but I just got hired at a firm in Chicago."

"No way?" I ask. How the hell can this be happening? First, he's on the same train as me, then we're both architects, and we're both from Oregon, and now we're both moving to the same city. What the hell? What next?

"Yes way."

"Are you excited to move?" I ask, bouncing in my seat.

"Yes. I wish I could go back home, but I know that Chicago is where I need to be if I'm going to make a name for myself."

"I feel the same way about Chicago being where I need to go to make it in this field. Though I'm a little nervous moving from a small town to a big city." But I'm glad I'll know at least one person.

"It won't be that bad. It will take some getting used to though."

"Yeah. I hate going into Portland. There are too many people, and I don't like all the traffic."

"Well, you better get used to it. The traffic in Chicago is worse than Portland. You may just have to learn to walk everywhere," he suggests.

"Or take a taxi or uber or lyft?"

"If you want to put your life in those crazy people's hands you can."

"*Close to the office* just moved to number one on my list of must-haves for my new place."

"Maybe I can show you around?"

"Or get lost with me!"

"Or get lost with you," he replies. "That sounds more fun."

I remember that I never asked him what firm he got a job with. "What architect firm are you going to work for?"

"H&S Architect and Design."

"Now you're joking. There is no possible way that we both got hired at the same firm."

My heart's pounding. I'm like a girl with a school yard crush, excited that maybe this could turn out to be something real and not just a fling. But also scared that working together might get in the way of a relationship. And here I go getting way ahead of myself and feeling things I don't normally feel so soon, or ever, for a guy.

"Are you saying that's the firm you're going to work

for also?" he asks.

"Yes. As long as they didn't make a mistake hiring multiple people. I hope it isn't a competition and one of us is going to lose our job right away. I don't mind competition, I just don't want to move across the US only to find out the job is temporary."

"I got the impression they were looking for two to three new architects to help with the expanding business."

"Well, that makes me feel better. But you forget, you're actually getting hired as an architect, and I have to finish my internship then take the test. They said if I do as well as they expect I will get offered a job with them."

I don't know what I'd do if I moved only to lose the job to a guy. Architecture is so male dominate it's scary. A lot of women don't make it in this field, and I want to prove to myself and other women that they can do it. This is my passion. I know what I'm doing. But if I was to compete against other males, it would be me to go first no matter how well I did.

"Do you have a place to stay yet?" he asks.

"No. I've been looking online at places for rent, but I'm nervous to rent before I see. You never know if you're seeing the real pictures or not. I'd hate to rent a shed when they show a luxury apartment."

"I hear you there. Too many people scamming people. I've been staying in Chicago for a couple of weeks. I decided to go to Chicago and look at places before coming here, and I ended up putting down a deposit on a nice two-bedroom condo in a secure building. I know we don't know each other well yet, but if you'd like to crash at my place until you find your own, you're more than welcome. Or you could be my roommate if you want to go that route."

I want to say no, but it really would be beneficial to have a roommate. Plus, he's hot and a gentleman. But what happens if he's not who he is here? Then I'd be stuck. Maybe I could move in on a temporary basis to make sure we're compatible.

"Let me think on it. I don't really know if I want to go the roommate route or not. I've had one since college, and it might be nice to have my own place." I can't come right out and say yes or no. If I say yes, then I'm going to look needy, and if I say no, it may hurt his feelings, and I don't want that because I really do like him.

"Sorry to interrupt, but this is your stop," the cab driver says. Then he gets out and opens my door for me.

"Thank you. You've made my day with how generous you are," I say and hand the guy some money, leaving plenty for a tip.

"You're welcome, ma'am. Have a wonderful time." He gets back in the cab and takes off.

"Holy smokes. This is amazing," I say to Ryker as I gaze at the castle. "I don't even know how to put into words how beautiful it is."

"It is amazing. The best part is walking around and reading about the history of the place. They have exhibits in the upper caves of the castle, and it just so happens that one of the exhibits happening now is *Architectural Development of Devin Castle*. We'll need to go check that out now, because we have the last tour time for that. Then we can walk around and see everything else," Ryker says.

My brain's on overload. The pictures don't do this place justice. It's one of those times you wish you could show the world through your eyes so they could see it as if they were there in person.

"Look at this place, Ryker. Thank you for bringing me here," I say in awe.

"Don't thank me. This was one of the places you wanted to see."

"Yes, but I didn't know about the exhibits. I thought they were closed down."

"They did close for a brief time to fix up the structure and make sure it was safe for the public."

"So, again, thank you for being here with me," I say. I feel like a broken record saying 'thank you' so much, but I'm thankful for everything he is doing for me, and I don't want him to think I'm taking his generosity for granted.

I stand there looking like an idiot because I'm not sure where we're going first. I want to see everything and doubt I'll get to. Although our first stop is the easy part since we're going to the upper caves for the exhibit tour.

The tour was a brief recollection of the history of Devin Castle. There's so much history in this place. Architecture is only one of my loves, but learning the history associated with the buildings is astonishing. There's so much to learn. While the tour was short it gave me time to see the other exhibits without having to worry about getting left behind.

"Did you enjoy the tour?" Ryker asks.

"Yes!" I squeal. "I not only loved the architect part but the history too."

"The history of the place definitely gives you a better understanding of it," he says.

"True."

I wish we didn't have to be out of here by a certain time. Though I doubt I'm allowed to go searching through all the caves.

"Can we go into the caves around the castle or are

those closed off?" I ask a woman with a name badge.

"The only one that is open right now is the upper caves where the exhibit is," she replies.

"Thank you." *Man, I wish I could explore more of the caves.* "Ryker, do you want to walk the grounds some more, or are you ready to move along?"

"We have a little time if you want to look around more," he responds.

"I don't know what we have planned for the rest of the evening, but if we could head back to the hotel and get a nap and a shower to cool down that would be great."

"We have time for that. Let's call a cab and head back then."

The cab ride is quiet. I'm exhausted. This trip has been a blast, but we've been go, go, go the whole time. I need a day of relaxation, but that isn't going to happen until I get home. Even then it won't be much because I have to figure out where I'm going to stay in Chicago and also finish getting all my stuff packed.

Those were the last thoughts I had before I'm being jostled awake.

"Annaliesa, wake up. We're back at the hotel," Ryker says with his hand gently pushing back and forth on my shoulder. "I would carry you inside, but I don't think you'd react to that very well, and I didn't want anyone to think I drugged and kidnapped you," he says, opening the door and getting out then reaching his hand into the back seat to help me out.

"I appreciate you not carrying me through a hotel lobby."

I don't believe I fell asleep in a cab. I don't normally sleep in cars. I guess I had a shoulder to lean on.

"When do we have to be ready for our next adventure?" I ask Ryker as we head into the building.

"I'd like to head out around seven, so we can grab dinner first. I promise not to keep you out too late since you're tired."

"Well, I can stay out later if I can get a thirty-minute cat nap in before we have to leave."

"You can nap while I shower and get ready. Does that work for you?"

"Yes. Thank you."

The elevator to our floor is slow. The doors take forever to open, causing me to freak out that they aren't going to open and we'll be stuck. I don't want to get stuck, but maybe it wouldn't be so bad being trapped with Ryker.

Once in the hotel room I kick off my shoes and fall face first onto the mattress. "Wake me in thirty if I don't wake up myself."

* * * *

The nap was exactly what I needed this afternoon. I would've been sad to miss out on this experience. It's what I imagine Bourbon Street to be like, just not quite as wild and crazy.

Ryker planned our evening around the nightlife here in Bratislava. There are people everywhere on the streets. You can hear music coming from several bars and nightclubs. People are dancing on the roads and sidewalks.

"How do you know about this place?" I ask.

"My buddies found it, and they like to come here whenever we come this way. They're big into the party scenes. I like that it's not as loud as being in a club, and it's easier to talk to people. I'm not a big dancer, so talking is what I'm left with. Good thing I'm not scared of introducing myself to strangers."

"Well, you're going to have to dance with me. You can't bring a girl to a club, or outside of a club with music, and not expect to dance with her."

He better not tell me I can dance alone and he'll watch.

"I wouldn't dare," he says, holding his hand over his chest, faking to be hurt by my comment.

"Then let's get another drink in you so I can convince

you to dance several songs with me." I wink at him.

The drinks are flowing, and the music is fast-paced.

"Let's dance!" I grab Ryker and start moving my hips to the beat of the music.

Ryker says he's not a big dancer, but he can move. He isn't having any trouble keeping up with me, and he's not breaking my toes.

"And you say you don't like to dance. Why not? You're good at it."

"It's just not my thing. Like some people hating sports, I dislike dancing, but maybe that's because I haven't had the right partner."

*Smooth talker.*

"Maybe," I say and continue to dance to the beat, swaying my hips from side to side.

This is turning out to be one of the best nights of the trip. The only thing that would make it better is if Kenslie was here to experience this with me. I know she's going to be jealous because she's always wanted to go to Bourbon Street. That's okay; one day she'll have to come back here and check this out. It's definitely something you don't want to miss out on if you're into some fun.

The music turns to a slow song, and Ryker spins me around so I'm facing him. He pulls me close to him, and our eyes connect. There is something in them that I can't look away from.

"I've been wanting to kiss you all night. May I?" he asks.

I've never had a guy ask if he could kiss me. They always just lean in and go for it. Like a sneak attack.

"Yes," I say breathlessly.

He leans down as I lean up, and our lips connect. It isn't a forceful kiss. We're exploring each other. He slowly swipes his tongue across my bottom lip, asking for entrance into my mouth.

I've never been kissed so thoroughly before. He knows how to kiss. When he breaks away we're both breathless.

"That was...wow," is all I can say.

"Wow is right," Ryker responds.

"Maybe we should do that again sometime," I say then wish I could take it back. It makes me sound stupid.

"I'd very much enjoy that. Now that I have permission, I'll be doing it as often as I can," he says.

Lord have mercy on me. I don't know how I'm going to make it the rest of this trip with him and not let temptation overcome me.

"Are you about ready to get out of here?" he asks. "It's two AM, and we have a day of traveling and sightseeing to do."

"It's really two AM already? Time flew by." I seem to be losing track of time a lot these last couple of days. Ryker is the reason.

We walk back to the hotel and enjoy the peacefulness of the night. The party scene is still going, but the farther away we get the quieter it is. It's nice that we don't have to fill the silence with useless chatter. I like that we're comfortable enough with each other that we don't feel the need to talk just to avoid the quiet.

"Would you like to use the bathroom first?" Ryker asks me as we enter our room.

"Yes, thank you."

I grab my toothbrush and jammies and go into the bathroom. I hurry through my nightly routine and head out to the bed. I'm going to sleep like a rock tonight.

"Oh, and don't forget I'm building a pillow wall to keep you away tonight," I say as he's walking into the bathroom.

He laughs. "You tell yourself it's for me, but it's really for you. I'm the one that woke up with you tangled around me."

He doesn't let me answer because he shuts the door on me. He's right though; I did wake up wrapped around him.

It felt nice. So nice I don't think I want to put up the pillow wall. Last night was one of the best night's sleep I've had in a while, and I'd really like to sleep well again tonight.

Ryker comes out of the bathroom and checks the door and turns out all the lights. "I see you didn't make a pillow wall."

"Nope. I wouldn't want to miss a chance at getting to snuggle with a warm pillow."

"Well, get on over here then," he says, holding the covers up so I can roll over toward him.

Laying in his arms should feel awkward since we haven't known each other long, but it feels safe. It feels like I belong here.

"Good night, Ryker," I whisper.

"Night, Liesa," he responds.

He's never called me that before, but I really like it.

# Chapter 11

*Kenslie*

*Prague to Bratislava*

I can feel the blood rush from my face as my mouth goes dry. I'm speechless as I watch Anna stare at me as *our* train takes off without *me*. I was supposed to be on that train. We—Anna and I together—should be on that train. My stomach falls, and I feel hopeless. I can't seem to catch a break. We're halfway through our vacation—*our* vacation—and we have spent little of it together.

"At least I know we'll have seats next to each other on the flight home," I say solemnly. "This trip is turning out to be a bust."

"Babe, don't say that. It's still an amazing trip. Think of everything you've seen. Anna would want you to have a good time. And it didn't exactly look like she was alone," Everett says, trying to comfort me.

Then his words hit me.

"What do you mean she wasn't alone?" I turn to him, concerned.

Anna is a tough cookie, but the idea of her spending her trip with a total stranger, who may not have the best intentions, is horrifying.

"It looked like she had a guy with her." He shrugs.

"I'm sure it's fine. She didn't look like she was being held against her will."

"How do we know that?"

"Come on, Kenzie. You think Anna would let that happen?"

I press my lips together as I consider his words. *No.* There is no way in hell Anna would let some creep hang around with her. And with that thought, I relax, almost a little happy that she isn't traveling alone. Maybe she's even having a good time? I'm not exactly having a horrible time. Things aren't going as planned, but I'm not letting it put a damper on the trip. I paid for this, and I deserve this.

"You're right. And maybe she's even seeing the sights too. We both deserve this trip, even if we aren't together for all of it." I give him a halfhearted smile.

"You do deserve this trip." He pauses and smiles. "Now, let's get our tickets for the next train. I think they have trains leaving every thirty minutes."

"Perfect! Maybe we can catch up to her after all."

"And when that happens, are you going to send me packin'?" Everett asks, grabbing my hand and locking our fingers together.

My heart sinks as I look up into sincere hazel green
eyes. The soft side of Everett peering through them, and
deep into my soul; in my heart, where he belongs.

"I don't know what I'm going to do with you, Everett,"
I say, taking a step forward. I push up on my toes and place
a chaste kiss on his lips.

Soft lips that feel like home send a sizzle through my
body. Life is so complicated, yet being here in this moment
with Everett feels so right, even as guilt ridden as I might
be. I'm being torn so many ways. Everett or Anna? Everett
or work? The only thing I can find that is missing from these
things is *me*. Here's my chance to really think about what I
want, who I am, what kind of person I'm really going to be.
Life is defined in every step we take, and I'm finding out
quickly that this trip is more than that; it's a journey for
many reasons.

"I love you, Kenslie. But you know that."

"I know," I reply, taking my lip between my teeth. I'm
not ready to say it back. Not just yet. "Let's get those
tickets, please."

Everett only nods, leading us toward the ticket counter.

\* \* \* \*

I'm relieved at the very quiet, relatively short, train ride
to Bratislava. Everett's hand stayed tangled with mine, his

thumb occasionally rubbing against it soothingly. Our connection was never lost, and in that symbolic thought I wondered if we're strong enough to work through this.

*Ugh.* I shake the thought from my head. I'm in desperate need of a hot shower; this has turned out to be a very long day.

"Next stop, Bratislava," the announcement says overhead.

"Let's look around the area for a little bit, and if we can't find Anna, let's just go to the hotel I have booked."

"Maybe she went straight to the hotel?" Everett adds, hopeful.

"No, she couldn't have. I booked it, so the room's in my name. I'm not sure if she even knows which hotel I booked."

"So much for planning every detail," Everett scoffs.

"We didn't exactly plan on getting split up," I say curtly.

Grabbing what few items I have with me, I stand. I'm eager to get off this train.

\* \* \* \*

It was almost eleven PM when we made it to the hotel. I was beat from a long day of sightseeing and emotionally drained from missing Anna yet again. Everett convinced the concierge to change my reservation from a room with two beds to one bed with an upgraded view of the city. At first, I was hesitant at the idea of one bed, but the pull I feel toward him isn't lost, even with what's happened with our relationship.

What is happening with our relationship? We hadn't really talked much about where we are with that and where it's going. He mentioned not wanting to lose me, that the reason he made this trip was to express some grand gesture, but as of yet that hasn't happened. But I'm finding it hard to stay angry with him, and I'd be a fool to think that we would really stay the night in separate beds.

I run my hands over my neck, trying to relieve the stress tensing up.

"I'm going to go take a hot shower," I call to Everett as I unload what little items I have stored in my bag. I pause a minute. "Do you think they offer a laundry service in this hotel? I'm running out of clean clothes."

"Maybe. You did pick a pretty swanky hotel. Why was that?"

I shrug. "I was in charge of tonight's stay, and with us mostly sleeping on trains and plans to stay in hostels, I thought this might be a nice treat. Plus, it's right in the middle of the city."

"Why don't you go take that shower and I'll call down and see if they offer laundry service. Just leave the clothes on the bed."

"Everett offering to do the laundry. You really are trying to win me back, aren't you?" I tease.

An awkward silence fills the room, and I instantly regret my words. At some point before this trip is over we're going to have to have a real conversation. I give Everett a flat smile before I turn to the bathroom.

Turning the brass handle of the shower brings the water to life and the sound is a soothing distraction. I slip in, letting the hot water cascade over my body as I relax into it. The hot water bites at my skin, washing away the worry and doubts I've held onto since I saw Everett at the station; since I made the terrible decision to jump off that train. Leaving Anna for Everett. I scold myself. How could I so easily leave my friend, but I won't give up a job for the man I love? A heavy sigh escapes, deflating my body.

I'm startled by a knock on the door.

"Hey," Everett says as he steps into the bathroom.

I'm not fazed by the intrusion. We lived together for years; there isn't anything to hide.

"Sorry. I just wanted to let you know they have a service. They just picked up our clothes and will have them ready and delivered at the door at seven AM."

"Thanks," I call from the shower.

"Kens." Everett says my name, before a long pause.

"Yes?" I finally ask.

"I'm coming in."

I'm startled by the candid action, but it also makes my stomach flutter joyfully. The intense intimacy of our showers together had always been something I cherished. It was where all our best talks happened, and *other* stuff. I try to erase the smile on my face, but I'm certain the blush is showing on my cheeks.

The curtain pulls back, and half of my shower stall is now consumed by his large frame. I can't help but appreciate his sexy body as my gaze runs from head to toe. He's just as I left him, and there the lust consumes me. I'm trying my best to hold back. I need answers, and I'm not going to miss out on my chance.

Everett's hands touch my shoulders, running down my arms before placing them on my hips. He pulls my willing body a step closer to his. I look up, getting lost in his eyes; in the silent connection between us.

"Talk to me. What's happening between us? Why are you really here?" I manage the soft words.

I watch his body move as he inhales then lets out a

heavy exhale. "I'm here to win you back."

He opens his mouth to say something else, only to close it again. He's holding back on me. I can see it, but I'm tired.

"What does that mean? You want to get back together? Are you willing to move with me?"

He shakes his head, breaking our eye contact. "I don't want to move. In fact, I hate the idea."

My heart sinks to my stomach as the hope floods from my body. I feel a lump in my throat as tears prick at the edges of my eyes.

"Why are you doing this to me?" I struggle with the words. "You already know I love you. I don't want to be without you, but this job is a chance of a lifetime for me. I'd be a fool not to take it, and you have to know that."

"I do. Which is why, if you'll let me, I want to come with you. I want this back." He pulls me tight against his firm body, his strong arms holding me in place.

"What? You just said you didn't want to move."

"Sometimes we do things we don't want to do, but we do them for all the right reasons. And you're the perfect reason."

"No," I say firmly, trying to twist out of his hold, but he doesn't let me. "I'm not forcing you to move just so you can resent me later. That's no way to live."

"I need you, Kenslie. I'd hate myself for losing you over my damn pride. It's not living without you. And that's the reason I want to move—to be with you. For better or worse."

That's all I need to hear. Pushing up on my toes, my lips desperately seek out his. I wrap my arms around his neck, and my body pushes into his, quivering as our sexy places align. The familiarity of solid arms roaming over my back and ass only ignites our kiss, deepening it. I need this. I need him more than he knows, in ways he can't imagine. And here he is, giving me everything.

Firm hands are under my ass, swooping me up. Instinctively, I wrap my arms around Everett's waist. His lips are wild on mine as I try to keep up with the eager lust resonating off of him. He releases my lips and I pull back, gulping in air, but the warm sensation of his mouth locking onto my hard nipple has me gasping in ecstasy. Maybe it's only been over a week, but I'm desperate for this joining of our bodies...this release that connects us again. My head's cloudy with thoughts, but my body reacts as I rock my needy core against him as he's moved to my other breast, licking and nipping at it.

My head falls forward against his body, landing in the

crook of his neck, giving me the opportunity to place kisses there. Making my way up toward his ear, I take the lobe in my teeth, tugging playfully. A moan rattles through Everett's chest and radiates against my body. I can't wait anymore. This foreplay is turning into punishment as I try to keep the friction against our bodies going.

"Please," I beg.

No other words are needed. His hand wraps around my ass, hoisting me up just a smidge before I slowly settle back down on his hard, thick shaft. The sweet pull inch by inch into my wet center nearly has me coming undone. I'm not sure anymore if it's his moans or mine echoing in the small bathroom; I'm lost in a daze of fervor. He lifts me up just enough to pull me back down, slamming his hard cock deep inside, grazing that special spot just ready to come undone. Throwing my head back as the pleasure sears through my body, Everett takes the opportunity to pull my nipple back into this mouth, tugging as his thrusts become erratic. My chest throbs, and I know my release is near.

"Don't stop. God. I'm so close. Everett," I plead.

Both of his hands are on my ass now, and I steady myself with my hands around his shoulders. He holds me close to his body as his thrusts continue, and I rock my clit against his base. *One more. One more. One more.*

"Yes!" I yell, and my body shakes as I come undone.

Blood whooshing in my ears mutes the world around me, but I can still hear the vocalization of Everett reaching his own orgasm. His head rest against my shoulder as we enjoy the glorious after-shock of the release of our pent-up sexual tension. After a minute I squirm out of his hold, letting my feet hit the bottom of the shower, but I keep my arms steadied around Everett for support, not yet ready to break our connection.

"I love you." The raspy whisper of words comes out, and he wraps his arms a little tighter around my waist as the hot water continues to shower down on our entwined bodies.

* * * *

I wake to a soft kiss just behind my ear, sending a luscious sensation down my spine. A giant smile breaks across my face as the memories of our make-up session, *sessions*, come back to me.

"Good morning, beautiful."

"Mmmm. Good morning," I reply, turning in his arms. "Wait? What time is it?" I ask, sitting up abruptly.

"It's a little after eight. I grabbed our clothes already. They're on the dresser."

"Thanks, babe. We should get up and get going," I say, stretching my arms overhead. My body is still tingling from last night. I might just love this man more than ever.

*Oof.* I'm wrapped in muscle and pulled back to the bed, turned on my back with the giant of a man on top of me.

"I had something else in mind." Everett kisses me. "Let's stay in, order some room service, and get a late check-out."

"Come on. How many chances do we have to see a city like this? We can't miss it."

"The city will still be there when we're done. How many chances are we going to get like this? Just us, alone in an awesome room, in a foreign country, no worries, no cares in the world. Let's just take it."

My heart flutters, and I smile up at the man I love. I run my hand over his stubbly chin.

"This is getting long," I say.

He leans down and gently rubs the prickly hair against my cheek and neck, tickling me.

"Just say yes." His mouth is a whisper against my ear, our bodies synced up perfectly in the plush bed, and deliberately his core grinds against mine.

I'm a puddle of lust, and there is no refusal at this point. A full day of making up is just what I need, and he knows it.

"Yes." I happily concede.

Page 144

# Chapter 12

*Annaliesa*

*Budapest and Vienna*

Waking up wrapped in a pair of arms should scare me, but I know whose arms I'm in. Ryker's an amazing man. It's too bad that we're meeting here in Europe. I can see Ryker as a person I can share my life with, but that's going to be hard since we both have new jobs. I know we're both moving to Chicago and can pursue something, but can we compete at work and make a relationship work? Why am I even thinking this? Maybe he isn't interested in more than a whirlwind Europe affair.

"Morning," Ryker mumbles, pulling me closer to him. "It's too early for you to be thinking so hard. Should I get used to waking up and hearing the wheels turning in your head?"

"Sorry. It's a bad habit of mine. I tend to wake up early and think about everything that I need to do and fix." *Does he mean what I think he does here? He wants to wake up with me long-term?*

"Don't apologize. Just let go and enjoy this trip. You have many days, weeks, months, and years ahead to worry."

Rolling over so I can look at him, I say, "I know I do. Like I said, it's a bad habit. One I've been having trouble breaking, but I've been better since this trip." *More since Ryker walked into my life.*

"What dare I ask were you thinking about?" he asks.

Do I want to tell him the truth or just part of the truth? Do I want him to know I'm starting to have feelings for him? How can I have feelings for him when I haven't known him but a few days?

"You're doing it again." His voice breaks into my thoughts.

I sit up so I don't have to look into his mesmerizing, emerald green eyes. "Sorry," I say, exasperated. "You want to know what I'm thinking about? Well, here it is—I'm trying to figure out how I can possibly have feelings for you when we haven't known each other a week. I'm thinking about the fact that I think you're incredible and the perfect boyfriend material, and I hope we can continue whatever this is we have going on once we get back stateside and move to Chicago."

Suddenly, Ryker pins me to the bed.

"Eek!" I scream in surprise.

Laying on top of me, Ryker says, "There's no time limit on when you can start developing feelings for someone. If you had asked me last week, I would've said it takes longer than a few days, but I've been feeling this pull toward you since I met you. I want to see where this...whatever you call us...goes once we return home. I want to know what it's like to be able to talk shop with my girl and not have her eyes glaze over from boredom. I want to learn new things and teach things to you. This isn't just a fancy hook-up to me."

Hearing him say that is just what I need. I don't even think before I lean up and kiss him. However, then I hesitate a bit because I remember that nasty little thing called morning breath and I'm not sure how he feels about it. I instantly have his answer when he presses his tongue against my lips for me to let him enter.

I don't want to rush us, but this kiss is making me hot, and it's hard not to rub myself against him. It's a good thing he's leaning above me, or I would be trying to climb him like a tree.

Before things go too far I break the kiss. "Wow," is all I can get out.

"Yeah, something like that," Ryker says and rolls over onto his back.

"Maybe we should get ready for the day and head to Budapest before going to Vienna," I suggest.

"Good plan. Why don't you go shower and do all your girly things and then we can go?"

"Ha. All my girly things. I can be ready in fifteen minutes tops, and that includes taking a shower and fixing my hair."

"I don't believe it."

"Well, I'll just have to prove to you I can do it."

"Sounds good. I'll be holding the door open for you at exactly..." He pauses and looks at his watch. "Six-eighteen. Time is ticking away, gorgeous."

I hop out of bed only to have Ryker smack my ass. "Ouch. That was mean."

"Just trying to get you moving faster." He laughs.

Oh, I'm going to show him moving fast. I'm not some high-maintenance girl who takes hours to get ready.

I rush to get everything done in the shower and throw my hair into a messy ponytail on top of my head. I glance down at my watch and see I have time to spare. *Yes!*

I walk out of the bathroom, and Ryker's dressed but reclining on the bed. I casually walk over to my backpack, slip on my flip-flops, and head to the door. Once I get it open, I say, "Looks like I'm holding the door for you to make the exit. Better hurry or I'll be leaving you." I walk through the door and wait for him by the stairwell.

"Holy shit, I didn't think you'd be ready in fifteen minutes, much less ten. Did you even wash?" he asks.

"Yes, want to smell me?" I lift up my arm and say, "Have a smell of my almond cherry blossom deodorant. I even shaved my armpits, so they aren't poky."

"No thanks, I'll take your word for it. But you've just impressed me more than you already have. I've never met a girl who can get ready and out the door in that time, and I grew up with sisters. Even when they woke up late they still took their time."

"Well, now you can't say that anymore because you've met me."

And I'm not going to let him get rid of me anytime soon.

* * * *

I wanted to stop in Budapest today even though it's risky. I know that Kens doesn't know I'm here, but I really didn't want to miss it since it's on the way to Vienna and this trip is about seeing as much as we can.

I looked online at the best places to go, and Ryker and I picked Vajdahunyad Castle. This was one as architects we couldn't pass up. The Vajdahunyad Castle was designed to showcase landmark buildings from all over Hungary. Since it used buildings from different time periods there are four very different architectural styles. Another really cool fact about the Vajdahunyad Castle is it was originally made out of cardboard and wood, but in 1904 it was rebuilt using stone and brick.

"Ryker, this place is a dream come true. I could spend days in here and still not see everything I want to. I feel like a kid in a candy store."

"I agree. I've never seen this much beauty in one place," he says.

I glance over at him, and he's staring at me. "I'm not talking about me. I'm talking about this castle. How can you not be excited about this place? Oh, let me guess...you've seen it before?"

"Um. Actually, I haven't."

"What? You've been here before and just happened to miss one of the best architectural buildings?"

"I've never been to Budapest. We've always skipped it. Now I don't understand why. And I was being serious about all the beauty in one place. This castle has a lot of beauty and so do you. You can't hold it against me for wanting to let you know how beautiful you are."

How can you fault a guy when he's so sweet and he's complimenting you? You can't.

"Let's look around some more. We're on a time frame

if we want to get on the bus to Vienna. We really need to make sure and get there before dinner time. There are things there I'd like to see too."

"Your wish is my command," he says and takes a bow. "Lead the way, m'lady."

What a gentleman. Again, I'm thankful that he got on that train and helped me out when Kens so foolishly got off the train.

Before I know it, we're rushing to get on the train to Vienna. We spent way more time checking out the castle than planned. We should've already been in Vienna. *Crap!* Another missed opportunity to find Kens. I'm beginning to think we won't connect until we fly back home.

"Ryker, which way? I don't remember how to get to the train station," I shout in frustration. This is one of those times I hate my lack of direction.

"Let's grab a taxi. It'll be faster. Then we can make the next train instead of waiting around," he suggests.

"Great idea."

If we miss the train at three, we won't be able to get out of Budapest until eight tonight. When I bought the tickets, the lady said the early evening trains were often full, and she wouldn't recommend riding those. We decided to go with the three PM time so we can get to Vienna today. This way it won't put a damper on what I'll be able to see in Vienna, so we can make it to Ljubljana on time. I don't want to miss any stops, but I'm thinking we'll miss Graz tomorrow.

Pulling into the station, we have ten minutes. That should be plenty of time to get on the train since we already have the tickets. "Hurry, Ryker. I don't want to miss this train."

"I'm hurrying," he says, throwing the money at the taxi driver. "Sorry. Keep the change." Then he chases after me. "Good thing I had cash. I forgot you can't use cards in the taxis here," he says as we run to board the train.

"Can I see your tickets please?" the attendant asks.

"Yes," I say, pulling them out of my bag.

He looks at the tickets and then tells us we can board.

"Thank you. Have a wonderful day, sir," I say.

"Thank you," Ryker adds.

"You're welcome. Have a good time in Vienna."

Once we find our seats I let out the breath I didn't realize I was holding. "Boy, I'm glad we made this train." I glance over at Ryker. "What are you doing?"

"I was sending a text to my mom. She's been texting for the last two hours, and I don't want her to send the whole European army looking for me. Sorry, it was rude of me to not tell you first. I can't stand when people are on their phones when someone is right there next to them."

"Good evening, travelers. We are departing the station now and expect to arrive in Vienna at six-twenty this evening. Enjoy your travels," the attendant says over the loudspeakers.

I turn my attention back to Ryker. "It's okay. I'm sure your mom is worried about you."

"She worries, but not as much as some parents. She likes me to send a text or two every couple of days. I don't think I've messaged in three days now. I've been busy courting a pretty girl."

"Oh, whatever. Don't blame me. Next thing you'll be telling me I have to go meet your parents."

"That's a great idea. Let me tell my mom I'm bringing the girl of my dreams home with me," he says with a wicked gleam in his eyes and a big-ass grin on his face.

"Don't you dare," I say, grabbing for his phone.

Looking down to make sure he didn't text his mom anything about me, I can't help but swoon when I see the way this man talks to his mother. "If you treat all women like your mom, you're going to be an amazing husband one day. Not many people our age have this kind of connection with their parents. It seems a lot are yelling and telling them to butt out of their business. I love seeing this type of connection, because I have it with my own parents. The only reason my mom isn't blowing up my phone is because she hates texting and she thinks I'm with Kens and knows we didn't add a ton of international usage to our phones. We pay a flat fee per day, but that only allows for limited calls and internet usage."

"Well, you can use my phone if you'd like to touch base with her," he offers.

"I'm not sure that would be a good idea. Kens doesn't have her phone, and I don't want her parents freaking out."

"I didn't even think about that. That's probably a good thing. But when we connect with Kens you can use my phone to call your parents. Let them know how amazing the trip has been and how you had the best-looking man you've ever laid eyes on to guide you." He winks at me.

"Cocky much?"

"Only telling the truth. Are you denying I'm the sexiest man you've laid eyes on?"

"You really are too much. I'll admit you're good-looking, but the sexiest... I mean, you can't really compete with Chris Hemsworth. Though with that hair you're one step closer." Ryker is pretty damn fine. His long hair he has in a manbun most days and the small beard on his face is a huge turn on. I never really thought I was a beard lady, but he can pull it off.

"Lies. It's all lies. I'm better looking than Chris, and you know it. You just don't want to admit it, but that's okay. I'll be the winner in the end."

"Winner? Is there a competition going on? Where's Chris at?" I question, looking around, hoping he doesn't see the smile on my face.

"Haha. You're so funny."

"I thought I was." I look outside the window to see if we can see anything. I have enjoyed seeing all the beautiful landscape around here. "Do you know if there are any landmarks we'll be able to see from the train?"

"I don't think so, but it's all beautiful," he says.

"Yes, but I was hoping to take a cat nap. We're going to be running once we get to Vienna. I just hope the Austrian National Library is still open. That place is one of the top on my list to see. I love a good book, and when I'm not working I have a book in my hands. There's something to be said about getting lost in the pages. Living in a different world for a few hours."

"I think it's open later than six. If not, we may have to stay the night in Vienna so I can take you there tomorrow. I would hate for you to miss one of the top places on your must-see list."

"We can't stay in Vienna."

"Why? Is it because you don't want to worry Kens?" he asks.

"That's the main reason. The other is where will we stay? It seems we've been staying in hotels more than was planned. Though you can't really sleep on a train ride that's only two to three hours. I mean, even a five-hour train ride doesn't allow for much sleep."

"I've only paid for one hotel, so I'm not sure about this staying in more hotels than planned, but we can sleep on the trains if that'll make you feel better," he says, then continues on. "Now, for Kens, I don't know how to answer that. Is she going to be waiting for you at the library or will she already be heading to the next stop this evening?"

"That's just it, I don't have a clue where she is or where she's going. I don't even know if she's in Vienna right now. Maybe she got lost or something."

"Stop. She's with Everett. I'm sure she's fine. Let's not freak out. You will meet up with her soon."

"Yes, we will. We have to since we only have a few days left of our trip. She'll at least be on the seat next to me on the flight home."

"You'll see her before then. It's just taking longer than planned. I'm sorry about that."

"It's okay. Let's take a short nap so we can hit the ground running when the train stops."

"Okay. Sleep well."

I drift off to sleep faster than I thought I would. It isn't always easy to sleep sitting up, but Ryker allows me to rest my head on his shoulder.

"Liesa, wake up. We're in Vienna," Ryker says in my ear.

I slowly sit up straight and stretch my arms over my head. "Sorry, I slept like the dead. I didn't realize how much I needed that nap," I say to Ryker as I'm grabbing my stuff.

"It's all good. I took a nap too. I was more tired than I thought. I just woke up about five minutes ago."

That's good that I once again didn't bore him. It seems I fall asleep a lot on him; in the cab, on the train.

"So, first stop library?" Ryker asks.

"Please. That's the main place I want to see. If we don't see the other places, I'm good with that. Then we can even get on the eleven PM bus and head to Graz tonight."

"We can. We should see when the library closes and maybe eat first since you'll probably close the place down."

"Let's grab a taxi and ask. I'm sure there's something close to the library."

Ryker gets us a taxi, and we end up eating at a little

café next door to the library. Much to our surprise the library is open until nine tonight. That gives me plenty of time to explore it and get to Graz tonight, so we can get to Ljubljana first thing tomorrow.

"Do you read, Ryker?" I ask.

"I'm not a big reader. Never have been. I'd rather sit and draw things."

"I can understand that. I've been a reader since I was a kid. I go a little crazy if I go long periods without reading. I'm actually shocked I haven't read yet on this trip. I usually read before bed to help me unwind from my busy days."

I'm pulled from our conversation as we walk into the library. "Holy shit! I didn't realize this place was so big and had four museums also," I say in awe.

"Yes, there's a lot more than just books here, but there are a lot of those too."

"Do you think we'll have time to see it all?" I ask, sounding like a kid on Christmas morning wanting to play with all their toys but not sure which one to start with.

"If we hurry, we can see most of it. Or at least I hope so."

This place is huge. I can get lost in the architect alone. Throw my two favorite things together and I'm in heaven. "Do you think they'd let me sleep here tonight?" I ask, not really expecting an answer.

"We actually have tours where you can stay the night. It's kind of like *Night at the Museum*, but the museum doesn't come to life," someone in a museum uniform says.

"Really?" I ask excitedly.

"When do you do this?" Ryker asks.

"We're doing it tonight and tomorrow night this week, and then again next Friday and Saturday."

"Do you have any tickets left for tonight?" I ask without thinking.

"Liesa, are you sure you want to do this? We're supposed to head to Graz tonight."

"I really want to do this. It's a once-in-a-lifetime opportunity. I can always catch Kens in Ljubljana or in Italy. Please?" I ask, though I'm not sure why. This is my trip. I don't need his permission. "Aren't you the one who told me I needed to go with the flow and not be such a stickler to schedules?"

"I just wanted to make sure you were okay with the possibility of not finding Kens until Italy."

"I wish she was here with me, because she'd love this as much as me, but she isn't here, and I'm not going to miss this opportunity."

"Then I'll go get us the tickets, and I'll let you get lost

in some books. Don't go too far though. I'd hate for you to lose someone else."

I don't even know how long Ryker is gone because I can't stop looking at all the books. I've always wanted to own a library. One day I want a library in my house with a fireplace and a big, stuffed armchair that I can relax in while I read.

Tonight is going to be the best night of my life. I'm going to be surrounded by architect, books, and a very good-looking man who's working his way into my life one minute at a time.

# Chapter 13

## *Kenslie*

"We keep missing Anna. I honestly thought we would have found her by now. We are looking for a needle in a haystack!" I say, letting out the heavy breath weighing me down.

"Not really. I mean, c'mon it's Anna. She must have planned this whole trip exactly to the tee. You've told me places you both wanted to visit, and we've tried to find her there. Do you think she might have changed her mind and ventured to another place? Besides, she was with a guy on the train, right?"

Panic hits me. I can't stop thinking about *that* guy, the guy she's with. It's so out of character for Anna to pair up with a stranger in a foreign country, let alone change her plans. Unless he's charmed her into it. What can she know about a man she just met? Terrifying thoughts run through my head; drug trafficking, human trafficking, murder, rapist. *Oh God!* I cover the gasp escaping my heaving chest.

"Babe. Don't overthink this."

Everett pulls me into his strong arms, encompassing me. This is the spot I normally find comfort and reassurance

in, but not this time. I'm too worried about Anna. It's my
fault. I got off that damn train! *Stupid. Stupid. Stupid!*

"She looked fine. Besides, the guy looked American."

"What?" I whip my head up, glaring at him. "What
does that even mean? Like there aren't horrible
Americans?"

"Okay, okay. I'm sorry. That was a thoughtless
comment." Everett exhales. Stepping back, he places his
hands on my shoulders. "Anna is a great girl. She's strong
and brave, and crazy about following a plan. I'm sure she's
on track. It wouldn't make sense for her to stray. I'm sorry I
even mentioned it. Let's keep looking." Everett pauses,
placing a kiss on my nose. "But let's not forget to enjoy
ourselves too. C'mon, let's think about this. Where are we
going after this?"

"Umm…" I run my hands through my hair, twisting the
ends, and try to think through my cloudy thoughts. "From
here we go to Ljubljana."

"Okay, and how were you going to get there? Were you
planning on staying the night here and leaving tomorrow?"

"Fuck." I shake my head. "The one thing we didn't
plan on was us getting separated. We'd talked about taking a
car service called Daytrip. It would make it a four-hour trip
and not a seven-hour train ride. Then we were going to find

a hostel to stay in."

"Fine. Let's go with that plan. Although, I'm not sure about the hostel thing. Wasn't there a horror movie about that?"

"Chicken." I smirk. This big, strong man unsettled by a scary movie.

"Hey now. I'm just being safe."

"Don't worry, I'll protect you. Besides, we can't keep staying in hotel rooms that run over two hundred dollars per night. I'm on a budget. Remember, I'm moving when I get back. That isn't cheap."

"Right," Everett says with a flat expression on his face.

I slightly regret the comment. We've discussed him wanting to come with me, but none of the details. Not how things are going to look, not the logistics. And a piece of me still worries that there might be a hint of resentment on his part. But I want to trust him, I want him with me. I want our life together to continue.

"Guess what?" I say with the chipper tone, needing to change the mood.

"What's that, honey?"

"I'm going to let you buy me lunch. I think my problem is I'm hangry." I giggle.

"Lunch it is! And after that where would you like to

go?"

I feel a coy smile pull across my face. "I'm not sure you can handle it, big boy," I tease.

Everett rolls his eyes at me.

"The Viennese Prater, which is essentially a large theme park with rides and a variety of other corky things to check out."

"You think you're so funny. I'm not scared of rides."

"Nope, just a hostel full of college travelers."

"I'm not scared!" Everett says with a serious tone, squaring his shoulder.

I try to hide the smile at his petulance. I step in close to him, pushing up on my toes to wrap my arms around this neck. I feel the familiar action of his arms wrapping around my waist.

"I know. But if I don't give you hell, who else will? You're a big, scary dude."

"And don't you forget it!"

Everett's voice is rough, full of testosterone, and I'd be lying if I didn't admit how much it turned me on. My body buzzes at the feel of his, and I can see in his hooded eyes that he feels the same. I push up further, landing my lips on his.

Our embrace escalates, and his hands rush up my body,

holding my face as his mouth overwhelms mine. I submit to his pace, letting him take the lead. I rub my body against his, feeling a wet fire burning between my legs.

A whistle from behind us finally causes us to break our intimate embrace. Our eyes meet, and the blush on his cheeks is sure to match mine. We laugh a minute before he takes my hand in his and leads us off to find food.

\* \* \* \*

"I can't believe I let you talk me into this." I try to hold back the shake in my voice.

"Now who's scared, honey?" Everett chuckles as he moves his arm, wrapping it around my shoulders.

"Stop!" I demand. "You're shaking the carriage."

I roll my eyes at the mocking smile on his face.

"We're over two-hundred feet in the air! And to be honest, I've never thought Ferris wheels were very sturdy. Like, why do these little seats have to move? And what happens if we get stuck? Or it breaks, and we fall?"

Everett scoffs, "What if you get hit by a bus crossing the street? What if the brakes go out in your car?"

I stare at him, my mouth hanging open at the horrible suggestions.

"Don't." His hand gently caresses my cheek. "The point is that bad things could happen at any point in time.

Don't let that hold you back from enjoying the moment. Let yourself live a little before this short life is over. You of all people should know that—I can't imagine the things you'll see working in the ER."

"Look at you being all insightful."

I lean into the nook of his shoulder, giving into the moment as my gaze takes in the most amazing view I've ever seen. I want to keep this memory forever. The way the blue sky meets the landscape of this foreign land, the way my body melts into Everett's, the way my heart beats hard in my chest, full of more love than I ever thought possible.

"I'm glad you're here. I love you," I whisper.

We sit in silence as the Ferris wheel continues to take us around. It may be minutes before Everett moves his arm from around my shoulder, causing me to sit up. I give him a questioning look as he takes my hands in his, turning his body toward mine as much as he can for the small space.

"Kens, we really need to talk about our future."

I know he's right, and I knew this was coming, but I was hoping we could keep pushing it back until after the trip.

"I want to come with you. I don't see a life for me without you."

I'm almost angered by the sincerity of his words. I feel

backed into a corner. I don't want to be the bad guy, but if we're going to really talk about this, then it all needs to be put out there.

"I don't want to be without you either, but I don't want to live life with resentments. What if we never move back to Oregon? What if after my first year I get an offer at a bigger hospital and I want to move again? It's not fair for me to ask that of you. I don't want you to go into this with false hope."

"My job can move. Sure, it's not simple, but it's not like I would have to find a whole new job. I'd just have to find new clients, and I already know how to do that."

"I guess I'm still trying to wrap my head around how quickly you changed your mind. I want to make sure it's real and not just because breaking up is hard."

I lower my head, pulling my hands out of his and twisting them anxiously in my lap. I don't want to look up into his eyes. My words are painful to say, but I'm not strong enough to witness the truth of them in his eyes if I'm right. Breaking up with him almost broke me. I'm not strong enough to do this on-and-off business.

I feel the deep breath and heavy exhale moving from Everett, and like that, our carriage comes to a stop. There's a clicking noise as the security bar comes undone, and the ride operator gestures us out, offering me his hand. Solemnly, I accept, stepping out. I don't have to look back to know Everett's following me.

"Slow down," he calls.

I can't run from this conversation, even as much as I want to. It needs to be settled once and for all. Stopping, I turn to face him, my arms defensively crossed over my chest.

"I have a response for your questions, you stubborn woman. You leaving was the worst thing that's ever happened to me. And I never thought for one second that we'd break up. You asked me about marriage, and I didn't have an answer—I'm not sure I have the right one now either. What I do know is that I don't want us to be apart, ever. Marriage down the road, sure, but we're still figuring out our lives, let's do that."

I'm utterly shocked by his admittance. Everett takes advantage of my stunned state and closes the gap between us, taking my hands in his.

"I'd never regret living our lives together, but I'd sure as hell regret losing you. I'm not that fucking stupid to not know a good thing when I have it."

I can't hold back the smile peeking up on my face as I roll my eyes at his comment.

"You almost did, you dummy," I say playfully.

"No, I didn't. I would have figured it out sooner or later, and there would have been nothing that could stop me from getting you back."

I swoon at the romantic declaration. Isn't this what every woman wants? A man to fight for her, to prove his love. And I'm one of the lucky ones who gets to have it.

"All right! It looks like *we* are moving." I shrug my shoulders and shake my head. "There is so much to do when we get back. We need to find a place to live and pack our apartment up and have our furniture shipped."

"Wait." Everett furrows his eyebrows at me with question, "You don't have a place yet?"

"Well, no. I budgeted to stay in a hotel for the first week while I looked for a room to rent. I'll be making more money at that job, so I could afford my own place, but I didn't want to live alone in a new city. It just sounded lonely."

"You were going to move in with a stranger!"

"That's what the week was for, to meet them first and make sure it was a good fit. It's not like I would consider a guy roommate. So, just calm down."

"I guess it doesn't matter now anyway."

"Right." I lean in, giving him a kiss on the lips. "Hey, it's getting late. Let's grab a snack and then schedule our ride. I wanna get a move on so I don't miss Anna again."

"Sounds good," Everett replies before slipping my arm in his as we walk out of the carnival-esk park.

* * * *

"Honey."

The gentle word whispered against my ear wakes me. Opening my eyes, they meet Everett's, and my heart beats fast in my chest. This man, what he does to me, God.

"We're here."

"Where exactly? Did you ask the driver for a suggestion for a good hostel?"

Everett scoffs as I sit up, stretching my tired muscles.

"There's no way in hell I'm staying in one of those places. Shared bedrooms and community bathrooms…nope."

"I'm on a budget," I protest.

"You might be, but I'm not." He shrugs a shoulder.

I roll my eyes at him. It's too much effort to argue with this man right now. It's been a long, exhausting day. And the idea of a hot bath sounds really nice.

"Fine. Thank you. But you, sir, are moving across the country, so you might want to consider a budget."

"I'll take it under advisement." He chuckles before opening the door, helping me out of the compact car.

I take in my surroundings as Everett pays the driver and thanks him. This service is great for foreigners; the drivers are required to speak English and have to pass a multitude of background checks, or so the website says.

"Let's get checked in, and then is there anything you'd like to do tonight? There is still some daylight left."

"You know, maybe it sounds silly, but I'd like to do some clothes shopping." I giggle. "Packing *this* light," I say as I throw my bag over my shoulder, "isn't really for me."

Everett chuckles. "I have to admit, I'm surprised you agreed to it, and that you haven't done more shopping along the way."

"Shut it," I say, giving him a playful push. "Let's go, and then we can shop 'til I drop!"

"We?"

"Yep. You have talked yourself into a shopping trip. Besides, you might want to get some fresh clothes. Who knows, this Eastern European look might be for you." I wink.

The pale on Everett's face is enough to have me laughing hard. This trip has definitely taken a turn for the better. And I plan on keeping it that way.

# Chapter 14

*Annaliesa*

I didn't plan this very well, but I'm excited we stayed at the library. It really is a once-in-a-lifetime opportunity.

"So, Ryker, what do you think of skipping Ljubljana and just heading to Italy? I know they have an early train. It'll take around thirteen-ish hours, but then we'll be in Italy tomorrow, and maybe we'll be on track to finding Kens. If we hit Ljubljana first, that will be a five-hour train ride, and then from Ljubljana to Italy it'll be another eight-ish hours, and that's not including any time to sightsee in Ljubljana." I pause, taking in a breath, trying to gage his response.

"Liesa, this is your trip. I'm just along for the journey. If that's what you want to do, that's fine with me. It doesn't sound like you'll have much time to sightsee in Ljubljana if we head there. If we do, you'll be a day behind on getting to Italy. I'm guessing Italy is a place you really want to spend your time."

"I feel like I'm missing out on something by not going everywhere on the itinerary," I huff.

"Hey, the important thing is, are you having fun, are you experiencing things you wanted to, are you doing what you want and not what someone else wants you to?"

"Yes, I'm having the time of my life. I'm experiencing more than I ever dreamed of, and I'm doing everything I want to do. I just have a hard time not following the plans. I feel like I'm letting myself down by not doing everything. It's hard to explain to someone who isn't so OCD about their schedule. It's something I'm trying to break free of, but it's hard."

I don't want Ryker to think I'm a stick in the mud because I'm having trouble breaking out of my comfort zone, but I've spent the last twenty-two years living by a list and a schedule. I can't change overnight, or even in a few days.

"Hey, don't stress. If you want to go to Ljubljana, then let's do it. I don't want you to stress over this and not have fun the rest of the night. You've already seen so much and experienced a lot more than most people." He pauses like he's debating if he should say more. "And if I have anything to do about it, this won't be your last trip here."

Ohmygawd. Here I am stressing, and he's promising me another trip to Europe. How did I get so lucky to end up finding him?

*Thank you, Kens, for getting off the train!*

"Then let's head to the train station and get a couple of

tickets to Italy."

"Sounds good."

Let the fun begin. No more getting inside my head. I have an amazing man with me, and he's going to bring me back to see everything I can't see on this trip.

* * * *

"I'm so happy that agent told us about the train from Wien Meidling Station that cuts the trip almost in half. I don't have to spend thirteen hours of the day on a train."

"Yes, that's nice. What do you want to do for the rest of the day though?" Ryker asks.

"Well, since we spent the night in the library I don't need to go there. What would you like to see?"

"Do you trust me?" he asks.

"Yes." Seems silly he'd ask me this. If I didn't trust him, he wouldn't still be with me on this trip.

"Then let me plan our day," he says, rubbing his hands together and giving me a mischievous look. "Why don't you go grab a table at the café around the corner, and I'll be there in a few minutes."

"Okay," I say. "Wait, do you want me to order for you or do you want to do it yourself?"

"Surprise me, but we'll need something to eat and drink."

Walking down the street, I can't help wondering what he's got up his sleeve. I'm happy he's with me on this journey. I can say with a one hundred percent certainty that I wouldn't be enjoying this trip without him. I'd still be sitting in the train station in Germany or I would've flown to London and just waited there for Kens, but I got lucky and ran into Ryker.

I'm not sure what to get for Ryker so I just order him a coffee and a muffin. I've learned he drinks black coffee. *Yuck!* I need at least some cream and sugar. I'd much prefer a mocha though. Can't go wrong adding chocolate to your coffee.

"Can I get a black coffee and a caramel mocha iced with two of your muffins, please?" I ask the barista.

"Do you want chocolate chip or banana nut muffins?" she questions.

"One of each, please."

I hand over the money and step to the side to let the next person order.

"You about ready?" Ryker asks in my ear, causing me to jump.

"Ryker, you can't go doing that to me," I say, grabbing my chest. "You almost gave me a heart attack."

"Sorry. I couldn't help myself." He grins.

"Meanie," I say, then stick my tongue out at him.

"Careful with that tongue. I have better uses for it." He winks.

Holy shitballs. I've got a lot of better uses for my tongue too. *Where are these thoughts coming from?* Oh, that's right, from me. The girl who hasn't had sex in over a year because she's been committed to school and hasn't had time for a relationship.

"We don't have time to eat here. We need to get a move on. We have to be somewhere by six forty-five. That gives us just enough time to get there since it's a little after six-thirty."

"Where are we going?" I inquire.

"That's for me to know and you to find out."

"Fine. You and your secrets."

"Oh, trust me, you'll love it. Let me just say it'll make up for us having to miss Ljubljana."

Now he has my interest piqued. I can't wait to see what he pulled out of his hat for us.

* * * *

We pull up in front of a rustic-looking hotel.

"What are we doing here? Are you planning on locking me in a room all day and putting my tongue to good use?" I ask. *Holy shit!* I can't believe I just said that.

"While I'd love to lock you in a room with me all day, that isn't in the cards for us," he says with a wink. "We're catching a bus from here. Don't worry, you're safe with me for now," he throws over his shoulder as he exits the cab and reaches out for my hand. "And no more questions. You said you trusted me, so just prepare to be blown away."

He's surprising me at every turn. I don't know what I did to deserve such a great man. Though he isn't mine. But I want him to be. That scares me, because I don't like to rely on anyone. He's managed to help me loosen up and realize I don't have to be in control of everything. I'm starting to really like this new me.

"I can't wait to see what you planned for us."

"Let's go. We don't want to miss the bus."

We get on the bus and sit up front. I'm giddy trying to figure out where we're going. It doesn't take long for the tour guide to announce it.

"Welcome aboard the day trip to Salzburg. We'll be experiencing Salzburg, the wine country of Wachau Valley, and the mountains and lakes of Salzkammergut. Once we get to Salzburg you'll get to see Mozart's house and the Mirabell Gardens."

"You've gotta be kidding me, Ryker?" I say in disbelief. This was somewhere I wanted to go to, but we

didn't have time to fit it in. I can't believe that he did this
without knowing.

"Did I do something wrong?" he asks.

"No, I'm just in shock that this is the trip you'd pick. I
wanted to go here, but we couldn't fit it into our trip. It
seems that you always know what I want."

"It's really easy. I listen to what you say, and we like a
lot of the same things. I want you to have a trip to
remember. I want the best for you."

How can I feel so strongly for someone I just met? It
seems his feelings are as strong as mine.

"Let's make the best of this day. Because tomorrow
we'll be in my dream place. But I don't want to think about
that right now—I want to enjoy what we're doing today."

I'm so excited for this trip. I cannot wait to see
everything that this trip offers.

"Wow, Ryker, this is amazing."

I can't stop staring out the window. Everything is
gorgeous here. The rolling hills, the mountains, and the
lakes. Seeing the grapes go for miles and miles is another
thing I don't see often back home.

Once we arrive in Salzburg the tour guide announces
we've reached our destination. We are told we'll have three
hours to do whatever we want or we can go on the tour of

Mozart's house and then explore after.

Exiting the bus, I tell Ryker we have to check out Mozart's house first.

"As you wish, m'lady," Ryker says.

I grab his hand and thread our fingers together as we walk to our destination.

We forego the tour so we can explore the things we want and not be on someone else's time frame.

"While it was cool to see Mozart's house I wish we could have watched *The Sound of Music* instead. I know most people want to explore, but I'd love to see a show of it."

"That would be great to see. Maybe you should mention that to the company. I wonder if anyone else has ever said it to them."

"Maybe they don't offer watching the show because of the time limit before boarding the bus back. They can't really extend it any more than it already is without it being an overnight trip."

"True, but maybe it's something they can offer if they have enough interest," he responds.

"Maybe, but let's not worry about that now. What are you going to feed me?" I ask.

"How the hell can you be hungry? I'm still stuffed from

breakfast."

"Stuffed from coffee and a muffin? Are you serious?"

"It's only been a couple of hours."

"I don't know why I've been so hungry. Maybe it's because of all the food options. I love trying new foods," I respond.

"Well, who am I to turn down a woman who's hungry? I do love that you like to eat. I can't stand those girls who only eat rabbit food and drink water. That isn't attractive to me. What do you want?"

I love that I don't have to worry about liking food with Ryker. I would never date a guy who put me down for eating.

"Surprise me. The only thing I request is coffee. I need something to keep my eyes open."

Sitting at the café I can't help but think about Ryker and how he's been amazing for me on this trip. He's opened my eyes. I don't always have to be in control of everything. And sometimes it's okay to not have a plan.

"Hey, what's got you thinking over there?" Ryker interrupts my thoughts.

"You," I respond honestly.

"I'm worried now." He laughs.

"Don't worry. It was good thoughts."

"Oh, really? Now you must tell me what you were thinking."

"I was thinking about how you're good for me. You've shown me it's okay to step out of my comfort zone. That I don't have to have everything planned to a T."

"Well, I'm happy I can be of assistance. It's good to just go with the flow every now and then. But it's also good to have plans. It's hard to find the balance. Sometimes that's why you need someone that helps balance you out," he says.

*Are you offering to be that person for me?*

"I'm happy that you were on that train when Kens got off. It was meant to be."

"I'm happy it was me too. You could have been left alone or with some creep."

While Kens and I had joked about getting separated, we didn't think it'd become a reality, but I couldn't help but think about all the bad things that could happen to us if we did get split up.

"So, what time do we need to meet back at the bus?"

"In about forty minutes."

"Let's go explore a little more before we load the bus."

I can't believe how beautiful it is here. The buildings are magnificent, not something we see back home, and the gardens are full of flowers that I wish I could have at home, but I have a black thumb. I've killed plants that people claimed were impossible to kill. I laugh whenever someone tells me 'you can't kill this plant', because I've killed an aloe plant and a cactus, and they are supposed to be hard to kill.

"We better start heading back to the bus. We don't want to miss it," Ryker says.

On the bus ride back to Vienna I have trouble keeping my eyes open, but Ryker is thoughtful and tells me to sleep. I feel like that's all I do when we're together on a bus or train. But he's always there to hold me. This is something I could get used to.

"Liesa." Ryker shakes my shoulder. "We're back in Vienna. It's time to make our dash to the train station to head to Italy."

At the mention of Italy, I pop up. I'm excited for Italy. It's one of the places I've been most excited to visit.

"I can't wait. I just hope that I can sleep the night away, but I have a feeling it's going to be like a kid trying to sleep on Christmas Eve...near impossible."

"I have something to help you sleep," Ryker says under his breath.

"Oh, do you now? Care to elaborate?"

"How about I show you when we get on the train?" he

asks.

Do I want him to show me? I really do. It wouldn't be a one-night stand, because I'm positive it would happen for the rest of this trip, but would it last once we got to Chicago?

"Don't go making promises you can't keep," I respond to him.

"Oh, beautiful, I don't make promises I can't keep. I also don't say things I don't mean."

He grabs me, pulling me to him, and kisses me. This isn't our first kiss, but man he takes my breath away. I don't know how long we stand there kissing before he pulls away, resting his forehead against mine.

"To be continued," he says. "We need to grab a taxi and get on the train."

"Okay," I say breathlessly.

It's a quiet trip to the train station, but it's not awkward. It's a much need reprieve for me. I need to decide if sleeping with Ryker is really the best option. I can't come up with any good reasons to not sleep with him. This is where Kens would say to quit over thinking it, just let it happen naturally.

\* \* \* \*

"I can't believe we got a bedroom on the train. It's

going to be so nice to actually have a bed to sleep in," I say.

"Don't get too excited yet. Just wait until you see the bed. We'll practically be sleeping on top of each other."

"As long as I'm on top, we'll be good. I think you'd suffocate me if you were on top." And not because he's fat. He's muscular in all the right places. I can't wait to trace his abs and V with my tongue.

"Oh, I'm sure I wouldn't suffocate you, darling. You may be breathless though." He winks at me.

"Get your mind out of the gutter." I shove his shoulder.

"That isn't what you were saying earlier."

He's right. I was imagining all the things he'd be doing to me.

"Holy shit, you weren't joking," I say as we open the door to our room. "We both barely fit in the room."

"They don't have a lot of room on these trains. They can't make each room huge. Plus, most people just sleep since we're on the red-eye train."

"True. I'm going to use the restroom and then head to bed," I tell Ryker.

Going into the bathroom, I get ready for bed and take a little extra time to make sure I look good. I have an idea of what might happen; not for sure, but I need to be prepared.

"It's all yours," I say, sauntering out of the bathroom in

my sexy shorts and tank.

Ryker's jaw drops, and he hurries into the bathroom. I hop into the bed and slide toward the wall to give him some room.

I wonder what's taking him so long, and the longer he takes the more nervous I get. I'm not sure why I'm nervous. It isn't like I'm a virgin. Yes, I might not do one-night stands, but I know Ryker.

"Quit thinking so hard, beautiful," Ryker says, climbing into bed, facing me.

"Ahhh. You have to quit scaring me."

"If you weren't always in your head, I wouldn't be able to walk up unannounced."

True. I'm always in la-la land around him.

He pulls my chest against his chest, and his strong hands start massaging my back. The tingling sensation is causing goosebumps to form all over my body. Without warning, he pulls me on top of him so I'm straddling him.

"It's easier to massage your back this way."

Slow hands rub up and down my back. With each pass his greedy hands find their way lower and lower, until he slips his hands inside the waistband of my shorts.

"Ryker," I say, though I'm sure it's more of a moan.

"Liesa."

"What are you doing to me?"

"Making you feel good. Just feel, don't think," he says, then shuts me up with a kiss.

It's hard to think when his tongue is massaging my mouth. He's thrusting his tongue into my mouth at the same pace as he's moving my hips against his impressive bulge.

Breaking the kiss, I moan, "Oh my God!" I don't want to let go so fast.

"Just feel." He moves my hips faster against him. Rocking his hips up in time, pushing me down on him. My thin sleep shorts and his boxers are the only barrier preventing him from slipping inside me.

"I'm coming," I cry out.

Ryker kisses me again, muffling what he can of my scream.

When I stop screaming out, he breaks away and says, "You need to be quiet or the whole train will hear us."

Shit! I forgot where we are.

"Sorry," I mumble. "It's hard to be quiet when you make me feel like that."

"Then I'm doing my job right."

Yes, he is. Now it's my turn to show him what I can do for him.

Leaning down, I press my lips to his. He's still hard as

a rock, pressing against my stomach. So I know he didn't get off like I did from our little make-out session.

I slowly peel my lips away from his and sit up. Running my hands down his toned, smooth chest, I scrape my nail over his nipple, causing him to shudder. I continue following his abs down to his V. I move down so my tongue can follow my hands.

His sharp intake of breath tells me he's enjoying what I'm doing to him. So I continue working my way down his body, placing kisses as I go. When my hands reach his boxers, he pulls them away.

"Not now. Not the first time. I won't last long if you touch me with your hands or your mouth. I'm too worked up from watching you let go," he says, pulling me up and crashing his lips against mine.

His hands are working their magic again, slowly working their way under my shorts. Why didn't I take them off when he was in the bathroom?

Leaning up, I start to shimmy out of my shorts. Once they are by my knees I use my feet to get them the rest of the way off. *Sexy, I know.*

"Help me get your boxers off," I say breathlessly.

"Wait," he says, looking worried. "I just realized I don't have a condom with me. I wasn't planning on having sex."

*What? You've got to be fucking kidding me.*

"Sorry," he replies.

"Oh shit, I said that out loud, didn't I?"

"Yes, and I'm really sorry, because I don't want to stop."

I don't want to stop either, but I will not be having sex without protection.

"Neither do I, but I'm not on the pill and—" I don't get to finish before he's kissing me again.

"It's all good." He rubs his hand over his face and takes a couple of deep breaths. Then he pulls me down on top of him and kisses my forehead.

"You don't want me to take care of you?" I ask.

"No. Tonight is all about you. But we're going to be remedying the no-condom situation as soon as possible."

Wow! He can't be real. What man would turn down a blow-job?

It's nice that the awkward tension I was feeling is gone and I can enjoy being wrapped in his arms without the pressure. He's considerate unlike any other man I've ever know. I'm looking forward to getting some condoms, so he can make me his.

"Sleep, beautiful. We have a busy day ahead of us

tomorrow."

"Good night."

As I'm falling into dreamland I swear I hear him say, "I can't wait to make you mine." But I don't respond because I'm lost to sleep.

# Chapter 15

*Kenslie*

I stretch my arms over my head as my body is cradled by the cushy bed and thousand count Egyptian cotton sheets. In this moment, I'm thankful for Everett's insistence on a hotel room. *Everett?* Opening my eyes, I reach out for him, finding his side of the bed empty.

It takes only a moment before I hear the gentle roar of the shower. It sounds awfully inviting. Warm water, silky strong arms, hot, naked man… I burst out of the bed, quickly making my way to the bathroom.

The door is cracked open, a perfect invitation. What is it about us and showers? I giggle to myself. A quiver runs up my body, and the dampness of my panties is apparent. I strip my clothes off in record time and slip through the cracked door.

"There better be room for two in there, 'cause I'm feeling awfully lonely in that big bed."

His deep chuckle echoes off the wall as he pulled back the glass door. I'm stunned at the powerful man standing in front of me. He could be a statue with those hard, sculpted muscles. I'm one lucky lady.

"Get that sweet ass in here pronto."

"Wow, you sure know how to treat a lady," I tease.

"Just you wait. I'm gonna treat you just right."

My mouth is dry, and the anticipation is killing me. Wasting no time, I hop in the shower, ready to collect on that promise.

\* \* \* \*

"This is going to sound terrible, but I don't want to stick around here. Can we just leave for Italy straight away?" I pout as I continue to comb out my damp hair.

"Yes!"

"Wow, that was an eager response." I giggle.

"No, it's just that… I mean, who's even heard of Lube-a-whatever-the-fuck-this-place-is?" Everett shakes his head before turning to collect his items around the quaint room.

I roll my eyes. "Lots of people have heard of this place. Maybe we should stay, and I can try to impress some culture into your life."

"Wait a minute. Let's think this through…you wanna stay *here* over Italy? Pasta… bread…shoes?"

Everett's patronizing is annoying. And if that man can be stubborn, so can I.

"The shoes will still be there when we get there, and I'm sure *Lu-be-ana* has plenty of bread. So I've decided to change my mind. We'll be staying, and then we'll take the late train to Italy. It's a about an eight-hour ride, so we won't need an overpriced hotel to stay in."

"Look at you, making all the rules."

"You forget, handsome, this is *my* vacation, *my* rules." I shoot him a brazen wink as I saunter off to pack my stuff.

"Oh yeah? Your rules, huh? Okay, baby. For now."

I ignore his comment as I bustle around the room, making sure to collect all my items, careful not to miss any of the new pretties I bought yesterday. Especially the few delicate items I purchased to decorate our new place together, something to remember this time in our lives, starting fresh. I stop for a moment, and with a pleasant sigh, I run my hands through my hair. What a trip this has been. I could have never guessed that everything going so wrong would make me so happy. The smile across my face is almost painful from my current state of euphoria.

"Whoa!" I jump at the pat on my butt, and turn to swat at Everett, but he's too quick.

"Come on, honey, let's get going. What's on the agenda for the day?"

"Well, the original plan was to do some hiking and then see a couple of sights, but I'm not sure I'm in the mood for a hike."

"All right, no hiking."

"How about we go to the Ljubljana Castle and then take a stroll over the Triple Bridge area?"

"Whatever you say, teacher. Refine me with the cultures of this country," Everett says ardently with a clap of his hands.

I roll my eyes and shake my head with a smile. *Ugh, this man.*

We exit the hotel, and I soak in the warm sunshine. I've found the warm summer days to be a nice change to the Oregon weather. While summer back home can be nice, it isn't always predictable.

I straighten my new dress while Everett asks the doorman for a taxi. I love the subtle style of this dress. It's not something I've seen at stores back home, and I can't wait to show Anna. It's sleeveless, with a flowy boat neck that almost looks like a scarf. The dress hits just above my knees and has a loose fabric tie belt. It's a beautiful creamy beige, with an accent of white birds printed on the center of the bodice and a dark blue trim at the hem which matches the belt. I'm pleased we didn't go hiking, I was so looking forward to wearing this dress today.

"Car's here, babe," Everett says as he places a hand on the small of my back, guiding me to the waiting taxi.

"Hi. Get in." The driver rushes us, and I slide in the back seat, Everett following me. "Americans, no?" he asks.

I smile up at Everett as he clears his throat. "Yup, and we'd like to go to the castle, please."

"Of course, you must see the castle. I'm Anton. I know where all the Americans like to go."

"Really?" I chime in. "What else should we see?"

"Young people like you would like the Cirkus."

"There is a circus in town?" I ask eagerly, and I can hear the octave go up in my own voice. "A circus with performers or with animals?" I secretly hope there are animals, especially since we had to forgo the zoo trip at our last stop.

"No. No." Anton laughs. "Cirkus. It's a disco. Dancing."

Everett and I look at each other, chuckling a bit, and I feel like a naïve foreigner.

"Maybe we will." Everett shrugs his shoulders. "Where's it at?"

"Oh, not far. Will you be going downtown?"

"Yes, the Triple Bridge area actually."

"Perfect. Just ask around. You'll find it in no time."

\* \* \* \*

I feel the thumping radiating from the building, and the

electric energy of The Cirkus spills out in the street as the line of soon-to-be partygoers wait. Nightclubs haven't really been my thing since...well, ever.

"Couldn't we just find a nice little dive bar around here instead?" I look up at Everett, giving him my best puppy dog eyes.

"We could. But when will you have another chance to say that you've been to a disco? Come on, isn't a disco cultured enough?"

"Fine." I take a deep breath and square my shoulders as the line moves, letting us in.

I'm awestruck as the electric vibe intensifies inside the large building that looks like at one point in its life it was a warehouse. My hand squeezes tight around Everett's as he leads the way through the swaying bodies. A gaggle of girls sashay past us, tight party clothes painted on their bodies, with faces carefully masked in perfected makeup, and for a moment I feel insecure about my plain day dress. I give my head a shake, brushing back my hair and squaring my shoulders. I have nothing to prove to these people, and I'm determined to enjoy every ounce of this exotic outing.

I'm grateful when Everett pulls me against his side as we navigate our way through the crowd to the bar. The house bass music echoes off the walls, thumping around us as Everett flags down the bartender. The young, slender man makes his way to us, leaning over the bar with a nod.

Everett looks back to me with a questioning look. I haven't the faintest idea of the language here, and least of all what to order.

"Vodka?" Everett calls to the man.

"Americans?" the bartender asks.

I blush with a shrug. Apparently, we stick out like a sore thumb. I hope the accent is the dead giveaway and not our clothing style. *How embarrassing would that be?*

"We sure are," Everett replies boldly, pulling me tight against his body.

I smirk at his overcompensation of confidence, marking of his territory or setting the precedence that he can't be fuck with. *Yeah, it's hot.* But I like knowing that I'm safe in this unruly place, not having to worry about sleazy men trying to hit on me in a language that's beyond foreign. What language do they even speak here? *Stupid, unprepared American!*

The bartender shuffles down to the far end of the bar but it isn't long before he returns, setting down a champagne flute in front of me and a double shot glass in front of Everett.

"This for American. You not want vodka. Trust me."

The man nods.

Everett hands over his card to pay, and this gives us the opportunity to inspect our drinks while the bartender cashes us out. Mine is light, sparkly, but clear, and seems to have some sort of flower petals floating in it. It's elegant, and just what I'd expect from a place like this. Everett picks his up and gives it a sniff. It's almost layered, a dark red color sitting at the bottom, and the middle is the caramel color of tequila, and it's rimmed with what appears to be salt.

I tentatively take a sip of mine and am rewarded with a sweet, silky flavor with an after fizz of bubbles. I need to know what this is! This truly could be my new signature drink. I watch as Everett throws back his shot, and shakes his head hard, slamming down the shot glass.

"Wow. That has a kick!"

"Mine's amazing!" I giggle. *To hell with it!* I tip the glass back, finishing it off as if it were nothing but water. "Will you order me another one, please? I wanna dance!"

"Sure thing, baby. Just stay close." He winks.

I take a few steps into the crowd of sticky bodies and begin swaying with the rhythm. Everett reaches me with drink in hand, and I eagerly drink down half the glass before the house music goes silent, but not for long. The crowd erupts when a live band takes the stage. I finish my drink and join in with my fellow dancers, swaying, jumping, my body giving into the uninhibited dancing to the blaring rock music. Everett's arms are wrapped around me, my back to his front as we melt together in the crowd. His hands take advantage of the dimly lit club to wander my body, as gentle kisses are pressed into the nook of my neck. This is everything I hoped it would be.

A woman in a very seductive nurse's costume walks by, offering to take the empty flute out of my hand, and I let her. She then gestures for me to take something off the tray she's holding, and this I *am* familiar with: Jell-O shots. I take two, one for Everett and myself, but then Everett takes one of his own, and the woman winds her way through the throng of bodies.

"I got one for you," I say, turning up to Everett.

"And I got one for you." His eyes widen with a grin on his face. "Come on, baby, you got this."

I give into the peer pressure and finish off my two red shots and follow it up with his green one. I spin in his arms. *Whoa, too fast.* I wrap my arms around his neck for support. I feel the giddy grin on my face, the first sign that the alcohol is doing its job. It's been a while since I've drank this much in such a short amount of time. And I'm loving it! I feel free, weightless, carefree!

"Good girl." He winks at me playfully.

I feel my nipples harden, and the smooth ache of lust hits low in my body. That grin, these muscles, my lover.

"I want you," I purr, pushing up on my toes, my lips grazing his ear seductively.

"Here?" he asks, intrigued.

I love the effect I'm having on him. It's the same one he so often has on me. *Turnabout is fun!*

I look around, considering his question. "No, not here. I wanna dance. But if you're lucky, we could probably work something out on that long, long train ride."

"Whatever you say, baby. This is your show. I'm just along for the ride."

"That's damn right!" I shout playfully, twisting out of his arms and letting my body rock to the motion of the music.

I'm going to throw caution to the wind and dance the night away! This is how to live your twenties—not with your nose stuck in a book forty-hours a week. I fucking deserve this!

I squeal with delight as I raise my arms, dancing, twisting, and turning, joining the party. Everett's protective hands are gently on my hips, steadying me as I allow myself to get lost in the ambiance of it all.

* * * *

"Oh, babe, I haven't seen you this drunk in a long time." Everett laughs.

His hand is on my elbow as we make our way out of the humid club. The cool evening air is refreshing. Rejuvenating.

"I'm not drunk, I'm fantastic!" I put my arms out and twirl as we walk down the street. "I love vacation. I love this country. I love you!"

I stop and pounce on Everett, wrapping my arms around him. My mouth is sloppy on his, but I find satisfaction in his return of affection. I'm on a ride, and I never want it to end. Wait? My mind clears, ride…train. *Shit.*

I pull back from Everett, and I can feel the blood drain from my face.

"What's wrong?" Everett's eyes are full of concern. His cool hands are on my face, steadying me as I straighten my thoughts.

"We missed our train! We're going to miss a whole day in Italy. How stupid am I?" I pull out of Everett's embrace and stomp my foot like a child.

I feel like a fool. I got off the train and lost Anna, I haven't been able to find her, and now I've let myself get out of control and forgot the plan.

"Kens." Everett calls me gently.

"No. I'm thinking." I dismiss him. I'm chewing on my thumbnail.

If we get on the seven AM train and it's eight hours, we can make it there by three PM, and we haven't lost the whole day. But we have lost a lot of time to look for Anna.

"Kenslie." Everett's tone is sharp this time, and I turn to look at him. "Baby, we haven't missed our train. That's why I pulled you out of the club. It's time to go. Which is perfect, because you can sleep some of this off on the train."

"You're the best! Why can I always count on you?" I smile.

"You're awfully cute like this. I'll have to get you drunk more often at home," Everett whispers to me. He takes my arm, hooking it into the crook of his, leading us down the street.

I'm thankful when we don't have to walk long before Everett waves down a taxi. He opens the door for me, and I not so gracefully fall in, giggling as I go.

"Hey! It's the Americans!"

"Anton!" I squeal. "You found us! And we found the Cirkus!"

"So it seems."

"Hey, buddy," Everett interrupts, shutting the door behind him. "We need to get to the train station, and pretty quickly if you can."

"Oh, leaving so soon?" Anton asks.

"Yes. We have to find my friend. She's missing. I think she's in Italy."

"Well of course, that's where all the missing people go," Anton replies.

"Anton!" I scold teasingly.

"Can we please get going?" Everett asks, and the cab takes off, pushing my back against the soft cushion.

"All right, Anton. Tell me about you. Start at the beginning and don't leave anything out." A hiccup escapes, and I lean forward so I can listen intently. *Wow. Drunk me is very inquisitive. Go me!*

"I was born in Ljubljana in 1963…"

"What?" I sit up with a jolt. I see Everett's face, but it takes me a minute to realize that I'm still in the back of the cab.

"Kens, we're at the train station. We need to go so we don't miss our train."

"Oh. I don't even remember falling asleep," I say with a flat smile.

"I think my story put you to sleep. I apologize, miss,"

Anton calls from the front seat.

*Anton. Oh yeah.* "Thank you for the ride."

After paying, Everett helps me out of the cab. My footsteps are unsteady, but Everett catches me quick, holding me to his side.

"Just a little bit longer 'til we're on the train and you can sleep. Or…"

"Or what?" I'm almost afraid to ask.

"Well…you did mention something about sex on a train while we were in the club." Everett gives me a wink.

I roll my eyes at him and give a stern push to his chest. "You should have cashed in those chips with drunk Kenslie, now you're stuck with sobering-up, possibly-already-hungover Kenslie."

"Damn it. I'll have to remember that for next time." He laughs. "Come on, baby. Let's go, and you can sleep it off. Hopefully, you won't wake up in Italy hungover."

I'm excited for Italy, but man, I had a hell of a time in Ljubljana.

# Chapter 16

*Annaliesa*

*Italy*

I don't know what it is about sleeping in Ryker's arms, but I sleep better than ever before.

"Good morning, beautiful," Ryker whispers into my ear.

"Morning, handsome."

"You ready to start our adventure in Italy?"

"Yes!" I scream a little too loudly.

"I can see someone's excited. Our next-door neighbors may get the wrong idea about what's going on over here. Though after last night I doubt it'll shock them."

"Oh, hush. I wasn't that loud last night," I say as I feel my cheeks heating up. I really was loud. I've never been loud, but Ryker has this effect on me where nothing goes as it normally would.

"If that's what you have to tell yourself. I love that I can make you lose all your inhibitions." He smirks over his shoulder at me as he climbs out of the bed. "We need to get packed. The train should be arriving in Italy within the hour."

This is one of the places I've been most excited about visiting. I've always loved food, and pasta and bread are two of my favorites.

"The first place I want to stop is for Tiramisu. I don't care that we haven't eaten breakfast yet. That will be my breakfast this morning. I'm on vacation and can do what I want."

"Tiramisu it is then. You won't hear me complaining about having dessert for breakfast, lunch, and-or dinner."

"Good to know."

We don't have much to pack, so we're ready to go in no time.

"Do you think we'll find Kens?" I ask.

I feel bad that I'm having the time of my life, but I can't help but feel it was meant to be. I would have had a blast with Kens, but Ryker helped me let go of the control, allowing me to relax and enjoy my time.

"I don't know," he says honestly.

* * * *

"We're in Italy. I can't wait to see the Grand Canal, the sculpture of David, the Piazza della Repubblica, the Fountain of Neptune, Tuscany beaches and vineyards, and the Leaning Tower of Pisa."

"Slow your roll. We just got off the train. Let's get you

some Tiramisu and talk about a plan of where to head first. Plus, I need some coffee before I can even begin to think about all those places and how to fit it into two days," Ryker says.

"I'm excited. I can't wait to explore the area. It's been a dream to come to Italy, and it's finally come true."

"And I'm going to make sure it's the best experience you've had yet," he says, pulling me into his arms for a kiss.

I love when he kisses me. I feel treasured and like I'm the most important person in the world.

I pull away from Ryker and look up at him, saying, "I'm happy I get to experience this trip with you. I know that it wasn't in the plans, but sometimes the unexpected is better than the expected."

The way he looks at me makes me feel cherished; like I'm loved. It's too early to be in love with him, I try to rationalize, but that's what this feeling has to be. I get butterflies in my belly, my heart starts racing, and my breathing accelerates. If this isn't love, I must be having some major heart issues. I can see myself spending my life with him. He's everything I've dreamed of in a man.

"Thank you for letting me accompany you on this trip. It wasn't what I had planned either, but this is so much better than what I had planned. I wouldn't give up this experience for anything," he says, holding my face, so I can see the love in his eyes.

I don't know what to say to him, so I kiss him.

He breaks the kiss this time and says, "Get me some coffee, woman."

I'm happy that he changed the subject, because we aren't ready to start confessing our love for each other. I definitely don't want to say 'I love you' for the first time on a sidewalk in Italy.

"Fine, I thought I was sweeter than any coffee you could have."

"Coffee isn't sweet, it's strong," he replies.

"Haha. That's funny."

"Now with how much sugar and milk you add to it, it's like drinking a soda. Or wait, I should say you add a splash of coffee to your sugar and milk." He laughs at how I drink coffee if they don't have mochas.

"Better than drinking mud," I say, acting like I'm gagging.

He grabs for me, but I spin away from him. "Oh, you're going to pay for that comment, Liesa. I don't drink mud." He tries to grab me and fails once again.

I'm laughing and trying to catch my breath. "In your dreams, lover boy."

"I'm a patient man. I can wait you out. When you least expect it, I'll get you for that comment about my coffee. I drink mud." He mutters the last statement, rolling his eyes.

It really is funny how I can rile him up about his coffee. "Oh, don't be a poor sport. I did say I was sweeter than your coffee."

"I guess you did. Maybe I won't pay you back, but you'll never know," he says before pulling me into his arms, kissing me chastely. "Let's get this party started."

We find a quaint café and go inside and place our order. One cup of mud and one cup of pure sugar and two slices of Tiramisu.

"Oh my God, I didn't know Tiramisu could taste so good," I moan.

Ryker is sitting across from me trying not to laugh.

"What?" I question.

"It's a good thing you don't always moan like that when you eat."

"Why? Nothing wrong with appreciating the taste of good food."

"No, there isn't, but if you keep making those noises we won't be leaving the table for a while."

Holy shit, is he saying what I think he's saying? Is he getting turned on by the way I'm eating? I could totally mess with him and make it worse or even get some to go for tonight in our room. I think I like the latter better.

"Oh. I'm sorry you're having a hard time over there. Maybe you should try this and see how yummilicious it is," I say, holding out a fork full for him.

He takes the bite I offer him and says, "That is pretty good," then adds something to the end that I can't really make out.

"What did you say? I couldn't hear you."

"I said it was pretty good."

"No, you added something to the end of that." I give him a look like *you can't fool me.*

"I said that I'm sure you taste better." He says it with a straight face, not looking away from me.

Holy cow, now I have a situation. I don't believe he said that. I'm turned on and just want to head to our hotel. *Why do we have to be in Italy?* If we were anywhere else, I'd spend the day locked in a hotel room with him.

"Let's head out and take a tour of the Grand Canal," I say.

Ryker stands up and grabs my hand and pulls me to him. He leans down and kisses my forehead. "Anything you want to do we'll make it happen."

"Well, I'm not sure there's enough time to do

everything, but I'm going to hold you to bringing me back here one day," I say as we exit the café.

"I'll start planning it now, because it's going to take years of savings to fit in everything I want to show you."

He starts to lift his hand to get a taxi, but I grab his arm, saying, "Let's walk. It shouldn't be that far of a walk, and it'll be nice to see the scenery."

The walk to the canal is peaceful and quiet. The silence isn't awkward. It's nice that we don't have to fill the quiet with useless words.

"This is a perfect way to start our journey. I think I needed some quiet. We've had some crazy nights," I say.

"Some crazy, fun nights," Ryker corrects.

"Yes."

\* \* \* \*

"This would've been more romantic in the evening with the sun setting," Ryker says.

"It would've been, but then I wouldn't have gotten to see all the sites and bridges. If we had more time, I'd let you take me on a gondola ride through the canal, but this private water taxi is fine with me." I love that Ryker's trying to make this feel like it's our vacation together.

"You aren't like most women. Most would want me to make it as romantic as possible."

"Whoa. Hold up. Ryker, it isn't on you to make this trip about romance. The fact that we're here and falling for each other is enough for me. Us meeting and having the time of our lives is more than I hoped for. I don't need you to go out of your way to make everything about me. I want us to experience it together and for both of us to get enjoyment out of it. I know this trip was planned with my best friend, but I can honestly say that I'm having the time of my life, and I don't think I would be having this experience without you. You're what is making this adventure the best for me."

I hate that he's trying to impress me, but I also love that he cares what I think. He's a true gentleman and is always looking out for others. He's a keeper. One I'm going to hold on to tightly.

"I have to say this is the best trip I've had here, and it's the company and the fact that we both love architecture."

"Agreed. Now, where do we head from here? I'm not sure about locations of places."

"If you really want to experience the countryside, then we should rent a car and drive to Florence, Tuscany, and then Pisa before we head to Paris."

"Yes!"

"Wow, that didn't take any convincing."

"Why would it? You're giving me an experience that

I've dreamed of. And if I'm being honest, it's better than anything I've dreamed of."

He really has opened my eyes to love and that having someone to share these moments with are worth it. I now understand what Kens was always trying to get me to see with her and Everett. I just hope she's having the time of her life too.

"Let's go find a rental car and get on the road. There are a lot of things to see and people to do," Ryker suggests.

"That is one of my favorite things to say, and Kens always gets annoyed with me when I say it."

"It is fun to annoy people with that saying."

Flagging down a taxi, we hop in and ask the driver where the nearest rental car place is. He says it's a drive, but it'll be worth it, so we tell him to take us there.

* * * *

"We'd like to rent a car to take to Florence, Tuscany, and Pisa," Ryker says to the agent at the desk.

"Yes, sir. What size vehicle are you looking at renting?"

"We'd like a smaller car since it's just the two of us and we don't have much luggage."

"Okay. Let me look in the computer," she says and then starts typing away on her keyboard. "It looks like we have a

Fiat Panda available. It will be 39.69 EUR a day."

"Ryker, are you sure you want to do this?" I ask. "That's a lot of money on top of needing a hotel room." I hate that we've spent more money than I planned on spending.

"It's fine. I didn't plan on it, but I have the money, and it'll be worth it."

"Okay," I say meekly. I'll pay him back once I get on my feet in Chicago.

We get the keys and head out to the car. My gaze lands on what I assume is going to be our ride and I feel claustrophobic.

"This is a tiny car," I comment.

"It isn't that small."

"Um, yes, it is."

"What kind of beast do you drive back home?" he asks.

"I drive a jeep. I like to feel safe. I don't want to be on the ground with all the big vehicles and semis on the roads."

"I don't blame you there. You may even need the four-wheel drive in Chicago with the snow and ice."

I open the door and toss my bag into the back seat. I'm excited to go on this adventure, and I'm happy that I'm with Ryker and getting to experience not having everything mapped out.

"Where to first?" Ryker asks, pulling out of the parking lot.

"Food. Feed me, please," I respond.

"You and your food. I swear you're always hungry."

"Nothing wrong with that. I learned early on to eat several times a day. It's healthier for you than eating once or twice a day. Plus, being on vacation in a different country is making me eat more because I want to try everything."

"Let me see if I can find you somewhere to eat that has something you haven't tried before."

"Sounds good."

"Anything in particular you want?" he asks.

"Surprise me," I say, trusting his choice.

"I know the perfect place then."

We pull up to this cute little food cart, and I don't know what they serve. I have no idea what lampredotto is, but that's all that's on the menu.

"Welcome to Sergio Pollini Lampredotto," Ryker says, sweeping his hand out toward the food cart. "Would you let me order for you?" he asks.

"Sure," I reply.

Ryker walks up to the window and asks for two orders of their lampredotto, one with spicy red sauce and one with herbal green sauce.

"What is that?" I ask once he joins me while we wait for our order.

"I'm not going to tell you until after you try it."

"Boy, nothing like scaring me. I don't know if I want to eat it now."

"You're the one who said you'd try anything once. You going to back out on me now?" Ryker asks with a smirk.

"I hear a challenge in your voice. Don't you worry, I'm not going to chicken out. But I do require you to tell me what it is once I taste it." I don't believe he actually remembered that I said I'd try anything once.

"I can do that."

"Sounds good," I say, then decide we should make plans for where to go after we eat. "We should go see the Piazza della Repubblica after we eat this fancy meal and then maybe the Fountain of Neptune."

"I'm sure we can make that happen. I've never been to the Piazza della Repubblica, so it'll be great to experience it together."

"What? You mean that you haven't seen *everything* in Europe yet?"

"Not even close. There's a lot I haven't seen, but I've seen most of the big stuff."

"Well, maybe I should have let you plan the whole

trip." I gasp and quickly add, "Oh shit, I didn't mean to say that. It's not like we even knew each other before this trip."

"Hey, don't worry about it. I wish I knew you before this trip, but I'm happy I've met you now. It's been a great experience, and I'm honored to have been able to accompany you. I'm getting worried that things are going to change soon when we meet up with your friend." Ryker shakes his head. "Let's not get down. Our food is done. Let me grab it, and then we'll find a table."

"This better be the best food I've eaten," I say as we walk to a table. I have to admit it smells divine.

"Oh, trust me, it will be. Which one do you want?" he asks.

"The spicy one." Taking a bite, I'm actually shocked by the taste. "Oh my gawd, this is amazing. I don't think I've eaten anything with so much flavor."

"It is delicious. Do you want to try mine?"

"I don't know if I should. I love this spicy one, and I don't know about something that's herbal. I'm not about the healthy stuff."

He starts laughing at me. "There is nothing healthy about this meal."

"Fine, give me a bite," I say as I lean over the table to take a bite of his sandwich. "Yuck," I shout and try not to spit the food out. "There is no way that's the same thing I have. That's terrible." I grab a water and try to wash the taste out of my mouth. "That is disgusting. I can't get that taste to go away," I say, spitting into a napkin and then wiping my tongue on it. Not very ladylike, but I don't care at this point.

"It's not disgusting." He laughs when he looks up and sees what I'm doing. "Quit being a drama queen."

"You have bad taste in food. The one with spicy sauce tastes completely different. I'm glad I didn't try the herbal one first, because I never would've tried this one."

"Apparently, my taste isn't that bad since you're devouring one of the orders I got. But you may want to beat me when you find out what you're eating." He smirks and proceeds to eat the rest of his food.

"What is it?"

"Tripe"

"What is tripe? Do I want to know?" I ask tentatively.

"Probably not."

"Tell me. You said you would."

"It's cow intestines."

"*What!*" I shout louder than I should've.

"You said it was good. Or at least the spicy one."

"I don't believe I'm eating cow intestines." Ugh. *Why*

*am I freaking out over this?* It isn't bad. "Sorry. I shouldn't freak out. It's good, and that's all that should matter."

"It's okay. I should've told you first."

"No, you shouldn't have. I wouldn't have tried it otherwise, and I do really like it. It just freaked me out to think about cow intestines."

"I was freaked out the first time I tried it too."

"I think most people would be. Once you get past the idea and just think of it as food, it really is good. Though that green stuff is nasty."

"It is not. I happen to like this one the best. You should be happy I didn't order the bagnato. That's wet bread with some gravy. That one is nasty."

"Well, thank you for not ordering that one."

"You're welcome."

We finish eating and then throw our trash away and head to the car.

Once in the car I can't stop talking about Piazza della Repubblica. "I can't wait to see everything the piazza has. There are cafés, historic places, pictures, and I think maybe even a hotel we can stay at. Hopefully it won't be booked."

"Maybe we should head there first then, so we have a better chance at getting a room," Ryker says.

"Smart thinking."

"That's what I'm good for." He winks at me.

The ride doesn't take long, but I must have dozed off because Ryker is shaking my shoulder telling me we're here.

"Sorry, I didn't mean to fall asleep on you."

"No problem. If you're tired, you need to sleep."

"I was, but I don't want to sleep. I want to explore some more. I can sleep for a whole three days when we get back. Well, that is if I find a place to stay."

"You'll find a place, and if you don't, you can stay with me like I suggested a couple of days ago."

We pull into a parking spot close to the hotel. "Let's leave the bags and see if they have a room. That way if they don't, we can just look around and not have to lug our bags with us. It'll be nice to explore without carrying my stuff."

We walk into the hotel and are lucky enough that they have one room left. The only problem is it's a Plaza View room and they go for eight hundred US dollars a night.

"Here's my card," Ryker says, pulling out his card.

"Excuse us please," I say to the lady behind the desk. I grab Ryker's arm and whisper to him, "We're not spending that kind of money to stay here. We'll find somewhere else. I don't care if you can afford it. I'm not paying eight hundred dollars to sleep somewhere. We won't be in the room enough to enjoy it. I don't need fancy and glam for you to impress me. I'm fine with staying at hostels."

"I just want you to have the trip of a lifetime."

"This is. I couldn't have asked for a better trip. I don't need fancy hotels. I want to sightsee."

"Well, we sure have done plenty of that, and we still have more to see."

"We can see if there is a hotel close to the fountain," I say.

"Okay."

"Sorry, ma'am, but we're going to have to pass on that room. Thank you," I say.

"You're welcome. Sorry we couldn't accommodate you."

"No worries," Ryker says. He grabs my hand, lacing our fingers together, and leads me outside. "Do you still want to walk around here?"

"Yes. I want to check out some shops. Maybe I can find some trinkets to take home with me."

Ryker hasn't let go of my hand yet. I thought he grabbed it to lead me outside, but apparently not. It feels natural, like this is how we're supposed to be walking.

I don't realize I'm staring down at our hands until Ryker asks, "Is this okay?"

"Yes."

"Are you sure?"

"Yes. I was thinking how good it felt to have you hold my hand."

"It does feel right, but this feels even better," Ryker says as he pulls me to face him and he kisses me. It's a soft kiss, but it's just what I need.

"That's even better," I say.

We spend a few hours scouring shops for the perfect gifts for my parents. I find a cute set of hippo salt and pepper shakers for my mom, and a picture frame with all the tourist attractions on it for both my parents, and I buy my dad a book on the geography of Florence.

"Did you get everyone something?" Ryker asks.

"Yes, but I'll probably try to get them something once we get to Paris. I know my mom will want something with the Eiffel Tower on it."

"Most people do."

"Do you need to get gifts for anyone?" I ask Ryker.

"No. My family and I have come here enough we quit buying stuff for everyone. Now we just enjoy looking around. Every now and then if something jumps out at one of us we'll buy it for the other."

Once in the car we decide to find a hotel to sleep at for

the night before heading to the fountain. We're hoping we can find one close to it, but since we stayed at the Piazza so long there may be no rooms left.

We strike out on the first three places we stop. They were either booked or out of our price range. When we pull up to the fourth one I look at Ryker and say, "If this one is full, we're sleeping in the car."

"That won't be very comfortable, so you better hope they have a bed."

I really do. I'm actually exhausted and having trouble keeping my eyes open.

"Why don't you stay here, and I'll go see if they have a room?"

"Okay." I don't even argue, but then I think about how much he was willing to spend at the Piazza and know without me in there he'll probably spend an arm and a leg just so I won't have to sleep in the car. "Ryker, please don't spend too much on the room," I say, not sure if he can hear me or not because the door is already closing.

I must have dozed off again because he's back and saying they had rooms available and he got us one.

"Thank God," I mumble.

"I'm not God, but I'll still take the thank you," Ryker teases me.

Once we get up to our room I flop onto the bed. "I don't think I'm going to make it anywhere else tonight. A nice, hot bath and the bed are calling my name."

"Is that bath by chance calling my name too?" Ryker asks.

That just perked me up. "I think it is," I respond.

\* \* \* \*

I can't believe our time in Florence, Tuscany, and Pisa is up already. It went by way too fast. While I'm excited to head to Paris, it means that the trip is coming to an end. The sad thing is I haven't found Kens yet, and she hasn't been on my mind as much as she should be. I've been having the time of my life with Ryker. I really hope she's forgotten about me and is enjoying her time with Everett. Hopefully they're working out their differences and are going to be moving together when the trip is over.

"Ryker, what's the first thing you're going to do when we get stateside?" I ask as we head to the bus depot to return the car and begin our journey to Paris. The City of Love. A city I'm happy to get to experience with Ryker; a man I can see myself falling for. A man that I'm already falling for.

"Probably sleep for a day straight in my bed. All these train seats or beds and hotel beds are killing my back. And here I thought it would be easy since I'm so young," he replies.

"I agree. I was always told young people can handle sleeping on floors."

"I'm not saying I'm old. I'm just saying I love sleeping on a nice bed."

"Me too. Though I think you're old."

"Hey now. I'm not old. I'm only two and a half years older than you."

"That's what, seventeen and a half years in dog years." I laugh at his raised eyebrows and scrunched lip.

"Oh, I see you're a funny one today."

"I try," I say, taking a bow. "Now, back to you liking nice beds—you'll only have a couple more days of sleeping on unfamiliar beds and you'll be home."

I don't want this trip to end, because once it does we're back to reality. Will that include Ryker and I together, or will we go our separate ways? I know we'll be working together, and he's said I can move in with him, but is he only being nice?

*No, don't think that way. This isn't a fling. Ryker isn't that kind of guy, and you know it! Stop trying to sabotage a good thing.*

"What's the first thing you're going to do when we get stateside?" he asks.

"Well, I'm going to sleep for at least a day straight and then begin my search for places to stay. So, while you'll be living it up with the best sleep I'll still be sleeping in an unfamiliar bed. You'll be all rested up for our first day on the job, and I'll be this little crippled thing from all these uncomfortable beds. Oh, the travesty."

"You could always come warm my bed, and then we'd both be in the same boat," he responds.

"How do you figure? You just told me you loved your bed."

"There's no way in hell I'd be able to sleep with you in my bed. We'd either be naked, and no sleep would be happening, or I'd be hard as a rock knowing you were in my bed and I couldn't touch you, so I'd be walking into work looking like I hadn't slept in weeks."

"Oh."

I love that he's so honest with me. He doesn't hold back. I know where I stand with him, so I need to stop with the self-doubt that will only start this...whatever it is...off on the wrong foot.

"But it would be so worth it."

"That it would," I respond, because it would be.

I want him to know that I want him as badly as he wants me. Though I hope he already knows that after what's happened between us the last couple of nights. I don't know what to call this thing between us, but I don't want it to end in a couple of days when we fly home. I want to see where this takes us. I just hope he's serious about us too.

# Chapter 17

*Kenslie*

*Italy*

This is the Everett I recognize: quiet, introspective, almost brooding. I relax as much as I can while the gondola glides down the canal. *Italy.* I want to pinch myself; I can hardly believe that I'm here. And honestly, I should be taking in the captivating sights, but Everett has stolen my attention. His broad shoulders fill the opposite side of the narrow boat, and the curious look in his intent eyes as he scans the streets has me wondering what he's thinking about.

Is it the same thing I've been agonizing over the last several days? We've discussed that to death, we're in a good place. Still I wonder, if not for my leaving if we would have ever taken a trip like *this* together? Europe? Random hotels and sights off the beaten path? Of all the things I knew about him, I'm not sure if this would be his choice of trip. It's easy for me to imagine him some place tropical, no shirt, boardshorts hanging low on his hips, exposing that sexy deep v, bulging muscles kissed by the sun, and a beer in hand. My fingers itch to touch that firm body filling out his classic, basic tee that somehow doesn't look plain on him.

The boat rocks, and the driver steadies it as I move carefully to the other side. Everett doesn't say anything, only opens his arm, allowing me to burrow into the nook of his body. The warmth of our embrace has me yearning for the comforts of home; wherever that might be. We're in the most romantic city in the world, and yet all I want is to be back at home with some sense of normalcy. My head has been spinning since the day I left our apartment, essentially leaving Everett.

His strong hand reaches out and slides down my hair before tucking under my chin, lifting it gently up in his direction. I give him a sweet smile, but there's a passing look in his eyes, and his lips flatten for a single moment before he speaks.

"Would it be okay if I pick the next place we visit?" he asks.

I'm taken aback by the request, but how can I deny him this? He came all this way out here to find me and has been putting up with my demands and insistence on our quest to find Anna. I nod, which earns me a swift kiss to the lips.

"Rialto Bridge, *per favore*," he directs the gondolier.

My breath hitches in my chest at the request. *That* bridge. A place where lovers come to leave a lock inscribed

with their initials. One of a handful of *lover's bridges*;
there's a similar bridge in Paris—The Pont des Art—that
Anna and I had planned to visit. But in researching that, I'd
become familiar with many of them. And this one was just
as breathtaking.

This trip is bringing out the romantic side of Everett,
and I'm not about to complain. He's a superb boyfriend,
much more than people saw on the outside. When it comes
to business he's a straight shooter, with just enough charm
to work a good deal, but in the normal day-to-day grind he
plays everything close to the vest. I smile back on those first
months of dating, even the way he asked me out.


*"I'd like to take you out Friday," a gruff voice says
from behind me.*

*I whip around from my seat in the school library,
startled by the voice, and confused as to if it was even
speaking to me. A mountain of a man is standing there, his
gaze holding mine as he waits. I crinkle my eyes at him,
waiting to see if he's going to say anything more. If he's
going to realize that he has the wrong person.*

*"I'm sorry?" I ask.*

*I'd seen him on campus—he was hard to miss—but his
name escaped me. In a swift, albeit graceful movement, he*

*pulls out the chair next to me, taking the seat. His presence
alone seems to fill up the small table I'm at. The same place
I sit every day to study.*

*"I'm Everett," he says, resting his forearms on the
table and clasping his hands together.*

*"Hi. I'm Kenslie," I reply nervously as I look around to
see if I'm missing something that should be obvious to me.*

*"I know."*

*His calm, collect manner is impressive, but only
confuses me more.*

*"Okay? Can I help you?"*

*"Yes. I'd like to take you out Friday night," he says
again, so sure of himself.*

*I bite my lip to hold back the scoff wanting to escape. I
roll my eyes at the arrogance of the statement, but he's hard
to read, and the tone of the words hadn't come off that
way...cocky.*

*"You think so? Why is that?" I sit back, crossing my
arms over my chest, eyeing the man before me.*

*I'm not so meek that I can be intimidated by an
attractive man. While part of me is ready to tell him to piss
off, the other wants to hear what he has to say.*

*Everett leans forward before he speaks. "I've seen you
around campus, mostly here in the library, and believe it or*

*not, we've even had a couple of classes together. From that I've decided we should get to know each other."*

*"I'm not sure you're making a very good case for a date. However, you are sounding stalker-ish."*

*I'm torn between feeling flattered and creeped out. He's good-looking, but that doesn't mean he's a good guy, I rationalize.*

*"Everett..." I pause. "Does this usually work for you? I mean, is this how you go about asking women out? I'd be interested in hearing how well it works for you."*

*My heart patters hard in my chest when a small smile tugs at the side of his lips, showcasing his square jawline. His dark hair, fair skin, and those captivating green eyes tell me that line absolutely works.*

*"Yes... nine times out of ten, anyway. And today I'm certain it's going to work again, but not without a little effort." His mouth quirks in a smile at the edge of his lips. "Honestly, I've been trying to figure out how to ask you out for a month now. And I'm not creepy, I promise."*

*"Well, I guess if you promise," I tease.*

*I swoon a little at his revelation that he's been wanting to ask me out for the last month. Already in my sophomore year and I've not dated much. Maybe I've been missing the social queues, or just been too involved with my studies.*

*"This isn't a 'Netflix and chill' type situation, is it? I can tell you right now, that's not my style. You should know that upfront."*

*That handsome smile widens across his face, and I'm sure he's trying not to laugh at me, but I don't care. He might as well know what he's getting into...or not.*

*"I like that." He nods. "No, I want to take you somewhere nice. No house parties or bars. Just leave it up to me. I promise it will be a good time."*

*"If you promise. But that's two promises you've made now. You best be careful, I'd hate for you to turn out to be a liar."*

*My agreeance to the date changed the air around us, and his face lit up. My heart pounds hard against my chest with a special feeling that I can't quite define, but just knowing this simple act made this man so happy makes me feel good. Now I can only hope that he's everything he promised he'd be.*

My heart thumps as I swoon at the memories. We haven't been without our ups and downs, but Everett has been everything he promised to be.

"Babe, we're here," he says, pulling me from the thoughts.

I accept his offered hand, and he helps me off the boat. As the gentleman he is, he tips the gondolier before we make our way up the stony path to the bridge. The clamminess of Everett's hand doesn't escape my attention, and I wonder what has him so worked up. I bite my lip to keep from laughing at his nerves over the silly act of professing his love by placing a lock with our initials on a bridge.

"Do you have a lock?" I ask, breaking the silence, before nodding toward the street merchant. "It looks like they have some for sale over there."

Everett shakes his head. Interlocking our fingers, he leads us up the bridge to the peak. We move off to the side, both gazing down into the dark waters of the channel. The swift current is mesmerizing, relaxing me, as the people shuffle past us.

"I don't know how to say this, how to do this. I just..."

An uneasy feeling overcomes me, my stomach flipping as I watch the confusion battle on Everett's face. I want to step in and comfort him, but he's obviously struggling; something I can see he needs to figure out on his own. Whatever it was on the tip of his tongue needs to be his words, not me coaxing it out of him.

I can't handle the suffocating air circling around us,

and as much as I want to hear what he has to say, I offer him an out.

"We can always talk later. We only have a couple more days on our trip. Whatever it is, I'm sure it can wait," I say with a smile.

The darkness in his eyes recedes and is quickly replaced with a gentle, burning gaze that cuts me deep, taking my breath away. My heart pounding in my chest, whooshing in my ears, holds me hostage as time moves in slow motion, Everett drops down to one knee. My jaw hangs open while my mind connects the dots.

My body jerks back to motion, out of its paralyzed state. I grab Everett's arm, tugging him up.

"Get up," I demand in a low, stern tone.

I delicately canvas our surroundings and am thankful that it seems no one really noticed what was about to happen.

I let my hand fall from Everett's arm as he stands. My eyes feel harsh in comparison to the perplexed ones staring back at me. *So much for giving him an out.* I won't feel bad. I don't feel bad. I feel fucking pissed off!

"How dare you?" I scold in a hushed tone. "What are you thinking?"

I'm not here to make a scene, whether it be positive or

negative, but this can't wait.

"What was I thinking?" Everett retorts. "I was thinking that you were the one who brought up the idea of marriage just weeks ago. I was thinking that it was a good idea. And like a fool, I was thinking that a romantic bridge in Italy would be a great place to propose!"

Everett's shoulders are squared, and his voice is no longer hushed as he tries to make his point. The problem is that the points he's using are exactly why I can't say yes. And while my heart wants to soothe the embarrassment and pain I see behind his guarded expression, I can't bend on this.

"You must see why *now*, why *this* isn't right?" I ask, hoping he'll agree. That he can connect the dots.

Everett shakes his head, folding his arms across his chest, and rocks back on his heels. His eyes look everywhere but at mine.

I want to scream, I want to confront him, and console him. I want to dissect every piece of what we've said to each other, but my feelings hurt. My emotions are hyper-aware of every single up and down that's happened over the past minutes. He proposed...*almost.*

I bite back, my jaw clenching as I try to hold the emotion in. I take a deep, cleansing breath and release it. *I need to think.*

"I'd like to go back to the hotel," I say meekly.

He nods and turns sharply on his heels, stalking down the cobblestone road. I follow silently for the handful of blocks we walk until we're at a main fairway. It's only another minute before a cab is stopping for us. Everett opens the door for me and I settle in, but then the door shuts. My heart drops, and I have no words, only a pleading look directed at Everett. But he doesn't acknowledge me, he's busy giving the driver instructions.

"Kens," he says, and motions for me to roll down the window, which I do. "Go back to the hotel and wait for me there, okay? I won't be long."

I go to open the door to get out, but he pushes it closed.

"Go back to the hotel. Wait for me. Do not leave the hotel." He growls.

I can feel the blood rush from my face. *What have I done?* Thoughts are overwhelming my head, making me dizzy. Everett takes a step away from the cab, motioning to the driver to take off.

"Wait!" I call to him from the window. "Where are you going?"

Everett gives a somber shrug. "I guess I have a ring to return."

The air is sucked from my lungs, and the car lunges forward, pushing my back against the seat. I sit paralyzed as the words replay: *I guess I have a ring to return... I guess I have a ring to return... I guess I have a ring to return.*

\* \* \* \*

I quickly wipe the tears from my cheeks when I hear the hotel door open and shut. I take the washcloth from the side of the large, soaking tub I'm currently drowning my sorrows in and press it to my face; I hope it's enough to erase the blotchy signs of my crying.

I spent the first hour back in our room pacing, waiting for Everett to walk in. When that passed, I started cleaning. *Cleaning an already clean hotel room, that's rock bottom.* But I had to keep busy. By hour three I couldn't keep it together anymore. I sought solace in a painfully hot bath, and it was exactly what I needed. It was the only shoulder I had to cry on. *Oh, Anna, how I need you! I wonder if you know how badly I need you.*

A gentle knock on the door startles me, and I inadvertently splash some water out of the tub. I knew he was here, in the room, but I wasn't so sure he'd come to me. I guess somewhere in my mind I imagined coming out of the bathroom to a dark bedroom with Everett already curled up somewhere—maybe on the couch, but hopefully the

bed—asleep. I need to take full advantage of this
opportunity. I don't want to hurt his feelings, I don't want
my feelings hurt, and mostly I can't lose *us* again.

"It's open," I call, impressed with the tone of my voice
and how it doesn't sound scratchy from crying.

Everett creeps in, shirtless, barefoot, and with pajamas
hanging low on his sexy hips. He worked hard for that body,
and I always made sure to appreciate every single inch of it
whenever I could. *Well, when things were less complicated
with us.* He stands there a moment before I notice his eyes
skimming over my exposed flesh. Yes, he wants me too. A
smile pulls at the corner of his lip and I know he's aware of
my hardening nipples. I'm making no effort to hide my
body. There's nothing I'd hide from this man.

"It's time for you to get out of that bath." His voice is
deep as he gives the order.

Everett shuffles around the bathroom as I stand from
the tub, and when he turns back to me he has an oversized,
plush bathrobe in hand. No words are exchanged. I turn
around so he can help me into the robe. The soft fabric
against my warm skin sends a shiver up my spine. When
Everett's arms wrap around my front, fastening the robe, my
knees start to buckle. I'm caught by strong arms, and then
there's a warm breath at my ear.

"I've got you."

*Do you?* I question, but not aloud. My emotions are draining, and this moment of semi-normalcy is something I'm not going to pass up.

In one fell swoop, I'm in his arms and being carried out of the bathroom. Gently, he lays me on the bed. His body covers me like a blanket, but he makes sure to hold his weight on his forearms. His eyes stare into mine...searching for something? I'm captivated by the intimate encounter with no clue as to where it's headed. His hand slides up tenderly over my cheek, brushing back my damp hair, as he places a loving kiss on my lips.

"You have to know it's you." His words whisper, and I can feel the uneven beating of his heart racing against my body. The earnest tone is enough for a lone tear to escape, running down the side of my face.

"It's only ever been you," I promise. I'm overwhelmed with a need to be close to him at our raw confessions, and I wrap my arms around his neck, pulling him close.

The weight of his body presses me hard into the plush bed, and I feel as if we are melting into one, reclaiming what once was ours. His hard member pressing against the terry cloth barely covering my body has me aching for an intimate connection. I need him inside me. Rubbing against his great length, I'm pleased when he takes the hint and sits up on his knees.

Slowly, he undoes the robe, exposing my naked form, sending a chill of goosebumps and a hardening of my nipples as he takes in the sight. His hand cups my cheek, then deliberately and gracefully runs down my chest, past my breast, then sprawling wide against my stomach before reaching my throbbing core. Grazing past the neediest part of my body, his hand continues on its journey, tickling the inside of my thigh as its moves.

The bed shakes, startling me out of my lust-induced stupor, and I realize that he'd hopped off, stripping off what little clothing he had on. The dim lighting accentuates the sculpture of his body as he comes toward me, slowly as if I'm his prey, and I can't wait to be devoured. Strong hands rub my ankles before they are spread apart. They run up both sides of my legs as he settles his body between them.

Leaning forward, he kisses the tuft of my vagina, and I'm bucking up as the pleasure overwhelms me. His lips are on my pussy, licking and nipping at the sensitive spot. Warm fingers startle me as they press deep and hard into the heart of my core. I buck into his face as his fingers find a rhythm. I'm too close to my end and I don't want it to be this way. I eagerly grab at his hair, pulling him off of me.

"I need more," I pant. "I need you."

"Yes."

Settling himself between my opening, it only takes one swift plunge and I'm full. He's deep and thick, stretching me in the most amazing way, and I know I'm not going to hold on much longer.

"Go. More," I demand, wrapping my arms tightly around his body, egging him on.

With no further instruction, the pace has picked up, and with each thrust I throw my head back with an uninhibited moan.

"Oh God, Kenslie." His hands move to my hips, holding them in place as he grinds against me hard, and I'm gone.

My orgasm shatters through my being; the waves of pleasure are like nothing before, sending every nerve on edge. I'm acutely aware of the roar bouncing off the walls as his hands bite into my hips as he thrusts, finding his own end.

Everett gently falls onto me, his hot breath panting against my ear as we both come down from the ecstasy. My skin feels cool as he rolls off of me, but only for a moment, because he's pulling me against him, his front to my back. The bed shakes as he kicks at the blankets from the end of

the bed, pulling them over us as we settle into a blissful
slumber. I drift off knowing that even though I declined a
proposal, I know he's my end game; and I'm his.

* * * *

It's been an exhausting day in Milan. *The clothes.* Oh,
the clothes! I may have gone overboard, but only because
Everett insisted, and he bought me a medium-sized luggage
case with rollers. That's romance. Who needs a ring when a
man understands your need for clothes?

It doesn't seem like a pain in the ass to haul around the
case; our trip will be over in a couple of days. That thought
hits me. Anna and I should have been in Milan, shopping,
trying on clothes for hours, giggling and drinking fancy
champagne. I desperately hope she made it to Milan and had
a wonderful time—alone or not. And in this moment, I hope
Everett is right, that the man she's with is a good guy and
escorting her like a gentleman on her trip. *Wishful thinking.*

Besides, Anna would understand, how do I say no to
the clothes? I imagine it, "*I got these in Milan. Oh, this
dress, I think I got it in Milan. This Prada bag, Everett got it
for me when we were in Milan.*"

Shit. I sound like a bitch, *in my head,* I'd never say it
out loud. And honestly, I'm not sure how many of these
clothes I'll even have a chance to wear when we get home.

I'll be starting my career. It took me four years of hard work, but I'm ready as hell! But I can expect to live in scrubs. *I wonder if I can get designer scrubs? Oh yes, I got these in Milan.* I laugh out loud at the ridiculous thought.

"What's so funny over there?"

"Just being silly. I might be drunk off shopping."

"Really now? Does 'drunk on shopping Kens' make the same kind of deals 'drunk Kens' makes?"

"Hey! Why do you think I have to be drunk to be naughty?" I tease. "We could have a fight again—our make-up sex is pretty intense." I wink.

"Cute." He puts his hand under my chin and tilts it up. "But no," he says sternly.

"How many hours until we get into Paris?" I ask.

"I'd say we'd be in our hotel room by ten PM. We spent longer in Milan that I thought we would."

"And whose fault is that?" I give him a pointed look.

"You can't be saying it's mine? I didn't need new clothes," he accuses with a mocking tone.

"It *is* your fault. And I'll tell you why…you bought me a suitcase! You knew exactly what was going to happen."

Everett leans over, his hand gently caressing the side of my face before his lips descend on mine. His lips start off soft and gentle, but his hand wraps around my head, holding us together as our tongues tangle intensely as the tangible need grows. Warmth hits my panties, and I lean my body into his as much as I can in this damn seat.

He continues to take what I'm giving, and I'm aware of a soft moan escaping my lips. And then I'm aware that we're *not* alone. I pull back maybe an inch. Our eyes lock, and it makes my heart weak. So much emotion from a single look, and I can feel the dampness in the corner of my eyes. I sigh.

"I love you, more than you know. Even when it was touch-and-go there for a minute, I knew I'd never stop loving you." I pour my heart out.

"It was never touch-and-go. You were, *are*, mine. Always."

His lips are on mine again, and I know he's telling the truth. Ring or not, we belong to each other.

# Chapter 18

*Ryker*

*Paris*

I'm going out of my mind on how to keep Liesa from the Eiffel Tower tonight. She's dead set on going up there at night. I have plans for us to go up there tomorrow morning and then again in the evening before we leave Paris. And no, it isn't to propose to her. We aren't ready for that yet. I'm ready to call her mine. I hope to convince her to move in with me when she gets to Chicago.

"We're at Pullman Paris Tour Eiffel Hotel," the taxi driver says as he pulls up to a stunning hotel.

"Thank you," I say, giving him money for the fare and a tip.

Before we get into the hotel Liesa is saying how we have to go to the Eiffel Tower tonight and we need to hurry so we can be up there as the sun sets.

"Liesa, we can't go to the Eiffel Tower tonight. I have other plans for us tonight."

"But it's been a dream of mine to go to the tower at night. There's no guarantee that I'll be able to see it before we leave."

"Do you really think I'd let you miss that?"

"No, but I don't see why you can't change your plans."
She stomps her foot.

*Fuck, she's cute when she does that.*

"You'll like these plans too. Come on. Let's go put our
bags in our room, and then I can show you my surprise." I
grab our things and head to the check-in desk.

"*Salut*. How can I help you this evening?"

"I have a reservation under Annaliesa James."

"Oh, I see it right here. You have a room reserved with
a view of the tower."

"Yes!" Liesa responds with a little too much
excitement.

"You will be in room 524, and you should have a great
view of the Eiffel Tower from the balcony and also the
window," the desk clerk says as she slides our keys over to
us.

"Thank you," I say, grabbing Liesa's hand and our
bags.

"I can't believe we're here. I can't wait to see the view
of the tower from our room. I don't know why I paid extra
since I don't plan to do much more than sleep in the room."

"Let's go. We have plans tonight."

"Let's take the stairs," Liesa says.

"Why?"

"Because I don't like elevators."

"But this one has glass on three sides, and I'm told you can see the Eiffel Tower from it."

"You don't have to ask me twice. You just won me over."

Wow, I didn't think it'd be that easy to get her into the elevator with me.

"Look at this view. I really hope that we have this view from our room."

# Chapter 19

*Kenslie*

*Paris*

I spring off the train with a new-found energy. I'm in Paris! I've loved every stop along the way, even the unexpected ones, though they took me longer to appreciate. But honestly, what beats Paris?

I get to spend time with my man, and it's the best chance I have to meet up with Anna since I know where she's staying, and I know where she'll visit...multiple times, I can be sure of that. *Maybe.* I laugh to myself. I did leave out the part where you can no longer take the stairs all the way up the Eiffel Tower. I hope that mysterious man can convince her.

"Everett!" I squeal and take his hand, twirling myself around. "We're here, and we're going to find Anna, I just know it! I feel it."

Everett only nods with a smile on his face. I noticed that the closer the train got to Paris the quieter he became. Maybe he's worried about meeting up with Anna. She's bound to have a few choice words with him. *And maybe even me?* I cringe at the thought, but it passes quickly. I love

Anna like a sister, and sisters figure their shit out!

"Let's go. I know which hotel Anna is at! Let's see if she's there, if she's checked in." I rush my words as I pull Everett's hand to follow my haste.

I'm abruptly pulled back by the bull of a man whose feet are stuck firmly in place. I'm confused, and words escape me. I shake my head at him, giving him a questioning look. He opens his mouth, only to shut it again.

"Well?" I challenge.

He lets out a deep sigh. "Nothing. You're right, let's go."

It's now clear to me what's going on—he's pouting.

"Baby," I say, taking steps, closing the distance between our bodies, I reach my hand up and caress his cheek. "Just because I want to find Anna doesn't mean I don't want to spend my trip with you too. We've had a wonderful time, but I, *we*, need to finish it with her. It just wouldn't be the same. You understand, right?"

"Of course I do," he responds swiftly and places a chaste kiss on my lips. "And you know what? I think this time you're going to get your wish."

"That's the spirit!" I bounce with excitement. "Let's get a cab and get to the hotel."

\* \* \* \*

"What do you mean you can't tell us if she's checked in or not?" My tone is harsh with the man working across the counter, but I'm fed up with being one step closer to only go two steps back!

"Madam, I'm truly sorry, but unless you have a room number I cannot tell you if she's checked into the hotel. We are *the* premier hotel in Paris, and I could no sooner tell you if an American girl was staying here or the Prime Minister."

"You've got to be kidding me!" I slam my hands down on the desk, only to have the man shrug his shoulders at me with indifference.

"Fine! I'll sit in the lobby until I see her."

The man's eyes get wide before he speaks, "Again, madam, I cannot allow that."

"And why the hell not?"

I narrow my eyes at him, ready for a fight, but then I feel the warmth of Everett's body next to mine before he takes my hand in his. He's trying to comfort me, which maybe I need, but I want to keep my anger. It's been pent-up since I got off that forsaken train!

"It's obvious you're upset, but I cannot allow you to stay here and continue making a scene. I'll have to ask you to please leave now."

"Come on, babe, there are other places for us to look

for her. I think there's even a hotel close to here we can check into, and then maybe we'll bump into her that way."

My teeth grind together as I hold back words that would be said out of anger, and unable to take back once they were out. Submitting to Everett's request, I reluctantly let him pull me from the hotel. A deep inhale of the fresh air is welcoming, and I agree that Everett is right. There are still plenty of ways to track Anna down.

"Baby, you gotta get out of your head," Everett says.

He takes us off the steps of the hotel and pulls me into his arms.

"I love you, and I hope you remember there's nothing I wouldn't do for you. *Nothing.* And I *promise* we'll find Anna, and…" He pauses. "And when we do I hope you won't forget how much fun we've had together. You might have wished this trip had gone differently, but as of right now, I wouldn't change a thing."

"Everett," I say, pushing up on my toes and wrapping my arms around his neck. "I love you too. It's been an incredible trip, and nothing will ever change that. Thank you for coming for me, for proving your love. Don't worry, nothing is going to change once we find Anna. You might be a little bit of a third wheel," I say, laughing, "but you're familiar with that."

"Promise?" he implores.

My chest swells at the request, and I notice his soft eyes, backed by a darkness. There's something more to his words, and I can't put my finger on it. I want to ask outright what's going on, but I decide to take him at face value. After all, Everett isn't much for games. But my thoughts are haunted by his words. I'm missing something. Maybe he's going to try to propose again? *Please no more surprises!*

"Promise." I smile and press a tender, quick kiss to his welcoming lips. "Where to next?"

"Let's find a place to stay. We can walk around and see what they have, and maybe we can catch Anna while we're out?"

"Look at you...so smart."

Everett takes the luggage that I've been towing around, and with his other hand, he wraps my arm in the crook of his arm. We fall into a comfortable silence as we walk down the busy streets just blocks from the Eiffel Tower. I try to free my mind as I keep my eyes peeled for Anna, but every couple of steps I look up at the magnificent sight. It's more than I could have ever dreamed. I have so much to be thankful for, good, bad or indifferent, I'm a lucky lady.

\* \* \* \*

"I don't know why we can't go tonight," I pout. "I've

always wanted to see the Eiffel Tower at night. I know it's Anna's dream too. Maybe, just maybe, we will see her?"

Everett shakes his head, stalking toward me, his eyes skating over my body, sending a warm buzz up my spine. I don't want to be seduced right now. Right now I want to go, but man, he's hard to resist. I sigh. Pulling off his shirt, he tosses it on the plush hotel bed as he presses toward me, and he means business. We've spent this trip making up and appeasing our needy bodies, and now all thoughts of leaving the hotel have escaped my mind. He is the most handsome man I've ever met, and the inside is just as good. The thing I wanted to see—*what was it again?*—will still be there tomorrow.

Strong hands settle on my waist and warm fingers slip under my billowy shirt, sending every nerve on high alert. Rough, masculine hands push my blouse up over my head, and I allow it, holding my arms up for easy removal. Goosebumps scatter across my skin when he presses his lips against the sensitive crook of my neck, and I melt into his body. He pulls me tight against him, and his skillful hands unclasp my bra. I pull back just enough to slip it off, tossing it away. My hard nipples brush against his firm, smooth chest. Leaning down, Everett connects our lips and I easily open to him, our tongues intently exploring with passion.

I grin inwardly. *Discussion over. Sexy time go.*

# Chapter 20

*Ryker*

Waking up after an incredible night, I'm finally taking Liesa to the Eiffel Tower. She's been talking about it non-stop since we got up this morning. Seeing how happy she is makes me happy. I love that it's me she's sharing this trip with.

"Even though it isn't night I'm excited to see the Eiffel Tower. I can't wait to go up it."

"Even though you have to take an elevator?" I ask.

"We can take the stairs," she replies.

"You have some wrong information. There are only stairs up the first two levels, then to get to the top you have to take an elevator."

"What? Kens must have forgot to tell me that little piece of information."

*Probably for a very good reason.*

"Why would she do that?"

"Oh, that little bitch totally did it because she knows I'm scared and she wants me to go to the top."

"What? If you had known, you wouldn't go up?"

*Is her fear really that bad?*

"Well..." She takes a deep breath. "I don't know. I want to say yes, I would have still went up, but I have this irrational fear of elevators. I'm afraid I'm going to get stuck in them or that they will plummet."

I don't know what to say to make it better. I don't have a fear like that. I do know that they are real though.

"You do know that elevators have a call button for help. They also don't just plummet."

"How do you know it won't plunge to the ground, smashing to smithereens?"

"Because there are multiple steel cables that hold the cars up. They'd all have to break at once, and that isn't likely. There's only one elevator that has done that, and it was due to a plane going through the Empire State Building and severing all the cables in one car."

"Wow. Aren't you a bucket full of knowledge?"

"I try to be. I know that you know a lot of stuff too. More than most people." I grab her hand and pull her to me. "I'll hold your hand and make sure you make it to the top alive."

"Don't laugh at me. It isn't funny. This is a real fear. It's called elevator phobia. It's often accompanied by claustrophobia and agoraphobia. I think some of my fear is agoraphobia. Being trapped in a situation in which escape would be difficult or impossible."

"I'm sorry. I'm not laughing at you. I don't know what it feels like to have this type of fear. I want to help you get over this fear, or at least make it more comfortable for you."

"I don't know if I'll ever get over it, but with you by my side it'll definitely help," she says and grabs my hand. "Let's head on up so I can see the view. Plus, we should go now while I'm acting brave." She laughs.

We stand in line and wait for the elevator, and it looks full by the time we get to the front of the line, but the attendant tells us to load up.

"This one's full. Shouldn't we wait for the next one?" Liesa asks.

The attendant tells her that all the elevators are this full, so we can wait if we want.

"Liesa, let's just head up now. Come on." I try to get her in the elevator. We are never going to make it up there today if she doesn't just go. "You can do this. I'll be right by you."

"Fine, let's do this." She grabs my hand and leads me into the elevator.

I'm nervous and excited for her to see the top of the tower. I just hope it lives up to all of her dreams and expectations.

"Wow, that was a fast ride," she says, exiting the elevator in a hurry.

"See, you had nothing to worry about." I grab her into a hug, then spin her so my front is to her back. "Now, look out at Paris," I whisper into her ear.

I should have looked up first because...

"Oh my God. It's Kens." Liesa closes her eyes and rubs them like she's trying to make sure she's not seeing things. When she opens her eyes again she yells, "Kenslie!" and looks over at me and says, "It's Kens and her boyfriend Everett." Then she grabs me and pulls me toward them.

"Everett! Anna's here! Oh my God! Of course she'd be here. Where else in this whole damn trip would I find her!" Kens exclaims, rushing over to her friend.

"Kens, I'm so happy to see you. I have so many questions." Liesa runs into Kens's arms and they hug. More like jumping up and down screaming.

"Anna, are you having a good trip?" Everett asks in his normal calm demeanor.

"It's been okay, but it would have been better if Kens was with me the whole time," she smarts off to him.

"Ryker? Is that... What? Ryker, you're *here*?" Kens asks.

Oh shit, I didn't expect her to recognize me. We

haven't seen each other in a few years and I let my hair grow out.

"Yes, it's good to see you again."

I look over at Liesa, and her mouth is flapping like a fish. Open. Close. Open. Close.

"What?" stammers out of her mouth. "You know them?" she asks me.

"Liesa, I wanted to tell you so many times, but I didn't know how," I say. What an idiot I am. I should have planned for this better, but when Everett and I made these plans I didn't know that I'd fall in love with her.

"Maybe you should've tried harder. I don't believe you guys. How could you do this to me, Kens? You knew how much this trip meant to me, and you let Everett steal it away from me? I can't even believe this," Liesa says while wiping at her face.

"It wasn't like that, Anna. I didn't know. You know we broke up. I wouldn't have ruined this, I promise," Kens pleads with Liesa.

"What I do know is my best friend in the whole world let her boyfriend play me like a fool. He got his wish. I hope he's happy now, because my world is crumbling before me," she says, turning to walk away.

I can't let her leave. "Liesa, you can't leave."

"Watch me. Last time I checked I was allowed to do whatever I wanted. Now that I know I was a babysitting job to you I have no desire to see you. As far as I'm concerned, I don't want to see any of you for the foreseeable future. Unfortunately, I'll have to see you on the flight home. But after that, if I never see you guys again, that'll be too soon," she finishes and rushes to the elevator.

What do I do? Do I chase after her or give her time to cool off?

Before I can ask Kens for advice, she's yelling at Everett.

"How could you keep this from me, Everett?" Kens accuses and pulls Everett off to the side. I can't make out what she's saying to him, but she looks pissed.

"Well, this totally blew up in our faces. I never expected this reaction," I mumble as I watch Kenslie rush off toward the elevator.

"Fuck," Everett says, walking back to where I'm standing. "I messed up big time. I knew I wasn't exactly welcome on this trip, but I needed Kens to take me back. What do I do, man?" He's rubbing his hand through his hair, staring at me like I have all the answers.

"I don't know. I just lost Liesa too. I love her. It wasn't supposed to happen like this, but it did, and we better figure out 'operation win Liesa and Kens back', or we're both going home single."

"Let's get the hell outta here. I need a fuckin' drink. There has to be a bar around here somewhere," Everett says.

Alcohol isn't the answer, but it sure does make everything feel right at the time.

# Chapter 21

*Kenslie*

The Eiffel *fucking* Tower! I want to jump up and down with excitement, but I decide against making myself look like a fool in a foreign country. *A little dignity.* Everett wraps his arm around my shoulder and presses a kiss to the top of my head. I'm sure the anticipation is radiating off my body.

"We gonna stand here all day, babe, or you think we should go up?" Everett teases.

"Hell yeah!" I exclaim, dragging him with me as I rush to the line for the elevator.

I bounce from foot to foot. This must be the slowest line I've ever waited in. My body is cosmically pulled to the tower. It's a ridiculous thought, but maybe I'll be able to see Anna from the top. I want to scour the city looking for my missing friend like a *Where's Waldo* puzzle, but maybe, *just maybe*, I'm due for a little good luck.

The elevator is crowded, and the hum of the excitement among the many tourist is almost tangible. There's a special bond with these strangers as we're about to experience a world wonder, and in this moment, I feel sad...heartbroken.

There's a heaviness in my chest, but I manage to hold back the quiver of my lip. There are thousands of things in this world that I want to experience with the man I love, but this trip was to be a last hoorah of a friendship that has survived years, and a promise that we'll endure the miles apart.

Fingers clasp around mine, and I look up at Everett. Soft and caring eyes search mine, and I love that he knows so well that the wheels are churning in my head.

"Today's going to be the day, baby. I can feel it." He gives me a half-smile as we exit the elevator.

While the hopeful tone behind his words are genuine, I don't want to set myself up for yet another disappointment. I was sure I would have found her before now... *Wow.* My attention is drawn away from my dreary thoughts, and words cannot explain what I'm seeing.

"Oh, Everett." I tuck my arm into the nook of his arm and rest my head on his shoulder.

I feel a tear in the corner of my eye as we look silently out into the beautiful skyline. Nothing I have ever seen has prepared me for this moment. *There is nothing that could.* I take in a deep breath of the cool wind bustling around us and let it escape. I turn into Everett, hooking my arms around his waist.

"*Kenslie!*" I hear the faint sound of my name in the

wind. I look in the direction of the voice and my eyes narrow, trying to comprehend what they're seeing. My fingers pinch into Everett's arm

"Everett! Anna's here! Oh my God! Of course she'd be here. Where else in this whole damn trip would I find her!" I exclaim, pushing past him, rushing to her.

"Kens, I'm so happy to see you. I have so many questions," Anna says as we wrap one another in a giant hug, jumping and squealing.

I've never felt more relieved in my life! Anna's here!

"Anna, are you having a good trip?" Everett asks from behind us, in his normal calm demeanor.

"It's been okay, but it would have been better if Kens was with me the whole time." Anna shoots him some sass.

*Awww. I missed you!* My heart swells with relief, and for the first time in what feels like ages, my body relaxes. I have so many questions, but I'm so damn pleased that we're finally together again! I smile at her, and then look to her left, at the mystery man. My body slumps, and I pull out of our embrace. *What?* I look back to Anna and the proud smile on her face.

"Ryker? Is that… What?" I cock my head to the side, examining the man before me. "Ryker, you're *here*?" I ask.

His face falters and pales a moment, before he regains

composure.

"Yes, it's good to see you again." He smiles with a nod.

I'm completely confused. Why is Anna here with Ryker? Does she know? She can't know. We haven't introduced them yet. It had always been the plan, but it never seemed to come together. To me, Everett's cousin Ryker and Anna seemed like a perfect match. But *now*?

I turn my attention to Anna to try and figure out this whole messed up situation, but she beats me to the questions.

"What?" she stammers. "You know them?"

I try to respond, but Ryker speaks before I have a chance.

"Liesa, I wanted to tell you so many times, but I didn't know how," he pleads.

"Maybe you should have tried harder. I don't believe you guys. How could you do this to me, Kens? You knew how much this trip meant to me, and you let Everett steal it away from me. I can't even believe this." Anna wipes at her face.

She's crying? My head is spinning, but the dots finally connect. She thinks this was a set up. She must think this was the plan all along.

"It wasn't like that, Anna," I promise, pushing my way

toward her. "I didn't know. You know we broke up. I wouldn't have ruined this, I promise."

"What I do know is my best friend in the whole world let her boyfriend play me like a fool. He got his wish. I hope he's happy now, because my world is crumbling before me." Anna turns on her heels and heads toward the elevator.

I'm on my toes, ready to go after her, but not without a few choice words for Everett; all of which I know are going to end with some lame-ass excuse from him.

"How could you keep this from me, Everett?" I turn back to him before pulling him off to the side, demanding answers.

He rubs his hands on his jeans nervously and blows out a heavy breath. "I told you there wasn't anything I wouldn't do to win you back. We honestly weren't trying to ruin your trip. I just needed to be where you were. We hopped on a flight the day after you guys left and tracked you down. You weren't supposed to see us until Paris. But you did. And then the train fiasco."

Everett runs his hands through his hair and gives his head a hard shake.

"It was lucky that Ryker saw you get off and he hopped on," he continues. "I'd hate myself if I thought that Anna was truly alone with some strange guy on her trip. Ryker texted me and he and Anna had hit it off, just like you said they would." His tone is hopeful

"No...no...no! Don't you put this on me! I suggested we go on a double date, not trick her into thinking she met a nice guy at random. This is so fucked up! How could you?" I ask, and I honestly want to know.

I want to know the thought process of this man, but I fear even the best answer would never be good enough. My body goes still as I process the rushed words from his mouth. I feel the blood flood from my face and my mouth gape open.

"What do you mean Ryker texted you? You fucking lied to me about your phone?" I shout, catching Ryker's attention, and he looks over at us. I roll my eyes at the two very stupid men before me with sheepish looks on their faces.

*I can't even!* I just... *Ugh.* He opens his mouth to speak, and I hold up my hand to silence him. I don't want to hear it. I need Anna, I need to fix *his* fuck up.

"I'm gonna go get Anna. You can pick up your shit at the front desk and find a place to sleep tonight. I have a feeling Ryker might have space." I shoot them both a harsh look.

I can't wait any longer. Turning, I push my way

through the crowd and head after Anna. I manage to make it on the elevator down just before the doors close. She's leaning up against the wall, her arms crossed over her chest, and her body is gently shaking; holding back sobs, I assume. *I've been there.*

I scoot past the passengers, trying to be as delicate as possible as I make my way toward her.

"Anna," I say softly.

"No," she says sternly, looking up at me. "No. How could you? Why?"

"I swear I had no idea. I promise," I reply with all the candor my body possesses. "I would never ruin this for us."

"Then what the hell happened? How?" Her puffy eyes search mine, desperate for the truth.

And I know that look on my bestie's face; she's more than angry that we got separated, she's hurt. Her heart. Everett was right, they must've hit it off.

"From what I could stomach to hear from Everett it sounds like he and Ryker came after us. Everett wanted to make up. And I'd been wanting to set you up with Everett's cousin for a while now, remember?" I shrug my shoulders. "The idiot thought now was a good time for that. According to Everett, we weren't supposed to run into them until Paris."

Anna gapes at me, and I can only shake my head. The truth is hard to believe, but it is what it is. There is no going back now. I can't change what's happened, but I can try to turn it around. I hope Anna sees that we owe it to one another.

"I told Everett to find somewhere else to stay tonight. It's just you and me, lady. Let's take our trip back, please," I beg.

We reach the base of the tower. The passengers start to shuffle off, and it feels like an eternity of silence between us. I follow suit, solemnly stepping off, waiting for Anna. I can't rush this...her. This trip has been full of ups and downs. Everett and I have been through some shit, but my tough Anna, she looks like a crack might have been made in that tough shell of hers. I love her to death, but it's clear something big happened on her end of the trip, and I'm just going to have to wait for her to be ready to talk about it.

"Okay, fine. Let's go get my stuff," she offers, linking her arm in mine.

I rest my head on her shoulder a moment, taking in the intense episode we've just clawed through. The mood is heavy, but not dark. We're walking away from the tower, the past, the lost, but we're walking away *together*. Whatever light we're heading toward we're going to need

each other to get through; just because there *is* light at the
end of the tunnel doesn't mean it's easy.

# Chapter 22

*Annaliesa*

My heart's breaking, and while I want to be pissed at Kens, I can't find it in my heart to be. I honestly don't think she'd betray me like this, but right now I'm so emotional I can't even see straight.

"Hey, miss, you can't be in here," some hotel guy says, running up to us.

"What do you mean she can't be in here?" I ask.

"She was asked to leave yesterday for causing a scene. She isn't welcome here. Sorry, ma'am."

"What did you do, Kens?" I ask. She doesn't normally cause scenes.

"They wouldn't tell me what room you were in. I got a little upset," she says sheepishly.

"It's okay," I say to the hotel attendant.

Knowing she made that scene trying to find out what room I was in and if I was checked in already makes me feel good. *She was trying to find me.*

Turning to Kens, I say, "I'll meet you outside after I get my stuff."

Heading up to the room is bittersweet. I'm going to

miss this room. I loved seeing the Eiffel Tower light up out the window across from the bed. I hope Kens's room has a view.

I don't want to leave without saying some things to Ryker. While he broke my heart, he deserves to know that I was falling for him and that he started off something good with a lie. Even if it was a lie by omission. Grabbing the notepad and pen the hotel left on the desk, I write Ryker a note.

*Ryker,*

*I'm sorry I left the way I did, but I couldn't stay around any longer. I'm devastated, and you guys blindsided me. I thought we shared something special. Now I don't know if it was all just a lie or if it was real. I know where I stand, but I don't know where you stand.*

*Things are so confusing right now. I won't stay mad at you forever, but I don't know if we can ever go back to what we shared this week. We built our foundation on a lie, and relationships don't work when that's the case. All trust is lost, and you need trust to have a healthy relationship.*

*With love,*

*Liesa*

I hurry up and pack everything in my bag and head down to meet up with Kens. Hopefully, she has a room with a view, because I'm not sure I want to do much more than sit and veg out. This trip has been exhausting, and now that my emotions are running high the exhaustion is setting in.

"Anna, over here," Kens yells out to me as I turn in the opposite direction of where she's waiting for me.

"Oh," I say, shaking my head. "What hotel are you guys staying in since you got kicked out of this one?"

"Hey, it isn't my fault they wouldn't tell me if you checked in yet. I tried to tell them that I should've been a guest on the reservation and it still didn't work."

"Only you could get kicked out of a hotel in Paris." I laugh and go flag down a taxi to take us to Kens's hotel.

"Wait, we don't need a taxi. The hotel is only a couple of blocks over," Kens says, grabbing my arm, and then she jumps right back into our conversation. "Well, I really wanted to meet up with you. While I've had fun with Everett, I wanted to spend the end of the trip with you. This was supposed to be our trip."

"Well, it looks like we get to spend the end of it together." I sigh.

"What are you sighing about?" Kens asks.

"I know the guys are going to want to be with us. I

don't know if I'm ready for that, and I can tell by your face you want Everett to be with you too for this last leg of the trip."

"I do, but I also want time with you. You are important to me, and I can live a day or two without Everett."

"I'm not sure that's possible with Everett and Ryker around. I'm not even mad about it. I'm more hurt."

We walk into their hotel, and it's beautiful. I can't believe I didn't pick this hotel to stay in. Hopefully, the rooms are just as gorgeous as the lobby.

"What floor are you on?" I ask, hoping it's the first floor.

"We're on the tenth floor. And before you ask, yes there are stairs, and no I'm not taking them. You can if you want."

"Hell yes I want. I'll meet you on the tenth floor."

The walk up to the room is peaceful. I need this time to think. I want to run into Ryker's arms and tell him we can work everything out, but I don't want to be a weak woman either. I wasn't looking for love and this is why. It's confusing, hard, time-consuming, and heartbreaking. I can't even imagine what it'd feel like if we'd spent years together.

Exiting the stairwell, I spot Kens waiting in front of a room. Once we enter the room, I see that the view is nice, but not as breathtaking as my room. It'll have to do, because I'm stuck here now.

"Oh, here's your phone." I pull it out of my backpack. "It should be charged. I was hoping you'd try calling it from Everett's, but I guess he didn't purchase the international plan?"

"Thank you," Kens says, grabbing it from my hand. "What do you want to do for the rest of the afternoon?"

"Be lazy and take a nap."

"Really? We're in Paris," she says.

"I realize that, but I'm not in the mood to walk around and sightsee right now. I just want to think, laugh, and talk with you. Catch up on how your trip went, and then maybe we can go to the tower tonight in the dark," I say, hoping that last part will help with keeping her from wanting to explore.

"Sounds good, but I'm holding you to going out tonight."

"I wouldn't miss seeing the Eiffel Tower all lit up and standing on it in the dark. The only crappy part is I have to take that damn elevator again."

"It isn't that bad."

"You're a sneak too! Telling me there were stairs for the tower but not telling me that it's only for the first couple of levels."

"I knew if I told you you'd chicken out and not even want to go."

"It's not like it did me much good to go today. I paid to go up and didn't get to see anything. Well, I guess I did find you."

"Yes, you did. So that makes it worth it!"

"Ugh, why did the guys have to go and ruin this trip? Why couldn't Everett wait until we got back? So many damn questions. If he would have waited, I would have still met Ryker."

"What do you mean you would have still met Ryker?"

"We'll be working together in Chicago. He got hired as an architect in the firm that hired me."

"*What!*" Kens screams. "I can't believe that jerk. He really did play us both."

I hate that Kens is upset, but this is typical Everett. He goes after what he wants. He doesn't intentionally hurt people, but he doesn't always think of the effect his actions will have on others.

*Why the hell am I defending him?*

"Kens, I have no idea why I'm siding with Everett, but do you really believe he'd do this to hurt you? I think in his mind coming to Paris to win you over played out differently.

I bet he thought we'd just accept him trailing along with us, and he brought Ryker so he wasn't the third wheel."

"I have a feeling you're right. He said they weren't planning on seeing us until Paris, but I saw him first and ruined everything by getting off the train."

"It's all good. Everything happens for a reason, right?" I ask hopefully.

"Yes, so I guess we'll have to meet up with the guys at some point and get their story?"

"It isn't going to happen tonight. We need to make them work for it a little."

"Hell yes we do!" Kens agrees.

"I want to hear all about your trip, but I really am exhausted. Do you mind if I take a nap?" I ask, not wanting to upset Kens, but not having the energy to do much else.

"No, I may just join you so we can go have some fun tonight."

"Sounds good."

\* \* \* \*

A beeping sound pulls me out of my sleep. "What the hell is making that noise?" I ask the room.

"It's my phone," Kens says.

"Turn it off," I grunt while pulling the covers over my head.

"I will, but we should get up and get ready to head out."

"What time is it?"

"It's five. I figured we'd do dinner first and then head over to the tower."

"I need a shower before I can do anything. I feel like I've been hit by a freight train."

The shower is just what the doctor ordered. It wakes me up and leaves me feeling somewhat human again. Now to have some fun with Kens.

"Girl, hurry up. I'm dying to get on with our night," Kens yells through the bathroom door.

"Don't get your panties in a knot. I'm almost ready."

We decide to eat in the hotel restaurant and then walk over to the tower, so we can see all the cute shops around. Paris comes to life at night. Everything is lit up like the Fourth of July.

"I can't believe one of our lifetime dreams is coming true. We're in Paris together and we're going to the top of the Eiffel Tower at night," I squeal.

"I know. This is something we've dreamed about for years. I'm so happy we're getting to experience this together," Kens says.

"Me too. Now let's pay for the elevator and get that

ride over with," I say, pulling Kens up to the ticket booth with me.

The elevator ride isn't as bad this time around because we aren't packed in like a can of sardines. I like having breathing room when I'm in elevators. It also seems to be moving faster than it did earlier in the day. Or maybe it's just my imagination.

"You're going to love the view. I didn't see much before I heard you calling my name earlier, but what I did see was magnificent."

Once the doors open my jaw drops. The sight before me is better than anything I've imagined. It's better than pictures too. Pictures don't do it justice.

"This is worth the elevator ride," I say in awe. "I'm so happy I didn't let my fear keep me from seeing this." I also did it without having to hold Ryker's hand. Once again I'm back to relying on myself, and I have to do things on my own.

"Me too. I would've pulled you up here kicking and screaming though," Kens says, laughing.

I can't help but laugh with her. "That's what friends are for," I say to her.

"True, to force them to step out of their comfort zones."

"Let's take a picture." I grab my phone out of my

purse.

"Yes, I can't believe how few pictures I've gotten on this trip. With leaving my phone with you, to forgetting Everett had his, I think he took a few. I even bought a couple of disposable cameras, but I'm not sure how well those pictures will turn out."

"Well, we'll just have to take a ton now that we're back together. Pictures are nice to have, but this is a trip that I'm positive we'll both remember forever."

"True," Kens agrees.

"What the hell?"

"What?" Kens asks, looking at me like I'm losing my mind.

"Ryker is texting me."

I'm not exactly sure why this surprises me, but maybe it's because I thought he would've tried to get ahold of me earlier.

"Oh God, Everett is texting me too."

"Ryker is asking for me to forgive him. Look at these messages." I hold my phone out for her to see them.

*Ryker: Liesa baby I sorry.*

*Ryker: Pease forgives me.*

*Ryker: I real did fall for yous. It wasn't a joke.*

*Everything was really to me.*
   *Ryker: Please talks to me.*

I can't help but laugh at the messages, because there are so many grammatical errors. I wonder if he's drinking. If he is, will he even remember them in the morning?

   *Ryker: An apology is only the beginning of what you deserve. You deserve the world. Give me a second shot to show you how much you mean to me. I know what I did was wrong, but it felt so right. Please forgive me.*
   *Ryker: How can something feel so right and be so wrong? It can't. We're meant to be together. We're better together. You complete me.*

"Where the hell is he getting all this shit?" I ask Kens, holding my phone out to her as another message pops up.

"He has to be getting this shit off the internet," Kens states.

"Yes, but it's kind of cute." I laugh.

   *Ryker: I know words aren't enough, but I am truly sorry. Give me a chance to show you that I'm sorry. Action speaks louder than words. Please let me prove to you that*

*I'm the one for you.*

*Me: Step one, BE ORIGINAL and quit copying and pasting from google for your messages! PS I know you're copying and pasting because your grammar is correct.*

*Ryker: Thanks gods yous talks to me.*

"I can't believe he thought I'd accept words of others for his apology. Men can be so dumb. Plus, he's drunk. Thanks gods yous..." I can't even finish before busting up laughing. Drunk texting can get people in trouble.

"Yes, they can. Everett is blowing up my phone too, but it's more about all the dirty things he wants to do to my body. I don't think he's as drunk, because his messages aren't discombobulated like Ryker's."

"I'd much rather have those texts. These apology texts suck. I know I shouldn't be mad at him, but I'm still hurt. I understand in a way why he didn't say anything, and if he would have, then we wouldn't have bonded so much. For that I can't be mad, because I fell for him."

*Ryker: I'm sorry. I just wanted a chance to get to know you and for you to get to know me. If I would've told you, then we wouldn't have had all this time together. Time that I won't apologize for. It made me believe that there's a person for me. One that I can see myself spending the rest of my life with.*

*Ryker: Dose are me words. Azzhole types fors me.*

"Should I put him out of his misery?" I ask Kens.

"Yes!" she says excitedly.

"Fine, but they have to meet us for breakfast early since I know they'll both have a hangover in the morning." I can't help but laugh at this. I'm evil.

"Sounds good. Serves them right for drowning their sorrows in whiskey or whatever they're drinking."

*Me: Meet us in the restaurant at Kens's hotel tomorrow morning at seven if you want to talk. Tell Everett he better come too. He knows where we're staying.*

I send the text and turn the phone on *do not disturb* mode so I can take pictures and enjoy the rest of the evening with Kens.

# Chapter 23

*Everett*

"Fuck." I swear under my breath as I scrub my hands across my face, trying to work the early morning off of it.

Those feisty women knew exactly what they were doing when they insisted on a seven AM breakfast to 'talk'. Ryker got messed up last night, and while I wanted to keep up with him, it was clear that I was going to have to play 'good cousin' and keep him in line. But I didn't do enough to keep him from sending sappy text messages to Anna. I shake my head at the thought, sitting up in the plush bed.

My own texts weren't exactly anything to be proud of. I'm not sure I have a whole lot to apologize for, I thought I had preemptively done that, and I asked Kens to promise that she'd understand whatever happened next. Looking back now, it was my arrogance, and sure the couple shots, that gave me the illusion that everything was going to be fine, that she wasn't pissed at me. When my text messages went unanswered it had me guessing that the sexy texts I sent didn't go over well. Or... Maybe she was being a good friend and taking care of Anna? Did they go out and get drunk? No. They wouldn't do that and then suggest getting up early.

*Shit.* I sigh inwardly. The heavy snoring coming from next to me pulls me from my thoughts. Ryker. I give him a hard shove. If I'm miserable, he needs to be too. Besides, I already let us sleep longer than I should have. We're down to forty-five minutes to shower and get to breakfast, and I sure as hell know if we're one minute late we'll never hear the end of it!

"Get up," I order with another shove.

"What the hell, man?" He grunts, pushing his face back into the pillow, waving me off.

"It's your funeral. See if you get Anna to ever talk to you again if you blow off this breakfast."

I stretch my arms over my shoulders, twisting the tension out of my body. Ryker bolts out of bed, staggering with determination toward the bathroom.

"Don't take too long, asshole. We gotta go soon, and I need a shower too."

The only response I get is the slamming of the door.

\* \* \* \*

"So, what's the plan, dude?" Ryker asks as we pick up the pace down the lonely street.

"I guess groveling?" I shrug.

"Well, what's worked for you in the past? Maybe it'll

help me with Anna since they're friends."

"Kens and I don't fight. I mean, this trip has caused all sorts of hell, but other than this..." I shake my head.

*What are we going to do? What am I not going to do is the real question.* There isn't anything I wouldn't do to get that woman back. She's mine, and always has been. I have to prove to her that I didn't ruin their trip on purpose and show her that if we can make it through this we can make it through anything. *That's it.* Women love sappy shit like that. I'll just say that to her. After all, it is true.

"I think our plan of attack should be to separate them," I finally say. "Those two together are a force to be reckoned with, but maybe one-on-one we can get them to accept our apologies."

"Good thinking."

We turn the corner and half a block ahead I spot the girls sitting outside a quaint café jetting out of the side of the beautiful hotel Kens and I had stayed at a day ago. The morning is cool, but it looks like a promisingly warm day, Besides, knowing them they'll wanna take in as much of this ambiance as they can. Pulling out my cellphone, I check the time. There's no way in hell we're late. It's 6:55.

A hard slap on the back takes me out of my thoughts.

"Here goes nothing," Ryker says, walking past me.

"Or everything," I express under my breath.

Ryker takes the chair across from Anna, leaving me next to Kens. Before sitting, I bend down and press a kiss to Kens's cheek, satisfied when she doesn't push me away.

Ryker follows my lead, reaching across the table to place a kiss on Anna's cheek, but is rejected with a stern look and her hand pushing him away.

I stifle a laugh at his failed attempt but admire his bravery.

"You guys look like shit," Anna says.

"Feel as good as we look, I guess then," Ryker says with a nervous chuckle.

I roll my eyes at the unsuccessful attempt to lighten the mood.

"Well, good morning to you too." I shrug. "Have you ordered yet?" I ask, looking at Kens, who has yet to make eye contact with me.

"Just coffee," she says, twisting her cup around nervously before sliding the small menu over.

As if prompted, the waitress comes over, thankfully interrupting the awkward exchange.

"*Bonjour.*" She greets us with a chipper tone.

"*Parlez-vous anglais?*" Kens asks.

The waitress shrugs and waves her hand, indicating that

she may know a little. I point to Kens's coffee cup, and she nods, apparently understanding what I want. Ryker holds up two fingers, and she nods again. Turning, she shuffles away.

It's only a few moments before the waitress is back with the coffees. She pulls out her notebook, indicating she's ready to take our order.

Kens turns her menu toward the woman and points at the item she wants, and Anna does the same. The server jots down the order then gives Ryker and I a look, and I shake my head. My stomach gurgles at the thought of food. Today is a coffee breakfast kind of morning. Ryker agrees, handing the waitress the menu.

"Not eating?" Anna asks, leaning back in her chair, arms crossed over her chest.

It's clear she isn't going to do Ryker any favors by making this easy on him. But as long as I've known her she's always been a woman who made a man work for it. Don't get me wrong, Kens did too, but Anna always had her guard up a bit more. I admire that about her. She doesn't take anyone's shit, including mine.

"I had a pretty rough night, not sure my stomach can handle it," he replies.

"*You* did?" she scoffs.

I can't sit here and watch this anymore. It's time for me

to make a move. I swiftly stand up from my seat and take a step toward Kens, putting my hand out in a request for her to follow me. The seconds drag as she gives Anna a long look, I assume asking for permission in a silent conversation. But when her cool hand clasps my sweating palm a wave of relief washes over me, and I know I'm one step closer to something. Good or bad, at least we're moving.

She lets me tuck her arm into the crook of mine as I lead her down the block, out of eyeshot of our friends; we need a private moment. Satisfied with the quiet street we've turned down, I stop, but I'm taken aback when her small frame wraps around me. Her arms hold tight around my waist, her head resting on my chest.

"How could you?" Her meek voice croaks.

My chest contracts at the depth of her words. She's right—how could I? What answer could I have that would possibly satisfy that question? In that moment I feel like the biggest ass in the world. Sure, I felt like a jerk before, but nothing like this. It's clear that I've disappointed her.

"The only thing I can come up with is my own selfishness." I rest my chin on her head, trying to find the right words. "I couldn't see past my own hurt in losing you. It was impulsive and drastic, and I want to be sorry about the way things happen, but that would only be a half-truth."

"That's not good enough." She pulls back, her puffy eyes meeting mine.

"I know, but it's all I've got. The moment you left I didn't know what to do. My head has been spinning since you accepted that job, since you asked me to move with you. But that's not your fault. I didn't handle it like the man I should be. The man I want to be for you."

"Everett." She sighs. "You are the man I want. But...really...this was the best plan you could think of to get me back?"

I give her a half-smile. *Yes, you idiot, this was the best you could come up with?*

"It was rash, I admit, and maybe a little overkill. But I couldn't wait. I couldn't stomach the idea of you meeting someone, or trying to get over me with someone else."

"You really think that low of me?"

I pause. "No, I don't. But my man brain went off on its own, and thinking straight wasn't a possibility."

With another sigh from her pouty lips she leans back into my embrace.

"I love you, Everett, and I'm going to forgive you for ruining my trip with Anna. But you're going to have to fix the Ryker-Anna situation. That was low."

"I know. I'm working on it."

"She fell for him," she says, pulling away from me. "Tell me, honestly, does he feel the same way about her? This isn't a game. We can't cause her any more pain if it can be avoided."

I want to tell Kens that they can wait, that she's the most important person right now, that fixing all this shit between us is all I care about. I *love you, and I'm going to forgive you.* Her words echo, causing my body to relax. But she's right; if I care about her, that means caring about her friends, and Anna is important too. I went into this shitty plan with tunnel vision, and it's time to take off the blinders and make sure I didn't hurt everyone I care about, including Anna and Ryker.

"I think he does. Really." I nod solemnly.

"Good." She smiles. "Now kiss me and let's go fix this mess."

That's my girl. And in one fell swoop I have her in my arms. My hands tangle in her hair, my lips pressed against her lips, taking everything she gives as if this is our last kiss. But for some reason it feels like our first.

# Chapter 24

*Annaliesa*

Really? Kens is always bowing down to Everett. She was supposed to stay by my side and be my support. But all Everett has to do is hold his hand out to her and she follows.

How pathetic is it of me to be pissed that Kens actually has Everett? I've known forever that they'd end together.

I need to quit being a baby and just face this shit head-on. I can't dwell over what should've been. I need to move forward, and you can't do that if you're constantly looking in the rearview mirror.

"I don't know what to say to you that you don't already know," I tell Ryker.

"I really am sorry," he says, grabbing for my hand.

I pull my hand out of his reach. "Please, don't touch me." See, I can't even be a bitch right now. This is how much I've fallen for him. I want to hate him, but I can't. But my heart and head aren't really on the same page. My head is telling me that I can't trust Ryker.

This morning I was prepared to meet Ryker, but I thought Kens would be with me. Then she leaves me. I shouldn't be mad at her, but I need her support. Maybe I need to pull up my big girl panties and deal with it Anna style.

Kens swore up and down that she didn't have anything to do with this, but then this morning she just leaves with Everett, letting me deal with this alone.

"I'm going to get out of here. I can't do this right now," I say, standing and reaching into my purse to leave some money for my food.

"Please, stay and talk to me," Ryker begs.

"I can't. I can't do this with you. I'm so tired and hurt."

"You can't leave like this," he says, reaching for my hand again.

"You're not my fucking babysitter. I don't need one now, just like I haven't needed one this whole trip. I can and will do what I want. I'm tired of everyone thinking they can decide things for me. Let go of me." I jerk my arm out of his hand and run out of the café.

I know running won't solve any issues, but I need time to think. To figure out my feelings. If I don't think it out, I'm going to end up saying things I'll regret, and I don't want that.

Once I get away I hail a taxi and tell them to just drive. Now that I know Ryker isn't going to catch me I let out the breath I was holding. Not wanting to worry them, I pull out my phone.

*Ryker, Kens: I'm going to be fine. I'll meet you guys in London tomorrow.*

I hit *send* before I can rethink it and then turn off my phone.

"Can you take me to the Eurostar please?" I ask the taxi driver.

"Yes," he responds.

It's a good thing I brought my backpack with me. I have everything I need to make it through the airport tomorrow morning.

"Miss, we're here," the taxi driver says, pulling me from my thoughts.

"Thank you." I grab some money and hand it to him, telling him to keep the change.

"You're welcome, miss. Have a great trip."

There are so many things I want to see while in London. I can't wait to explore and just be me. Not having to worry about anyone but me and what I want.

First things first—getting the courage to take the Eurostar by myself. This is scary for me.

"Ma'am, can I help you?" someone behind me asks.

"N-n-no, thanks," I stutter out. *Way to make this person believe you don't need help.*

"Are you sure?" she asks.

"Yes, I'm trying to get the courage to get on the Eurostar," I sputter out.

"Oh, dear, it'll be fine. It's safe."

"I know. I've been on it. I'm just scared of enclosed spaces, and the fact that it's underwater just adds to the fear."

She smiles at me then says, "You remind me of my daughter. She hates enclosed spaces, especially elevators. That girl will take the stairs whenever they're available. It doesn't matter if it's twenty stories high." She chuckles.

"I'm the same way," I reply.

"Why don't you sit with me and tell me what you're doing going to London by yourself?"

"Okay," pops out before I can think about it. I know I shouldn't go with a stranger, but she seems harmless. She even shared something personal about herself.

"Let's go then. The next one leaves in five minutes."

Oh God, I'm not sure I can do this. Though it'll be easier with someone. Any time I'm forced to take the elevator, I always try to wait for someone to get on with me, so this isn't any different than doing that except I'll be chatting with this nice lady to help keep my mind off of things.

"Here's your ticket," the lady says as she holds out my ticket for me to grab. "I went ahead and got you one since you spaced out on me."

"I'm so sorry. I didn't mean to. Let me pay you back." I start digging around in my purse to get some money.

She reaches out and touches my hand. "It's fine, dear. I don't mind at all. I understand fear, but you're facing it head-on. You aren't letting it get in your way of going to London. Plus, you're doing me a favor by keeping me company."

"If you're sure." I take my hand out of my purse and take the ticket from her.

There's something about this lady that puts me at ease, like having my mom here with me.

"My name is Annaliesa," I tell her.

"That's a beautiful name. I'm Mary."

"Thank you for everything you're doing for me, Mary."

"You're welcome, dear. Let's take a seat and you can tell Dear Mary why you're alone, looking like your heart was just shredded in a grinder."

Am I really going to tell a stranger all my woes? Yes, because she's sweet, and she'll have an open mind to it all and won't have a biased opinion.

"Well, I could ask the same of you except for the 'heart shredded' part."

"That's an easy question for me. My family and I are staying in London for the week. But I can't seem to find a choux à la crème made the correct way there. So, I decided to head to Paris and pick some up. They are to die for. I get some with chocolate, chocolate and spun caramel, and some with just spun caramel."

"I haven't had one of those yet, but the food over here is amazing. So much better than back home. If it wasn't for all the walking I've been doing, I would have gained at least twenty pounds on this trip." I grin and then pat my stomach.

"You have got to try one of these then." She grabs one out of the box for me. "Oh, I should ask do you like caramel?"

"Yes. Who doesn't?"

"Only crazy people." She laughs and hands me one with chocolate and caramel.

Taking a bite, it practically melts in my mouth. "Oh," I moan. "These are delicious." I can't help but stuff more in my mouth.

"I take it you love it." She laughs again.

I love that she's so happy and laughs all the time. More

people need laughter in their lives. They're too busy focusing on life to have fun.

"I do love it, and I'm happy I didn't discover them before we left."

"So, tell me why you're alone and sad."

She's so easy to talk to that I just spill everything about the whole trip. I keep going and going. I tell her about Ryker and how he made me fall for him, but it was all a game to him. That he was just sent to babysit me so Everett could win Kens back.

"Sweetie, we need to get off the train, but I want to finish this conversation."

Wow, that went fast. I don't believe she let me talk the whole ride to London. I'm embarrassed that I shared it all with her.

"Don't be embarrassed. I'm happy you shared this with me. It'll help you think clearer now that you've shared it."

"Okay." We get off the train and head for a bench outside of the station.

"It's beautiful here. I love it over here," she says.

"It really is. I didn't get to explore London on our way through, but I'm happy I came early so I could explore some places here."

"We'll talk about those places soon. First, I want to talk

about you and your leaving."

"Okay, I know I shouldn't have just run off, but I needed time and space. I needed to feel like I was in charge of something on this trip."

"I know, dear. That's not what I was going to say. I was going to say how do you know this Ryker boy doesn't have true feelings for you? It sounds like he does."

"I don't know. I think he does, but I can't help but feel betrayed. What if he was forced to come on this trip? What if he's just acting like he likes me because he likes the sex?" I gasp. "Sorry, I didn't mean to say that last part."

"Stop apologizing. I have kids about your age. I'm not stupid." She winks at me and then says, "Maybe he was forced to come on this trip, and maybe he really does like the sex, but that doesn't mean his feelings aren't real. My guess is he didn't tell you because he was afraid to lose you. It doesn't always make sense why guys do what they do. Lying, even if by omission, is still worse than just telling the truth. But if he would've told you at the beginning of the trip would you have formed a bond with him?"

I have to shake my head in reply.

"I'm going to say that's a no. But here's the thing— you've met an incredible sounding man, one who seems to want to make you happy, one that you have a lot of things in common with, one that's willing to admit he was wrong. Not many guys will say they're sorry let alone admit that they were wrong."

*Holy shit.* Did I really just throw everything away because I was hurt? *Yes.*

"You leaving was a good thing. It gave you the opportunity to get out of the situation and see it in a new light. I'm going to ask that you finish taking the day for yourself. Do some sightseeing and then come to my house around five and eat dinner with me and my family. We even have an extra room, so you can stay the night too. Then I want you to meet up with your friends tomorrow and let them know that they're forgiven even though you're still hurting. Just because you forgive doesn't mean you won't still have some hurt."

"What? I can't possibly intrude on your family's vacation."

"Of course you can. I wouldn't have it any other way. Do you have somewhere else to stay?"

"Not yet. I was going to get a hotel room."

"Nonsense. You'll come to our place and stay with us. No more arguing about it. I'll have more goodies for you to eat." She throws that last line in like she knows the way to get me to say yes.

"Okay. Where are you staying?"

She points across the street.

"You're staying in a house?"

"Yes, we own a house here since we like to come a couple of months a year, and the kids like to come with friends if they can all manage time off."

"Okay. I'll see you in a few hours," I say, standing up and giving her hug.

I feel like I've known Mary all my life. She's one of those ladies that you feel comfortable with and who puts you at ease.

First stop for me is going to be Buckingham Palace. I have to see the guards everyone talks about. The ones that don't move. It's tempting to want to do something to see if I can get them to move, but going to jail in London isn't something I want to experience.

Once at the palace it makes me want to go exploring inside. I wonder if I can get a tour. Probably not last minute though. Walking up to the admission booth, I cross my fingers that I can get a ticket.

"Hello, ma'am. Do you have any tickets available for a tour anytime in the next hour or two?"

"We actually have one ticket left for the tour at two this afternoon. If you need more than one ticket, you'll have to wait for tomorrow afternoon."

"Perfect. I'll take it," I say to her and then scream *Yes!* inside my head. Luck is on my side today.

* * * *

The tour was amazing, but I didn't enjoy it like I would've if Ryker was with me. I couldn't help but think of all the tours we went on together and how we could talk about the architecture and understand each other and not bore the other. I miss that comradery.

Why does this have to be so hard? Why can't I just forgive them all? *Because you weren't given a choice in the matter.* But was Ryker? Did he just come along to placate Everett? Why am I so pissed at Kens?

Since I did some exploring this morning I decide to head to Mary's house. It's a little after four. She told me to come around five, but maybe she'll let me help get things finished in the kitchen.

"Hello, dear," Mary says as she answers the door.

"Hello. I hope it's okay for me to come to dinner still?" I ask hesitantly, hoping she isn't going to send me on my way.

"I wouldn't have offered if I didn't mean it. Please come in." She gestures behind her with the sweep of her hand.

"Wow!" I say as I walk into the foyer. I can see most of the space. There isn't really an upstairs, it's more of a loft. "This place is beautiful. I thought it was a two-story building from the outside. But instead it's vaulted ceilings."

"We love that. On the times we come here for Christmas we can get a nice big tree and don't have to worry it won't stand up."

"And Mary loves to get the tallest trees on the lots," someone says from behind Mary.

"Oh, hush, Max," Mary says over her shoulder, then to me she says, "That's Max, my husband."

"Hello, Max. It's nice to meet you," I say, holding my hand out to him.

"Hello, dear. You must be Annaliesa." He ignores my hand and pulls me in for a hug.

"Yes. Thank you for having me."

"You're welcome, dear. We wouldn't have it any other way. Back home we always have extras sitting at our table. Back when our kids were in high school we always had our table stretched to the max and had no less than twelve people eating."

"That's crazy. How did Mary cook for that many people? I can barely cook for myself."

Mary responds before Max gets a chance. "It's

something you learn to do. Now I'm having to learn to make smaller amounts of food. With the kids out of the house we don't feed so many people anymore."

"My mom says the same thing. Though we never had more than five or six at the table at once. And with me moving out of state after this trip it's going to be even lonelier for her."

"It does get lonely when the kids move, but we moms always find something to fill the time. She will manage, darling," Mary tells me.

I hope so. I'm going to miss family days with my parents. I've always loved being close to them. It's going to be a challenge moving and not knowing anyone."

"Max, take Annaliesa to the table and introduce her to the kids, and then come help me finish up, please," Mary says.

"Yes, dear." He kisses Mary's cheek, then he turns to me and says, "Be prepared to answer a lot of questions."

Questions? What does he mean?

As we enter the dining room Max says, "Marla and Marcus, I'd like you to meet Annaliesa."

"Please call me Anna," I say. It's weird to hear everyone call me Annaliesa.

"Is this the girl Mom found on the Eurostar this

morning?" Marcus asks.

"Yes."

"Why were you alone?" Marla asks.

"Because I left my friends." I don't get to finish
because Mary walks into the dining room, hushing us all.

"We are not playing one hundred questions. Leave
Anna alone. If she wants to talk about her problems, she
will. Otherwise, we're going to go about like this is any
other day."

"Yes, Mom," Marcus and Marla say at the same time.

Wow! It must be a mom thing to get their kids to go
quiet like that.

"Dear, you can sit next to Marla," Mary says.

After I sit down Marla says, "Hope you like pasta and
bread."

"Yeah, because that's all we eat when we're here,"
Marcus comments.

"Those happen to be my two favorite things to eat.
What would life be without all those yummy carbs?" I ask,
then rub my stomach, saying, "Yum."

Everyone at the table laughs, Max and Mary included.
Before I realize it my plate is overloaded with food.

"She fits in perfectly with this family, Mary," Max tells
her.

"She does," Mary agrees, then looks at me and says, "You've officially been adopted by us."

Oh my, she is the sweetest lady.

"Does that mean she has to do the dishes?" Marcus asks hopefully.

"No, that's still your job."

"What? That's not fair. If she's part of the family, she should have chores too," he whines.

"I can help do them. I'm almost done with my plate. I don't mind. It'll help keep me occupied."

"You'll do no such thing. You're a guest in this house."

"If you're sure," I say quietly.

I don't want to go to my room and be alone though. It'll give me too much time to think. Though thinking is what I should be doing. I meet up with Kens and the guys tomorrow to fly home.

"Marla, why don't you show Anna to her room?"

"Let's go, Anna," Marla says.

"Anna, feel free to take a shower and get cozy," Mary says.

"I'm exhausted, but a shower does sound wonderful."

"Nice meeting you," Marcus says.

"Night," Max says.

"Good night, dear." Mary pulls me in for a hug,

squeezing me.

"Night. Thanks again for everything."

Marla shows me to the room I'll be staying in, and before leaving she pulls me in for a hug and says, "It was good meeting you."

Once in the room I lay on the bed, instantly dozing off. I don't sleep long though. You know when you have a bad dream, but you can't recall what it was about? Well, that's what woke me up. Now, I'm lying in bed wide awake.

Falling back to sleep isn't going to happen anytime soon. Especially now that I'm thinking about Ryker and how I really miss him. I didn't realize how much I've come to rely on him being with me.

Without even giving myself a chance to think about what I'm doing, I grab my phone and pull up Ryker's information.

*Me: You awake?*

After sending the message I start reading through some of the ones he sent me. He's the sweetest guy I've met. I'm beginning to think that I overreacted.

*Ryker: Yes. Are you okay? Where are you? Can I see*

*you?*

    *Me: I'm doing okay. Missing you though.*

    *Ryker: I'm so sorry. I never meant to hurt you. I'd go back and change things if I could. I'd tell you all about Everett's plans. Though if I did that, I doubt you would have given me the time of day. So, maybe I wouldn't change things, because I can't live life not knowing how having you in my arms feels like.*

    *See?* Sweet as can be. He wouldn't intentionally hurt anyone.

    *Me: I wish I could be in your arms right now.*

    I shouldn't be engaging him like this yet. We still need to talk. Or do we?

    *Ryker: You can be. Tell me where you are and I'll come to you.*

    *Me: I'm already in London.*

    I'm happy I came and did this for me. I needed to get away and think and breathe. Let myself know I don't need others to be there with me to have fun and enjoy things.

Though I'll be honest, it's more fun with friends.

*Ryker: What? You got on the Eurostar alone?*

*Me: Yes. Why wouldn't I?*

*Ryker: Can we talk on the phone instead of texting?*

*Me: Sure.*

I barely have the text sent and my phone's ringing. I hurry to answer so it doesn't wake anyone up. "Hello," I whisper.

"Hey," Ryker says.

"Why did you ask about the Eurostar?" I ask.

"I'm doing great. Thanks for asking."

"Why would I ask that? We already talked about that."

"No, we texted that," he says. "Big difference."

"True, but I'm really curious as to why you'd ask me that question about the Eurostar."

"Hmm. Maybe because you don't like enclosed spaces."

"How do you know that?"

"It's just a guess since you don't like elevators, and the Eurostar is similar," he says with a pause. "And maybe Kens said something when I asked her if you'd head to London. She said no because you were scared to even ride the

Eurostar with her."

"Well, I did ride it, and it wasn't fun, but I had a nice person to chat with. They even invited me to dinner and to stay with them."

"What? You didn't go to dinner with someone, did you? You aren't staying with them now, are you?"

This is kind of fun. No doubt he thinks it's a guy.

"Yes, I did eat dinner with them, and I'm staying with them."

"You keep saying *them*, so I'm praying you really mean a *them* and you're not just saying that to throw me off from it being a guy."

"Ryker, really? Do I look like the girl who would meet a guy on the Eurostar and then instantly fall into his bed and then chat you up after?"

"When you put it that way, no," he mumbles.

"Sorry. That's my fault. I shouldn't have been so elusive. I was being a bitch."

I hate that I felt the need to try to rile him up. I really don't want to cause any more issues between us. I want to make up so when I get to Chicago we can pursue where our relationship is going.

"No, it's good. I just hate the thought of another guy being with you when I want to be with you."

"I want you with me too. I'm sorry I stormed away, but I needed time."

"Did you think?" he asks hopefully. His voice gets higher and I can hear the smile in it.

"I did. While I get why you didn't say anything, I still feel like you betrayed my trust. But if you had told me, then we wouldn't have spent the trip together, because I would've made sure you got me back with Kens and then I would've kicked Everett's ass for ruining our trip. We told him several times that he couldn't come with us. Then Kens and him break up and he still manages to worm his way into the trip. I guess I'm more pissed at him."

"You have every right to be pissed at him. He should've waited to confront Kens. If I wasn't watching you, then I wouldn't have gotten on the train, and then it would've been a real disaster."

Everett and Kens really weren't thinking. They were too caught up in what they wanted.

"When are you guys coming to London?"

"I believe we're doing breakfast at seven and then heading over in time to go straight to the airport. Kens wanted to get there a little early to hopefully catch you."

"Then I'll make sure to get there early."

"Can I come to you tonight?"

"I don't know if that's a good idea. I don't know how Mary would feel about me inviting you here. Plus, it's kind of late."

"It's not that late. It's only eight-thirty. I can catch the nine o'clock train and be there around eleven-thirty. If I have to, I'll rent us a room. Please say I can come tonight and see you. I'm coming tonight whether I get to see you or not."

*What?* It's only eight-thirty? I didn't sleep as long as I thought then. I'd also bet Mary and the family are still awake.

"Well, since you asked so nicely and weren't demanding..." I pause. "I'll ask Mary if you can stay here."

"No, please let me find us a room. That way we can be alone and talk some more, and then maybe I can convince you to let me make it up to you."

I can envision him now raising his brow up and down with a come-hither look.

"How do you plan to make this up to me?" I ask.

"I have my ways, and from what I remember you really like what I can do to you."

Yes, he does. Plus, I really want him to hold me tonight.

"Fine, text me when you get on the train so I know

when to meet you. I'm staying across the street from the station."

"Sounds good. I'll see you soon, beautiful."

"Bye," I say and get ready to go find Mary.

I decide I should take that shower now. I need to do something to kill some time.

Once I'm out of the shower I get dressed and French braid my hair. I grab my bag, making sure I have everything of mine, and I walk back out to where Mary and her family are playing games.

"Hello, dear. Are you feeling better?" Mary asks.

"Yes, but I'm going to be leaving this evening. My boyfriend's on his way to London, and we're going to get a room and talk."

"Are you sure that's a good idea?"

"Yes, he really didn't do anything wrong. He's a great guy. I don't want to lose him."

"I'm so happy you came to this conclusion on your own, sweetie. What I meant was, is it a good idea to get a room?"

"Oh. Well, Ryker didn't want to impose here, and he said it'd be better for us to have some privacy." I blush when I say the last part, because that makes it sound like we're only doing it for sex.

"Okay. He won't be here for a couple of hours. You know how long that trip is since you just did it this morning."

"Yes, and if it wasn't for those amazing treats, I'd question your sanity for making a two-hour trip for pastries, but if I were you, I'd make that trip too."

"Well, I have a couple more if you want one before you leave."

"Please," I practically moan my response.

"Let's go in the kitchen," Mary says to me, then to her family, "You guys go ahead and finish this game. I'm going to go talk with Annaliesa for a while."

"Okay," they say.

"Follow me, dear. I'd like to talk to you while I feed you."

I'm not sure what she's going to say, but it'll probably be similar to what my mother would say if she were here.

"Would you like something to drink too?"

"Yes, please, I'll take some water."

Mary hustles around the kitchen and sets down my glass of water and a plate for me and her filled with a chocolate and a chocolate and caramel choux à la crème for us both.

"I wasn't sure which one you'd want. Pick."

I had the caramel and chocolate one earlier and loved it but want to try just the chocolate one, so I grab it.

"Great choice."

"I hope so. I really enjoyed the caramel chocolate one earlier. Chocolate doesn't usually disappoint."

"That it doesn't," she says and takes a bite. I know she has more to say, so I just enjoy my treat and wait for her to talk.

"I know we talked a little bit about this Ryker guy and your friends. I just want to make sure you're doing okay and that you want to meet up with Ryker."

"I really do. I miss him. It's hard to explain, but I want to be with him. I feel empty without him. I don't think it was really his fault. It was more Everett's fault. He put us all in a bad situation."

"I understand those feelings. I have those feelings for Max when we're apart or even when we get into fights. You're in love with him."

"What? I can't be. Can I?" I question. "When I think it's love I tell myself it's too soon."

"Is it too soon?" Mary quips back.

"Yes. Wait, no. I don't know." I sigh and then look down at my plate. "All these feelings are new to me. I want to take the time to explore Ryker and me. I want to get to

Chicago and learn what he's like in everyday life and not vacation mode."

"I think that's a great idea. Let your heart lead you, dear. Stay out of your head. Communicate with each other. Don't go to bed angry with each other either. Life is too short to always be mad at the other. You lose so much time that way."

This is the best advice anyone has given me. My mom has told me the same about going to bed mad, but there's something about the way Mary is saying it that has me believing it.

"Thank you, Mary. For everything you've done for me. If it wasn't for me meeting you this morning, I don't think I'd be in the mindset I am now. I would have spent the day in a hotel room crying. You've shown me what it's like to learn and let go of things. For that, I'm honored to know you."

"Oh, sweetie, you're very welcome. I didn't do anything for you that I wouldn't have done for anyone else," Mary says as she begins gathering our plates. "Let's head out to the living room and wait for your man to come and get you."

"Sounds like a plan."

We aren't in the living room long before my phone is

going off. It's Ryker letting me know that he's five minutes out. I'm excited and nervous to see him.

# Chapter 25

*Kenslie*

"So?" I stare at Ryker deadpan, "What did she say? Where is she? Is she okay?" I bombard him with each question as he comes back in to the main room of the hotel suit.

"She's fine. She's already in London," he responds, whirling around the room and swooping up his items. "I'm going to her now."

"We are too!" I declare, following his lead, gathering my items.

"No." He stops in his tracks.

I'm confused as both men stand in front of me, cutting me off.

"Kens." Everett says my name with a soothing tone. "You gotta let Ryker do this on his own."

"Like hell I do! You didn't come here to win me back on your own! You fucked everything up, and now I've spent what should've been an epic vacation with my best friend— my best friend who is moving states away from me— without her!" I stomp my foot, knowing it's a childish act, but I'm pissed, and a full-on tantrum is okay with me.

"You're not the only one with something to fix. I've known her longer than you. I can't let a friendship fall apart over some guy." I flail my hands in his direction as I turn from the men, returning to my packing.

Everett's arms wrap around my body as his front presses against my back. "Kens, I know you want to be there for Anna, but this is bigger than you." He nuzzles his face into my hair, and it soothes my anger, but just for a moment.

I twist out of his hold, turning to face him with a step back. "You have some apologizing to do too! This is your fault! You've ruined everything. This is your fucking fault!" I scream. Hot tears rush down my cheeks, and I don't even know what to do. I'm emotionally spent. My body feels hollow and weak.

Once again Everett pulls me into his embrace, my sloppy, tear-stained face pressed into his chest as his strong hands gently run over my back.

"You're right. This is my fault. I'm not proud of it. Lately, I haven't been proud of much. I've never felt like less of a man in my whole life. But I will make this up to you. To Anna. I know she's important to you, and you're important to me."

I feel the heavy sigh from his body with the intake of breath, and with the exhale his shoulders slouch.

"Besides, who else around here would bust my balls? That girl scares the shit out of me. I don't wanna be on the wrong side of that."

I laugh, and pulling back, I roll my eyes at him. "That's exactly where you're at, sir. You better figure this shit out soon."

I shake my head and wipe the tears from my eyes. Everett is right about one thing—right now it's Ryker's time to apologize to Anna. I love knowing that she found someone who makes her happy, and I only hope that hasn't been lost.

"All right, Ryker," I call over Everett's shoulder. "Go see Anna. Make things right, or as right as you can."

I step past Everett to give Ryker a hug before his journey, but he's not in the living room.

"Ryker?" I call.

"Babe, he's gone," Everett explains. "There's nothing that could stop me from making up with you, and it looks like that's the same for him."

"What do I do now?" I ask. "Do we go too?"

"Of course we go too." Everett pauses. "Tomorrow. We leave first thing in the morning. Let them have tonight."

I want to argue, I want to insist that we leave right now, but I know he's right, and I hate it. But there isn't much we can do now. If she wanted to see me, she would've returned the million text messages and calls I left for her.

"What am I supposed to do in the meantime?"

"Well..." Everett saunters over to me, with that hooded look in his eyes. "You could let me spend the night apologizing to you."

I roll my eyes again. I'm not in the mood for more *I'm sorries*. But there is something...

"Fine. You can apologize with a full-body massage," I say with a hand on my hip.

Everett's eyes widen. "I can do that for sure, babe."

"Wait a minute..." I smirk. "A no-strings-attached, no-happy-ending massage. You get to massage me until I fall asleep. And then, maybe I'll accept this new apology."

The grin widens on his face. "You evil woman, always testing my patience."

# Chapter 26

*Annaliesa*

I can't believe Ryker came to London for me. I'm nervous that Kens is going to come with him. While I'm not mad at her, I really just want it to be the two of us. I want to know if what we have is real. I don't want to head to Chicago with us fighting. I want to know where we stand.

While walking away and leaving everyone today may seem childish, it wasn't. I'm a firm believer in taking a time-out and thinking things through. Speaking in anger only ends in me saying something I'll regret and can't take back. Once the words are spoken they are out there forever.

"Hey, beautiful," Ryker says as he pulls me off the bench and into his arms. "God, I thought I'd lost you," he whispers into my hair.

"Sorry," I reply.

"Don't be sorry. It's my fault for being so stupid and not telling you about Everett's plan to win Kens back."

I want to say 'Yes, it is,' but I can't. "It's not all your fault. Yes, we both did some stupid things, but if you had told me, then we wouldn't have had this time together. I would've made sure you got me back with Kens sooner. I'm happy that I had this time with you. I got to meet an incredible man and open myself up. I actually love the person I became around you. I wasn't this uptight, follow-the-rules-and-schedule person. I allowed myself to have fun and not worry about everything."

"It's not often a woman apologizes," Ryker says, and I slap his chest.

"Oh, hush. Take it now, because I'll make sure not to do it again."

He starts reaching for me and I dodge him before laughing. I love that we can still mess around and my little fit didn't change that. I'll have to remember to call a time-out when I need to think so that I don't risk losing Ryker.

"You ready to head to our hotel?" he asks.

"Yes. I've already said goodbye to Mary and her family. She wants to meet you one day."

"Oh, really? Is she going to give me hell for letting you leave on your own?"

"No, she wants to meet the man who's claiming my heart." Oh shit, I basically just told him I love him.

"I'd love to meet her. I'm so happy you found someone you could talk to. I'd also like to thank her for helping you," Ryker says, grabbing my hand and leading us down the road. "There weren't many places to get a room, but I did find somewhere close to the airport, so we don't have to get up too early to be there."

"Sounds good. I have a feeling we aren't going to be getting much sleep tonight."

"Then it's a good thing we have a long flight home to sleep on."

"Too bad we aren't on the same flight." I sigh.

"Why? So I could initiate us both into the mile-high club?" Ryker asks as he looks over at me and winks.

"I don't know if I'd be adventurous enough to join the mile-high club." It would be obvious to everyone what was happening, and the last thing I'd want is to get caught and in trouble when we depart the plane. I don't even know if you'd get in trouble for that, but I don't really want to find out.

"Well, I may have to see if I can convince you since I'll be on your flight."

"What? How?" I ask, practically screaming.

"I don't know how Everett pulled it off, but he must've known the flights from Kens. He said that things had to work out for everyone since he got us on the same flight as you ladies on the way home."

"How long did he have this planned? Was he planning this before Kens and him broke up, or was this a spur-of-the-moment plan?" I need to know this, because it'll determine if I'm truly mad at him or if he was just wanting his girl back. I can now admire him for wanting Kens back and going for her.

"He called me a day before you guys were set to leave. Apparently, he couldn't find a flight that would get us here the same day, so we had to wait until you hit Germany. His plan was to follow you guys and keep you from trouble and then get Kens to talk to him when you guys arrived in Paris, so he could be with her for the City of Love."

That makes me feel somewhat better that he hadn't planned to ruin our trip all along. It's kind of sweet that he wanted to come win Kens back in Paris. "Let's move forward. I really couldn't have asked for a better trip, and I need to let it all go so I can move forward with you. I have all the information I need, and I'm not mad anymore."

"If it makes you feel any better, I couldn't have planned a better trip if I tried. I've been here several times before and none have compared to this one." He spins me around to look at him. "You are the reason it was perfect." He leans down and kisses me.

He kisses me in the middle of the sidewalk, not caring that people have to walk around us. I love that he isn't scared to show his affection for me in public. So many men seem to be.

"How far is the hotel?" I ask, wishing we were already there.

"Not very far. A mile I think. Do you want to grab a ride?"

"Please. Normally, I wouldn't mind walking, but we've done so much, and I really want to get back to the room."

"Your wish is my command."

\* \* \* \*

We couldn't get to the hotel fast enough. By the time we got in the elevator I wanted to rip off Ryker's clothes. I've never been like this. But Ryker brings this side of me out.

"Babe, you need to slow down," he whispers against my lips, breaking the kiss.

"Why? Isn't it every man's dream to hook-up with a girl in an elevator?"

"Not that I'm aware of, but I could be wrong."

"I think you're wrong," I say, continuing kissing him and wrapping one leg around his hip as I begin to grind on him.

"Liesa," Ryker moans in my ear. "You have to stop. I'm barely controlling myself as it is, and I want to get you to the room before getting you naked. We're not doing this in the elevator where anyone can see you. I'm the only one who gets to see that sexy body."

Why is he the voice of reason when I'm throwing myself at him?

"Fine." I huff.

"Don't go getting upset. I have plans for you tonight. Plans that you'll very much enjoy," Ryker says as the elevator announces our arrival to our floor.

"Let the good times begin then," I say, rushing out of the elevator.

"Why are you in a rush?" he asks, barely containing his laughter.

"Ass," I mutter.

"Glad to be your ass," he replies.

"Hurry up and unlock the door."

"Gotta love when a woman's in a hurry to take my clothes off. Makes me feel good about myself," Ryker says as he finally pushes the door open.

"As if you need me to stroke your ego. I'm sure you have women beating the doors down back home trying to get in your pants," I say as we walk into the room.

"Not hardly. I'm not that easy, babe. Gotta make them work for it."

"Ass."

"You've already told me I'm an ass, or are you telling me I have a nice ass?"

"You're so frustrating."

"Oh, come on, princess, you know I'm just messing with you."

"Princess?" Ugh, I don't like that nickname.

"What? You don't want to be the princess to my prince?"

"Hell to the no. I want to be the Liesa to your Ryker. I want to be us. Not some fairy tale."

"My kind of lady. It's not often you meet a lady who doesn't believe in fairy tales."

I don't understand why parents show their daughters fairy tales. It gives them a false sense of reality. I will not teach my girls that the man is there to rescue you. Women can save themselves.

"Well, I don't believe that women need a man to be happy. I want to think for myself and not be told what to do. I don't need a man to rescue me, but it's nice to have someone by your side supporting you and encouraging you."

"I agree with you. I don't want to rescue my women. I'm not a white knight."

I'm so over all this talking. Slowly, I start taking off

my clothes.

"What are you doing?" Ryker asks.

"It's pretty obvious," I reply sassily.

"Yes, but we're talking."

"No, we *were* talking, and now we're going to have make-up sex. I have to see what all the hype about it is. Everyone is saying it's so much better than just sex."

"No pressure at all," Ryker says under his breath.

"Oh, don't freak out. I know it'll be good. Every time with you is."

\* \* \* \*

After Ryker rocked my world, he shocked me with saying, "Did you mean it when you said I was stealing your heart?"

*Crap!* I thought he either chose to ignore that comment earlier or he forgot. But either way, it needs to be said.

"Yes."

"Really?" he asks, rolling me over so he can look into my eyes.

"Yes. I don't know how it can happen so fast, but it is. I can't fight it."

"Don't fight it. Let it grow." He leans down and kisses me.

"Ryker," I moan.

"Liesa," he says back to me.

"How can I want you again?"

"Because you love me and can't get enough of my sexy body."

"True," I moan as I rock into him.

"You love me?" he asks.

"Yes. I thought we just went through this."

"No, you said that I was stealing your heart, but just now you said you love me."

*Shit!* "Yes, you are stealing my heart, and yes, I'm falling in love with you." There, I said it, and it feels great to say it. Hopefully he feels the same way and I didn't just scare him away.

"Fuck yes," he shouts then continues, "I love you too. I've been waiting for you to come to this conclusion for a couple of days now. I know you think it's too soon, but what I feel for you is something I've never felt before."

"Me either. I don't know why I kept trying to put a time frame on how soon it was acceptable to fall for someone, but no one knows how long it takes."

\* \* \* \*

We're in the car heading to the airport and my mind is wandering. I'm excited to meet up with Kens and Everett. After my talk with Ryker I know that Everett didn't maliciously plan to sabotage our trip. He was looking out for Kens and trying to win her back. He didn't intend to come face-to-face with her until Paris, but we all know how that played out.

I'm sad that the trip is ending. But also excited to start our new adventures. This is what we've worked so hard to make happen. It's time to start adulting!

"You ready?" Ryker asks, pulling me out of my thoughts.

"Yes!" I really am. I want to make things better with Kens. I don't want any hard feelings between us. I need her to know I'm not mad at her and that I love her.

"Let's go then," he says as he grabs my hand and helps me out of the car.

"Do you think Kens will be mad at me for not calling her last night?" I ask, letting my nerves control my mouth.

"No, she wants you to be happy. She wanted to come last night, because she was worried about you. She knows you're in good hands though."

Walking through the airport, I get more excited because I know we need this closure so we both go home having experienced the trip of a lifetime. It didn't go as we planned, but we both learned a lot about us, our love lives, and being happy.

"Everett, she's here!" Kens shouts out.

My eyes snap up and connect with hers. *Why isn't she running to me?* I look down and see that Everett is holding her back. *Why?*

"Hey guys," I say as I walk up to them, grabbing Kens into a big hug. "I'm so sorry," I whisper in her ear.

"No, I'm sorry. Are you okay?" she asks.

"I couldn't be better. We experienced the trip of a lifetime and I've grown so much and learned a lot about life. I had to learn to not rely on you as often as I do. Which is good since we're not going to be living close to each other anymore."

"I don't want you to not rely on me for things. I'm only a phone call away."

"I know. And don't forget we're only a short seven hours away from each other, if we meet in the middle."

"Oh, I know it. Once life settles down we'll have to plan a girls' trip," Kens says.

"Yes." Grabbing Kens, I pull her into my arms again. "Sisters for life."

"Sisters for life. Love you, Anna."

"Love you too," I say, pulling out of the hug. "Let's get back to our men."

# Chapter 27

*Everett*

I rake my hand over my head. I've been trying to save the last bit of energy I have left to rally for the flight. But I still have a few things I must fix before this plane departs. The awkward silence floats in the air as we walk toward our terminal with plenty of time to spare before boarding begins. I find myself feeling responsible, and I'm quite sure at least half of our group would agree, and for that I know I have some major groveling and apologizing to do...to Anna.

I'm beyond relieved that she and Ryker hit it off; otherwise, this whole situation would've blown up far worse than it already has. But it doesn't make it okay to barge in and ruin their goodbye girls' trip. I get to come home to Kenslie, and Anna has to say goodbye. I should've given them that. I take a big breath, exhaling heavily. *It's now or never, tough guy.*

"Hey, um...I'm gonna check something with the desk." I nod to the group. "Anna, would you mind coming with me? I might need some help."

The group turns and stares at me like I just grew a second head, but I ignore them, not letting it have a chance to kill my determination. The moments of silence press on, but I'm not giving up.

"Just come on. It's not like there's much more I can ruin," I say, hoping to lighten the mood.

She rolls her eyes at me as she brushes past me, heading to the desk. I give Kens a nod before turning to chase after Anna. I'm lucky Anna even conceded to come along without a fight. I don't have a chance to speak to her before she's leaned up against the flight receptionist desk.

"Hello there. How can I help you two?" the lady at the desk asks.

Anna shrugs her shoulders and gives me a hard look.

"Yes." I clear my throat. "Hi, there are four of us traveling together back to the States today, and I wanted to see about upgrading our seats to first class."

"Oh, yes, I see." The woman behind the counter smiles before she begins typing away on her computer. "So, we have a little bit of luck, first class isn't full. However, I can't get you all seated on the same row. I could probably work something out where two of you are in the row in front and the others are behind, would that be okay?"

"Anna?" I ask, "Is that okay?"

I get an eye roll and a reluctant 'fine', but I ask the woman behind the counter to go ahead and set up the new seating arrangement. I pass my credit card over and pay the upgrade fees and receive new tickets for our group.

"Thank you, sir. Ma'am. Enjoy your flight."

"Thank you," I reply, guiding Anna with me away from the desk.

"So? Am I supposed to be impressed? Thankful that you upgraded our tickets?" Anna stops abruptly, turning toward me with her hand on her hip and a death stare.

"No... I was hoping you'd see it as a peace offering, and an apology of sorts. Not that I'm trying to buy you off or anything..." I pause, collecting my thoughts a moment. "I've messed up a lot of things in life, but nothing as badly as I have with you. I mean, I thought I royally fucked things up with Kens when I let her go. And yeah, that was a huge fucking mistake, but she's it for me, and there would have always been a chance, I would have always found a way to win her back. But what I did to you..."

I let out a deep breath. I hate words, I hate having to apologize, but I'm better than my actions, and now I have to prove it. Kens is the only one I've ever let in, but I'm understanding that I owe Anna a piece of that too.

"Everett, let me save you some time here—"

"No," I cut in. "I have some things I need to say, and if you don't let me do it now, I'm not sure I will get the chance."

I pause, and she gives me the nod to continue.

"For all the time Kens and I've been together I've never really taken the time to get to know you. I guess I just figured you were her friend and that was that. But I'm starting to realize that I missed a chance to become friends with you. You're a huge part of her life, which makes you important to me too. I'm not going to lose Kens, and I'm sure as hell not going to put her in the middle of our shit, and I think you probably feel the same way. So..." I pause, rocking back on my heels with an exhale, trying to find the right words to end my speech. "My point is that I have a lot of making up to do with important people in my life, and I want us to be able to move forward from this. I can't stand the thought of you hating me for the rest of our lives, because that's how long I plan on being around."

"That's an awfully sappy speech."

"Maybe." I chuckle. "But I'm asking for this to be a changing point, the place where you forgive my stupidity. And hey, think of it this way—I get to spend the next fifty years paying for this. You get to bring it up at dinner parties, hell, our wedding one day as an embarrassing anecdote. And believe me, I won't ruin another girls' trip. *Ever.*"

I'm rewarded with a laugh with that last sentence, and I

can see her considering my words. I just hope she knows how sincere I am.

"Ugh," she retorts with an eye roll. "You're a jerk, but I see that charm Kens is always going on about."

She sighs, and I see her shoulders relax. Turning, she looks back to Kens and Ryker sitting in the basic airport blue seats.

"Besides, I guess this trip wasn't without...its souvenirs. Come on, let's get back."

She pushes me in the shoulder with a friendly tease, putting to ease the tension in the air. But I don't miss the warning under her breath as we walk.

"If you *ever* pull something like this again, I *will* rip your nuts off like they're a paper towel."

I scoff at the threat, but not too loudly; it's a terrifying thought, and one I think she might follow through with.

\* \* \* \*

Kens's head is resting blissfully against my shoulder as we push hour five in our long trip back to the states. We've settled into a comfortable silence as we pass somewhere over the Atlantic Ocean.

It's been an absurdly wild couple of weeks, and though they've been filled with ups and downs, it's hard for me to regret them. I feel closer to Kens. It was our first real fight, and man, it was one hell of a knock-down, drag-out fight. And the chase... *Wow.* But it's only made me realize how perfect we are for each other. It confirmed everything I thought I already knew; she is mine.

My mind wanders, recalling the moment on the bridge, the one where I got down on one knee, prepared to ask the most important question a man could ask. I shake my head at the thought of my damaged ego. I'm still having trouble wrapping my mind around why she was so upset at the timing. Surely I hadn't read the signs wrong? What could be more romantic than a historical bridge in a foreign country? Granted, it's not really my style, but from what I've learned from women in the crappy romance movies Kens forces me to watch, it's the grand gestures that make them memorable.

*Maybe that's why she said no, idiot.* I've never been anything but myself with this woman, why would she now want me to be something other than me? I didn't have the heart, or dignity, to return the delicate ring that sits protected in my jacket pocket. Right now, in this moment, I'm glad I didn't.

"Kenslie?" I ask softly, "Are you awake?"

"Mmm-humm," she replies, soothing her hand over my leg.

I shift in my seat, removing the ring from my pocket.

My heart is pounding, but I'm doing everything I can to steady my hands. I take her left hand in mine, without words, and slip the diamond on to her left ring finger. I feel her body stiffen against mine, and a breath hitch. My heart stops as silence surrounds us like a bubble.

"Say something," I whisper low, hearing the desperation in my voice when I can no longer take the silence.

Shifting in her seat, her blue eyes peer up into mine with the hint of tears glistening in the corners. A smile reaches the edge of her mouth, and her hand slides up my chest, resting on my cheek.

"This is the Everett I know." She sighs before glancing down at the ring.

Kenslie pulls away from me, still peering down that the ring, contemplating my offer from what I can make out. My body deflates when she slips the ring off, moving it to her right-hand ring finger.

"Not just yet." She takes my hand in hers, pulling it over my shoulder as she settles into the nook of my body. "So many things have happened, and we still have so much to come. This isn't no, it's just…not yet."

I squeeze her tight against my body, and while her words feel like another rejection stabbing my self-confidence, I know she's right. She wants time, and I'll take a *maybe* over a hard *no* any day.

"Fair enough," I concede.

"I love you, Everett."

"Me too, babe. Me too." I kiss her on the top of her head, knowing time is on our side.

# Epilogue

## *Kenslie*

*Six Months Later*

I take one last look in the mirror before spritzing myself with the final touches of perfume. I'm grateful for the two, full days off in a row. The twelve-hour shifts four or more days a week have been chaotic to say the least, and also incredible, my exact dream, but an actual night off is the exact thing I need right now. The timing couldn't be better. Things haven't been rocky, but Everett and I could really use the time to reconnect.

We've both spent the last six months rebuilding our lives in our new city. He's working on building back up his clientele, and I haven't slowed down one bit either. I've just passed my certification for pediatric emergency and am enrolled in more certification courses. Nursing is my passion, it's who I am.

*And Everett?* The thought of that man pulls me from googly-eyed daydream. Yes, he's made everything right. He's been right by my side, holding me tight on those nights I come home a wreck from seeing things that no one should ever have to witness, and here to celebrate my accomplishments. *Perfect* is a big word to live up to, but I'd say we are damn near close.

I fiddle with the beautiful diamond ring on the wrong finger. My heart patters. *It's time.* I slip it off and put it on my left right finger. I needed time, and I've had enough. I'm ready to solidify our lives together. I can only hope he still wants it too. He hasn't brought up the subject since the plane ride home for London when I told him I needed time. When I didn't say *yes* or *no*.

"You ready yet?" Everett calls from the other room.

I shake the curls in my hair one more time, pull my shoulders back, and do my best to keep the smirk off my face as I move through the apartment to meet him.

"Yes," I say as I step out to meet him.

"Wow, baby. You look fucking amazing," Everett says, rushing toward me. He wraps his arms around my waist, pulling me against him.

I giggle, enjoying the easiness of the moment. His face is nestled into my neck, and a soft kiss is placed into that sensitive nook. My body trembles with anticipation, but I have to keep my head straight.

"Everett!" I squeal. "Come on, we'll have plenty of time for this later."

I squirm out of his hold and laugh at the exaggerated

disappointed look on his face.

"Don't worry, big boy, we have all night. And I'm used to working all night, so I won't be tired when we get home." I bat my eyelashes at him, and he just shakes his head at me with a smirk.

"Fine." He grunts.

I strategically let him take my right hand as he leads us out the door to our date.

\* \* \* \*

The hostess shows us to our table in the dimly lit restaurant, and Everett pulls out the chair for me. We've had fun exploring places in our new city. And with my hours we've been subjected to, we've had lots of takeout. But this place by far is the nicest.

"This place is beautiful. Where'd you hear about it?" I ask.

"One of my new clients recommended it. I wanted us to go somewhere nice. I'm not sure I could handle another night of Chinese takeout."

"You could learn how to cook," I tease.

"Hey now…let's not get any crazy ideas," he teases. "Did you tell Anna that you passed your certification test?"

"Yes, of course." I laugh. "I think we're going to try to plan a girls' weekend away. If we meet somewhere in the middle, it's only about a seven-hour drive. I have a feeling that we're going to have a lot to catch up on."

"A lot can happen in six months for sure. Maybe I'll see what Ryker's up to, see if he wants to meet up?"

"That's a good idea. As long as you guys don't pull some dumb stunt and try to spy on us." I narrow my eyes at him.

"What! Us? We'd never…" he says, dramatically faking insult. "Okay…well, never again."

He reaches his hands out over the table, seeking mine, and my heart beats hard in my chest. I bite back the smile on my lip as I wonder how long it'll take him to notice. Everett's warm hands wrap around mine as his eyes narrow at me suspiciously. I hope that my face isn't giving too much away.

We sit there, eyes locked as if he's trying to search my mind to figure out what I'm hiding. His masculine hands soothe over mine, and in an instant, they stop. His right thumb swivels the ring on my finger back and forth as realization hits. He opens his mouth to speak, but no words come out. I've never seen him quite this stunned, and I'm worried that I might have made a mistake.

I'm relieved when the waiter interrupts our intense stare-down, but Everett doesn't let my hands go as the man greets us.

"Good evening. I'm Anthony, and I'll be your waiter tonight. Can I start you off with something to drink?"

"Yes," Everett answers, giving me a soft smile. "We'll have a bottle of champagne."

"Wonderful! Are you celebrating a special occasion tonight?"

"We are in fact—this woman just agreed to be my wife."

I hear the waiter mumble words of congratulations, but Everett's voice saying *wife* echoes through my mind. *Wife. His wife.* I've always been his, just as he's always been mine, but that word, it feels like so much more. My heart swells with love, and it's almost painful, but it's just perfect. Everything is the way it's supposed to be.

"*Husband.*" I test the word.

"Yes?" Everett responds.

I hadn't realized I'd said the word out loud, but I'm glad I did. The love beaming from Everett is contagious and a reward in its own. That man, the things he does to me, the shit he puts up with, and the love, which is unconditional. I'm a damn lucky woman.

"Thank you," I tell him.

Everett scoffs a little, trying to hold back a chuckle.

"I love you, Kenslie. I would have waited forever. But *thank you* for putting this poor fool out of his misery."

He lifts my left hand and presses a kiss to it, sending a warm sensation down my body. My insides are a jumble of emotion, and for the first time since moving the ring, I'm ecstatic. A ridiculous smile pulls across my face, and a warm blush hits my cheeks. I roll my eyes at my schoolgirl giddiness, but I can't help it. This is how one is expected to feel in this situation, and I sure as hell do!

"That's an awfully sweet smile on your lips. Did I do that?"

"I was just thinking…" I pause. "There's something I forgot to tell you. Everett Langley, I'd love nothing more than to be your wife. Yes, I'll marry you!"

# Epilogue

*Annaliesa*

*Six Months Later*

I can't believe it's been six months since I moved to Chicago and started my life with Ryker and my career. I couldn't have asked for a better place to work. I love my job and all the people I work with. It's a bonus that I get to work with Ryker. There are some ladies there that are jealous I snatched him up, but so far, we haven't had too many issues with them.

"Liesa, you're going to make us late if you don't hurry up," Ryker yells up the stairs.

"I'm coming." I hate dressing up. It takes too long, and I never leave enough time to get ready. I hate being late too, so now I'm a ball of stress.

"Not yet you aren't, but before the night ends you will be," he responds as I'm walking down the stairs.

"You better not break that promise, pretty boy." I wink at him as I grab his face and kiss him before walking by him and grabbing my handbag.

"Have I let you down yet?"

"Ummm." I pretend to think about it. "May…" is all I

get out before Ryker's pinning me against the wall, his hand in my hair, and his mouth against my ear.

"Better think really hard how you answer that question, sweetheart," he says then begins nibbling his way down my neck.

"We don't have time for this. You already said we'd be late."

"You made time for it when you questioned my ability to please my woman."

"Wait." I push against him. "You've never let me down. Every time with you is better than the last." I wrap my arms around his neck again and kiss him. Slowly breaking the kiss, I say, "We can't be late to the company holiday party or everyone will know what we were doing."

"Oh, they already know. There's no hiding the just-fucked glow you have almost every morning," he says, giving me a quick kiss and swatting my ass. "Hurry up, woman."

"I'm ready. Let's go and get the party started."

\* \* \* \*

Leaving the party, we hand the valet our ticket and wait for them to get our car. "That was the best holiday party I've ever been to for a job," I say, out of breath.

"It was," Ryker replies.

I can't believe that everyone not only got a bonus, but laptops. I didn't expect anything, but this company sure knows how to keep its employees happy. Their motto is 'A happy employee is a good employee. A mad employee is a dangerous one'. If they have disgruntled employees, there's a likelihood for errors at jobsites and possible injuries.

"Can you believe how lucky we are?" I ask.

"What do you mean by that?" Ryker asks.

"That we met each other in Europe, that we ended up getting hired on at the same architect firm, that we're still madly in love with each other, and that we don't want to rip each other's heads off on a daily basis because we spend so much time together."

"That's a good thing. I never thought I'd want to work with my girlfriend or wife, but I love having you around all the time. It's great that we have so much in common. Hopefully, it will make it harder for you to fall out of love with me."

"Like that could ever happen. You're my lobster."

"Well, you're my person," he quips back.

I love that he isn't scared to be open with me about his feelings. He often tells me he loves me before I tell him, and he's always showing his affection for me, not just when we're alone but in public too. He doesn't care what people think. He just wants me to know that I'm loved by him.

"That you are." Before I can say anything more the valet drives up with our car.

"Here's your car," the attendant says, getting out of the driver's seat.

"Thank you. Have a great evening and a Merry Christmas and Happy New Year," Ryker says, walking around to his side of the car as the valet starts to open my door for me.

"Thank you, sir. You as well," the guy replies.

"Thank you. Happy Holidays," I say, getting into the car.

"The pleasure's all mine. Happy Holidays," the valet says as he closes my door.

I hear Ryker growling. After we're both in the car I say, "Calm down. He was just being nice. It's their job. It's how they make tips. If you would've opened the door for me, then he wouldn't have had to."

"No tip from me for hitting on my woman."

"Really? You can't not tip him. He was being a gentleman."

"No."

"Fine. No tip, no sex," I reply.

"What? You can't withhold sex from me for being

upset that he was hitting on you."

"Why are men so territorial? He wasn't hitting on me, and even if he was, why does it matter? I'm coming home with you, and I only have eyes for you. If I got this way every time a woman hit on you, I'd always be pissed and fighting with you."

"Women don't hit on me all the time," he says with his brows scrunched and lips pressed together.

"Men are so blind," I say and throw my arms in the air. "Take me home."

There's no use arguing about this. We won't agree on it. I'd rather stop the argument than ruin my night. I have special plans for us and sex is one of them.

"Oh, wait you better at least give him something. I really don't want to ruin my surprise."

"Fine. If you must know, I tipped the guy, but I'll give him more if you want," he says, starting to get out of the car to give the valet a bigger tip.

I don't bother asking him how much because cheap is one thing Ryker isn't.

"Thank you. It means a lot to me that you'd make their night." I lean over and kiss him before he puts the car in drive and takes us home.

"There isn't anything I wouldn't do for you," he says,

grabbing my hand and bringing it to his mouth and kissing my knuckles. "And I'm sorry I was an overbearing ass. I just hate seeing guys look at you knowing that they want in your panties."

"Just because they want in my panties doesn't mean they're getting in them."

"I'd hope not," he says so low I barely hear him.

I don't know what's gotten into him tonight. He's being really strange. Yeah, he doesn't like when men hit on me in front of him, but the valet guy was just doing his job and being polite.

"Is everything okay? Did something happen that I don't know about?"

"Everything's fine. Maybe I'm just tired. It's been a long couple of weeks. Happy that we get two weeks off soon."

"I cannot wait. I'm so excited for you to meet my parents, and while I'm a little nervous, I'm also excited to meet your parents."

I'm happy that we're finally getting to meet the parents. We've Facetimed with each other's family, but we haven't met in person, and I can't wait to meet the people who gave me Ryker. He's an incredible person, and I'm positive I'll fall in love with them too.

"I know we leave in a week. We need to start packing."

Oh God, I forgot he's one of those people who's always on top of things. I'm so not like that. I'll be adding stuff to our bags as we're trying to walk out the door.

"Sure."

Pulling into our parking spot, Ryker turns to me and says, "Let's get upstairs so you can show me this surprise you have for me."

"Let's go, lover boy," I say, hopping out of the car and running toward the elevator. I cannot wait to show him what I got him.

"What's the rush? We have all night."

"I'm just excited to show you."

When the elevator doors open I'm shocked to see Margie, our housekeeper, leaving. "What are you doing here?" I ask.

"I bought some flowers last night for the foyer and forgot them this morning. I remembered you guys had that party tonight and thought I'd sneak them into your place before you got home."

"Oh, okay," I say.

I look over at Ryker, and he looks guilty of something. What the hell is up with him?

"I'll see you guys in a few days," Margie says, waving

at us as she walks to her car.

"That was strange," I comment as we get into the elevator.

"Not really. I remember coming home a couple of times in the evening to flowers in the foyer," he responds.

Why do I get the feeling Ryker's hiding something? Maybe he has a surprise for me too. Hopefully Margie didn't see something she shouldn't since I set up our room for him before we left. That's part of why I was running late.

"I know you have a surprise for me, but would you be willing to close your eyes and let me guide you into the house?" Ryker asks.

"Umm. I guess. What do you have planned?"

"I can't tell you that yet," he whispers in my ear. He's standing behind me with my back flush against his chest. He has a silk scarf in his hands that he's tying around my eyes. "Relax and just feel what I'm doing to you."

This is so hard to do. I'm eager to get inside and give him my gift, but he has other ideas. "Hurry, let's go inside."

"Patience." He swats my butt before unlocking the door and leading me inside. He stops us right inside the door and kisses me. "Looks like Margie put mistletoe all over this place. Guess I'll be getting to kiss you a lot," he says.

"Guess so."

"I want you to keep the scarf on for a few minutes while I go do something. Can I trust you not to peek?"

"Yes, though I really want to know what you're doing."

"You'll find out soon enough."

"Wait," I holler out. "You can't go into the bedroom or you'll ruin my surprise."

"Don't worry, I'm not going upstairs."

What's he doing? I haven't a clue what he has up his sleeve. I really hope he doesn't ruin my plans for us tonight.

I can sense him in front of me before I can feel him. "Take off the blindfold, Liesa," he whispers.

I whip the blindfold off and Ryker is down on one knee with the most gorgeous ruby and diamond ring with diamonds wrapped down the sides.

"Liesa, I didn't know what I was missing in my life until you. I thought I had everything planned out, but I was missing one big piece, and that was you. You bring so much joy to my life. I can't imagine it without you in it. I can see our little rugrats running around and wearing us out. Would you do me the honor and make me the luckiest man alive and marry me?"

Oh my God. How did I not see this coming? I didn't think he was ready yet. I knew he was going to propose one day, but not yet.

"Before I answer will you follow me upstairs?"

"Liesa, you're scaring me. Are you going to say no?"

"You'll understand in a minute. Come with me."

I lead him upstairs and into our room. On the bed is a heart made of rose petals. In the middle it says *Ryker, will you make me the happiest woman on earth and make me your wife?*

"What?" he asks.

"I know it isn't conventional, but I want to be your wife, and I want to call you my husband. I didn't know you were going to ask me to marry you or I wouldn't have stolen your thunder."

"Yes," he says, pulling me into his arms and kissing me. "I would love to make you my wife."

"Yes!" I shout. "I'm going to be Mrs. Ryker Matthews!"

# About Heather Carver

Heather Carver was born and raised in the Pacific NW. However, if she could live anywhere it would be a tropical beach.

She's a wife and mother of three children, who keep her quite busy with sports and activities. In her free time, she enjoys hanging out with friends, traveling, spending time outdoors, and exploring new adventures.

While Heather didn't become a book lover until her twenties, she's happy that she finally found the book world; finding it the perfect stress releaser, and a way to fill nights of insomnia.

Heather enjoys chatting with fellow book lovers, and you can connect with her on Facebook or via email.

Heather Carver's Website:

www.facebook.com/hcarverauthor

Reader eMail:

authorheathercarver@gmail.com

# About A.K. Layton

A.K. Layton has always been one to play by her own set of rules. In her youth she enjoyed writing poetry as it gave her a creative outlet that had no restrictions. Now, after years of reading all types of romantic novels she decided that she wanted to write stories her way. She pushed ahead as only a natural born Taurus can, with sheer stubbornness and determination.

She resides in Oregon with her husband and two children. When she isn't over committing herself for school functions, playdates, and volunteer activities she enjoys watching MMA fights, taking advantage of the beautiful Oregon Coast, and reading until the wee hours of the night.

A.K. Layton's Website:
www.aklaytonromance.com
Reader eMail:
aklaytonwrites@gmail.com

Made in the USA
San Bernardino, CA
27 November 2018